OF SPIRIT AND BONE

Legacy of the Wolves

The Prophecy Unfolds

Of Spirit and Bone

BY

Cheryl Matthew, PhD

Copyright © 2025 Cheryl Matthew, PhD

All rights reserved.

No part of this book may be reproduced, stored in a retrieval system, or transmitted in any form or by any means—electronic, mechanical, photocopying, recording, or otherwise—without the prior written permission of the author, except for brief quotations used in reviews, critical articles, or educational settings.

Cover concept and direction by Cheryl Matthew, PhD

Cover art generated by AI under the creative direction of the author

Published in Canada.

Printed in Canada.

First Edition

ISBN: 978-1-7782075-1-8

For rights inquiries, contact hello@thewolfstarpress.com

Disclaimer:

This is a work of fiction. Names, characters, places, organizations, and events have been fictionalized for the purpose of storytelling. Any resemblance to actual persons, living or dead, or to real-life events is purely coincidental. Some characters may be composites or inspired by a range of experiences, memories, and oral histories.

While the narrative and its characters are fictional, the spiritual practices, ceremonial visions, and healing work woven throughout this book are rooted in the author's lived experience and cultural truths. These sacred aspects are shared with humility and reverence—not to represent any specific Nation, teaching, or protocol—but to honour the personal and collective journey of healing.

This story is an offering. A path through pain, reclamation, and spiritual awakening. Healing is not linear—it is layered, ancestral, and alive. This book reflects that journey, and invites others to remember their own.

The author does not intend to offend, misrepresent, or appropriate. This work is shared in good faith—as an expression of story, spirit, and survival.

Table of Contents:

Preface 1
PART 1: Daughter of the Wolf 3
    CHAPTER 1: The Awakening of the Wolf 4
    CHAPTER 2: The Land Remembers 12
    CHAPTER 3: Cracks in the Foundation.......................................17
    CHAPTER 4: Reckoning 23
    CHAPTER 5: The Wild Ones..28
    CHAPTER 6: War Paint 33
    CHAPTER 7: The Bonfire Party...37
    CHAPTER 8: The NorKam Boys...43
    CHAPTER 9: The Calm Before the Storm...................................50
    CHAPTER 10: The Promise 57
    CHAPTER 11: The Heat Before the Fall......................................62
    CHAPTER 12: Prom Night 67
    CHAPTER 13: Graduation 73
    CHAPTER 14: The Mine & The Fight for Eagle Ridge.............78
    CHAPTER 15: The First Kevin Fight..83
    CHAPTER 16: Kai The Downward Spiral 91
    CHAPTER 17: The Fallout 97
    CHAPTER 18: The Fight That Changed Everything 103
    CHAPTER 19: The First Night Home 105
    CHAPTER 20: The Sweat Lodge & The Fallout:......................110

CHAPTER 21: Spiraling 116

CHAPTER 22: The Breaking Point 121

CHAPTER 23: The Calm Before the Storm 128

CHAPTER 24: The Campus Life & Kevin's Warm Embrace 133

CHAPTER 25: The Fight for Eagle Ridge 138

CHAPTER 26: The Occupation of Eagle Ridge 144

PART 2: The Wolves Becoming 151

CHAPTER 27: Mending Wounds, Building Resistance: 152

CHAPTER 28: A Last Hurrah & The Road Ahead After the Occupation 156

CHAPTER 29: Leaving the Land, Losing My Spirit 162

CHAPTER 30: East Van Life 168

CHAPTER 31: Rez Blues & Revolution: East Van NYM 171

CHAPTER 32: The Manifesto: 176

CHAPTER 33: The Lodge & The Manifesto: 183

CHAPTER 34: The Treaty Table with Empty Chairs 189

CHAPTER 35: UNDRIP Isn't a Dream.......................................195

CHAPTER 36: The Occupation...202

CHAPTER 37: The Shot Fired..207

CHAPTER 38: When River Returned 214

CHAPTER 39: Smoke & Paper..221

CHAPTER 40: Chairwoman of the Landless.............................226

CHAPTER 41: Albuquerque & The Storm Waiting to Happen: 234

CHAPTER 42: The Fire In My Throat 238

CHAPTER 43: Arrival in Albuquerque..245

CHAPTER 44: Maw'Tsain & The Wild Year in Albuquerque 250

CHAPTER 45: Maw'Tsain's Perspective 254

CHAPTER 46: Midnight Rodeo & Wild Nights 260

CHAPTER 47: Holidays with the Greyeyes 265

CHAPTER 48: Todd & The Peyote Church............................270

CHAPTER 49: Indian Kids Leadership Camp 276

CHAPTER 50: Jonathan, Harvard Law & The Hopi Prophecy 282

CHAPTER 51: Prayers in Death Valley....................................287

CHAPTER 52: The Skinwalker 291

CHAPTER 53: The Choice – Scholar or Warrior?....................296

PART 3: The Grizzly Sleeps..301

CHAPTER 54: Rising From Ashes...302

CHAPTER 55: The Unexpected News..310

CHAPTER 56: The Storm Before the Calm 313

CHAPTER 57: A Wedding, A Home, and a Growing Family 316

CHAPTER 58: A House Filled with Joy....................................319

CHAPTER 59: Loss, Grief, and the Breaking Point................322

CHAPTER 60: The Summer That Changed Everything..........325

CHAPTER 61: The Call to Come Home...................................331

CHAPTER 62: The Breaking Point...333

CHAPTER 63: The Showdown Over Salmon & Wine............336

CHAPTER 64: Aftermath – Numbing the Pain.......................339

CHAPTER 65: What Had He Done?...343

PART 4: Echoes of the Ancestors................................348

CHAPTER 66: The First Meeting—Hé Sá 349

CHAPTER 67: The Love He Couldn't Keep 371

CHAPTER 68: The Women Who Showed Me the Way Back 378

CHAPTER 69: The Prophecy and the Path Forward 383

CHAPTER 70: The Blood Oath 387

CHAPTER 71: The Karmic Unraveling 405

CHAPTER 72: Blood & Bone 409

CHAPTER 73: The Final Battle – Nea vs. Xtotl 415

CHAPTER 74: Climax: The Curse of Xtotl 424

EPILOGUE: Peace 438

Preface

Welcome, beloved one.

Of Spirit and Bone: Legacy of the Wolves is not just a novel—it is a remembering. A soul-deep journey across timelines and bloodlines, where the past howls through prophecy and the future is shaped by the ones brave enough to reclaim it.

This story was born at the crossroads of ceremony and survival, rooted in ancestral knowing and fed by the flames of personal transformation. Though the characters and events are fictional, the medicine carried here is real. You may recognize pieces of yourself—or your ancestors—woven between these lines. You may feel the spirits walking beside you as the veils thin. Set in a world that mirrors our own but pulses with the presence of the unseen, this tale walks between land and spirit, trauma and healing, sovereignty and surrender. It is shaped by Indigenous teachings, spiritual visions, and a lifetime spent walking with the wolf.

You will meet Nea, a woman torn between worlds—guided by the wild, betrayed by love, and called by something older than memory. Her path is tortured, sacred, and deeply human. She is not a heroine, but a mirror.

This book is for the ones who've lost themselves and fought to rise again.

For those who know their dreams are not just dreams.

For the ones carrying stories in their bones.

For those called to remember.

Take what you need. Leave what you don't. And walk gently—because what you are about to enter is not just fiction. It's my medicine.

PART 1
Daughter of the Wolf

CHAPTER 1

The Awakening of the Wolf

For months—no, for years—I dreamed of running barefoot through the forest, my body shifting in fits and jolts. My muscles stretched like taffy, my bones cracked open like thunder, and my skin burned, not with fire, but with becoming and becoming something else. Something ancient. Something wild.

The dreams always began the same way: the intoxicating rush of speed—the slap of bare feet against damp earth. Trees blurred past me like memories I couldn't quite reach. My breath came sharp and fast, my lungs burning with cold air, my chest rising and falling to a rhythm I didn't choose. Initially, it felt like freedom—like an instinct rising from some forgotten core of me. Something deep, something primal. As I remembered how to exist in my proper form.

But then—came the shift.

The bones in my hands twisted unnaturally, fingers clawing inward as if some force beneath my skin demanded to be let out. I watched, helpless, as claws erupted through flesh, blood spilling hot over my palms. My spine arched violently, a snapping pain blooming as the vertebrae twisted and reshaped themselves. My face stretched forward, my jaw tearing open as fangs shoved their way through my gums. I tried to scream, but what escaped my throat wasn't human. It was a guttural, feral snarl—raw and unrecognizable.

I fell. Convulsed. My bones shattered and reformed in seconds. The pain was exquisite. Blinding. And yet... necessary.

Then came the running again. Always the running. Faster this time. Stronger. Paws instead of feet. Fur instead of skin. The scent of prey in my nostrils. The wind is no longer against me—but of me.

This was the dream. My dream. Over and over. A loop I could never escape. A lesson I hadn't yet learned.

I had always been... different.

As a child, I felt the world more sharply than others, not just in terms of emotions but in the unspoken, the invisible. Rooms carried energy. Trees whispered truths. People's sorrow seeped into my skin before they even spoke. I didn't have words for it then—I only knew I carried more than just my feelings.

My father, my Daddio, was the only one who didn't ask me to dull myself. A tall, sweet, silly cowboy-Indian with dark eyes full of knowing. He carried himself like a man who had seen pain and chosen to greet it with laughter. The kind of man who shook hands with strangers like cousins and made even the angriest logger grin by the end of a conversation. When he was home from the camps, the whole house shifted. It brightened. It softened. I was never afraid of the dark when he was around.

My mother was a different kind of woman. Beautiful. Strong. With eyes that had seen too much. The Indian Residential School had stolen her childhood, and the years with my father—his drinking, his wandering—had nearly stolen the rest. She loved us. She cared for us. But she lived like a woman who had built a fortress around her heart and had long forgotten where the door was.

Still, she taught me things my father didn't. About the old ways. About the spirits. About what it meant to be seen by the other world.

Some of my best memories were out in the bush with my dad. Fishing in the early morning mist, hunting under golden autumn leaves. He'd teach me how to track, listen, and wait. There was a rhythm to it all. A respect. He'd tell stories while we waited—of old warriors, shapeshifters, and wolves who were once men. Stories, I thought, were just legends until I began to dream.

The dreams started slowly. A flicker in my subconscious. A single paw print in the snow of my mind. But by the time I turned fourteen, they were relentless. Night after night, I didn't just *see* the wolf—I *was* the wolf. And in those dreams, I wasn't always a girl. Sometimes, I was a man, a mother, something with no name. A spirit. A shadow. A hunter. A guide. Something that existed beyond the lines of gender, beyond time. Something old. Something sacred.

Then, one night, the dreams bled into the waking world.

I opened my eyes—or thought I did—but couldn't move. I was suspended in that space between sleep and wakefulness, that liminal realm where the veil between worlds thins. My limbs were heavy. My chest is tight. The air around me buzzed with energy, thick and electric. The walls of my room seemed to breathe.

And something was in the room with me.

I couldn't see it. Not exactly. But I felt it. A presence—tall, dark, not human. It stood by my bed, silent, watching. Its energy pressed in around me like water. My body screamed to run, to flee—but I was frozen. Fear surged in my blood like lightning.

I remembered what my mother had said. "If a spirit ever comes for you, and you're afraid—*pray*."

So I did.

I repeatedly closed my eyes and forced the Lord's Prayer into my mind, each word a shield. I summoned every drop of courage and imagined my spirit rising, standing, *pushing back*. I slowly shoved the presence away with invisible hands, not with strength but with will. It resisted. Then relented.

And just like that—it was gone.

The air shifted. The pressure lifted. My limbs loosened. Exhaustion wrapped around me like a blanket, and I fell into a deep, empty sleep.

I didn't wake up until morning.

Downstairs, everything looked the same. Sunlight streamed through the kitchen window. My mother was at the stove, flipping eggs. The scent of bacon and coffee filled the air. But I wasn't the same. Not anymore.

She turned when she heard me, her eyes scanning my face. "How did you sleep?" she asked.

I hesitated. "Not great," I said. "I... there was a spirit in my room. It stood beside me. I prayed, like you told me. And I pushed it away."

She froze. Then, she slowly turned to face me, wiping her hands on a dish towel. Her voice was low. "I know," she said.

I blinked. "What do you mean, you *know?*"

"I saw them," she said. "Two wolves. One black. One white. They stood at your bedside last night. You were swatting at them in your sleep. And then... they left."

My knees nearly buckled. She hadn't been in the room. She hadn't seen me struggle. And yet... she *knew*. She *saw*.

At that moment, the world I thought I knew unraveled at the seams.

I was no longer just a girl with strange dreams. I was part of something older, sacred, terrifying, and beautiful. And I wasn't alone.

That moment marked the beginning of everything.

In the following weeks, my mother spoke to me in ways she had never spoken to me before. She told me of spirits she'd seen in her childhood. Of the times she felt her dead brother beside her, of the figure who once stood at the edge of the reserve road, beckoning. She told me the stories she'd never dared say aloud.

And I listened. And I asked questions. And I read everything I could—on spirit guides, mysticism, Wicca, astrology, meditation, the unseen laws of the universe. I wandered through the library as if it were a holy place. Knowledge became a lifeline. But so did silence. Because this wasn't something I could talk about to friends. To teachers. To strangers.

This knowing was too wild. Too raw.

By then, my father was sober. He had come back to us after years of drifting. My parents had stitched their lives back together with trembling hands and quiet forgiveness. Our home, for once, was still. But I... wasn't. I was vibrating and changing and seeing things I couldn't unsee.

I was a girl standing between worlds—one foot in the ordinary and the other in the sacred.

And the first time I met my *seméc*, my wolf spirit guide, I did not meet it with understanding. I met it with fear. With trembling limbs and a soul unsure if it was being chosen or cursed.

It would take time to understand that fear and power are siblings.

Learning that my path wasn't punishment but invitation would take time.

And that night, when the wolves came to my bedside, it wasn't just a visitation.

It was a *calling*.

And I would never be the same again. It was time to visit Grampa Oliver.

Grampa Oliver. The name alone made my stomach flutter. He was the one they called the Old Wolf, the medicine man who never left the ridge and spoke with spirits as easily as most people breathe. The *mélems`tye*, the wolf, was in my lineage. I'd only met him a few times at family gatherings, but even then, I'd felt his eyes reading me like he knew something I didn't. Like he *remembered* me from another life.

I had never been to the sweat lodge before. Not because I hadn't wanted to—but because I hadn't been *ready*. There's a difference. Readiness isn't about age. It's about memory. It's about waking up to what's always been inside you.

When we arrived, the air around the lodge was thick with the scent of sage, smoke curling through the trees like spirits returning home. Grampa Oliver stood barefoot in the dirt, a bundle of cedar in his hands. His face was lined with years and wisdom, his eyes dark as soil, as old as stone. When he took my hands, his grip was firm but kind.

"So you've been running with the wolf," he said, voice low, ancient. "And now you want to know why."

Inside the lodge, the heat swallowed me whole. Steam rose from the glowing stones, the scent of cedar and sweetgrass swirling like a song. My breath came in shallow gasps as Grampa sang. The songs weren't in English, but my soul understood. They were the words of my ancestors, calling me home.

The fire cracked and hissed, casting shadows that danced on the curved walls. As Grampa's voice grew stronger, something inside me broke open. My body trembled. My vision blurred. I felt her—*the wolf*. Not just inside me—but all around me. My skin burned, but I wasn't afraid.

That night, the dream returned. But it wasn't just mine anymore.

I wasn't running alone.

Beside me ran the wolves of my bloodline—women and men with eyes like mine, spirits fierce and untamed. I recognized some of their faces from photographs and old stories. Others I had never seen but knew by heart. They were guiding me, surrounding me, keeping me from straying too far from the path I hadn't yet discovered. We ran together through a forest older than time, chasing something I didn't yet understand.

But I knew this:

This was the beginning.

Not of the dream—but of *remembering* who I was before the world made me forget.

CHAPTER 2

The Land Remembers

The river was alive.

I had always known this even before I understood what that knowing meant. Even before the wolf dreams. Before the spirits. Before I knew my feet walked in two worlds.

As a child, I would lie on my back beside the water's edge, arms splayed, eyes closed, letting the hum of the current wrap around me. I would listen—not just with my ears, but with something more profound. Something in my bones. There was a rhythm in the river, a pulse beneath the rush of water that matched the beating of my heart.

I didn't have the words back then. I just knew the river carried secrets. That the wind didn't just blow—it *spoke* that the reeds bent low not with the weight of the breeze but with reverence. As if bowing to something unseen.

The land didn't just exist.

It watched.

It remembered.

It reacted.

The Elders had always said that.

"The land watches. It remembers. It reacts."

Our house was around a bend in the road down from the ballpark, nestled in the valley along the North Thompson River. Where Kamloops was dry and semi-desert, we lived in a lush paradise of tree groves, green as far as the eye could see, fresh from the river that fed life and the land. Fields of grass and hay, horses, cattle, and chickens surrounded us. Our garden was located below the house. Down from there was our haystack, which was fed by the family fields north and east of the house as far as you could see. The train tracks to the west of the house were a constant reminder of how, rather than "giving" crown lands to the railroads, they cut them across reserve lands for "free" as often as possible, further reducing Native lands. The constant sound of rail brakes was a continual nuisance that felt jagged and out of place against the quiet, peaceful backdrop. To the east of the farmhouse was Eagle Ridge, massive in size, looking down upon our lands like an iron warrior. At the base of Eagle Ridge was a poplar grove, and when the winds moved through the valley, that sound was like a beautiful orchestra of silvery green leaves in my ears. It was as much a part of my home as the river. I would often just lay out in front of the house, listening to the sounds of those leaves, whispering stories of thousands of years in this valley. Those trees, all of the trees, the lands, were my family as much as my blood relatives. I could live anywhere, but in my blood and my bones, this valley would always be my home.

I used to think it was a metaphor. It is a poetic way of reminding us to be grateful. To tread gently. But now I know it wasn't poetry. It was a warning—a truth carried in the marrow of those who came before me.

Daddio had spent decades cutting down trees.

Like all the men in our family, he was a logger. That was the way of things. The forest gave, and the people took because they had to. Not out of greed. Out of necessity.

But Daddio was different.

He never took it without acknowledging the cost. He talked to trees before he felled them. He taught me to offer tobacco, to speak words of thanks, to place my hand on bark, and to say goodbye.

"You take what you need," he would say, "and you thank it. You leave enough behind so the land doesn't stop giving."

I remember standing with him on a ridge once—maybe eight or nine years old—watching the fallers below. I remember the thunderous crack as a fantastic pine gave way, its groan as it toppled. That sound haunted me. It still does.

"Do you love this land, Daddio?" I had asked him, my voice small.

He didn't answer right away. He looked at the sea of trees, smoke curling from his lips. "Yeah, baby," he finally said. "I love it. That's why I gotta do better by it."

And he did.

He changed. I watched it happen in real time. He started spending less time cutting and more time listening. He walked the bush with Elders, asking questions most men his age were too proud to ask. He learned the names of every plant he once stepped over. He remembered the stories behind each animal track. He stopped taking the land for granted—and started offering himself to it.

That kind of love—the kind that doesn't want anything in return—was the deepest thing he ever gave me.

That morning, I woke before the sun and followed the path to the river—setétkwe.

Sacred ground.

My great-grandmother had built her *sqilye*, our sweat lodge there, in the clearing by the river. The Grandfathers, the stones used for the sacred fire in the lodge, were old; the same Grandfathers sat along the riverbank like a fence, keeping the good and bad spirits out. Older than my family's memory. She used to say they were alive too—that they carried the voices of our ancestors, that when they heated and cracked in the fire, they were speaking.

I had grown up playing there, building forts from driftwood, making dolls from grass, and leaving gifts for the little people my mother warned me not to anger. I never saw them, but I felt them.

That morning, the air was strange. Still. As if the world was holding its breath.

I knelt beside the river and pressed my palms into the damp soil. Normally, I'd feel the buzz of life humming back—a quiet recognition between me and the land. A heartbeat returned my own.

But not today.

The energy felt muted. Off-key.

I dipped my fingers into the water.

I could see the spirit of the water behind my eyes, familiar white glowing ripples, but the pattern was wrong. It was off.

Not just off—*wrong*.

Setétkwe's power was *pure* and unbridled. But now... it felt disturbed. Like something sacred had been touched without permission.

A knot twisted in my stomach.

I pulled my hand away and scanned the riverbanks. Nothing looked different. But everything *felt* different. The same way birds go silent before a storm. The same way your skin prickles before bad news.

I had felt it for weeks—this growing sense that something was out of balance. That something old was stirring and or unraveling.

That afternoon, the Elders called a meeting at the community hall.

No formal invites. You just knew to come. If you had ears, you would have shown up.

CHAPTER 3

Cracks in the Foundation

The road to the community hall was dusty, winding toward the ridge where the trees grew sparse, and the world felt wide open. River and I drove in silence, windows down, the warm breath of summer moving through the truck's cab.

The wind carried the scent of pine resin and cut hay from our family's ranch below—scents so familiar they lived in the marrow of my bones.

Eagle Ridge rose in the distance like a sentinel. The sacred mountain. The one they wanted to gut.

"If a miner sets foot on that mountain, he'll lose his kneecaps," I said flatly.

River didn't laugh this time. He grinned, but it was tight, hollow. One hand on the wheel, the other tapping absently against the steering column in a syncopated rhythm that gave away his tension.

"You and me both, sis."

We had been making that same joke for weeks—maybe months. But today, it wasn't funny anymore.

Eagle Ridge wasn't just a mountain—it was a memory. It was medicine. It was home.

It had been there before our family, before the treaties, before they tried to name and number the land into squares, lots, and deeds.

Daddio and Grampa ran Texas Longhorns past there every summer, baled hay under its wide shadow.

I had my first ceremony in the valley below, the river running thick and clean as Grampa chanted prayers that stitched my spirit back into the land.

And Great-Grandmother had made offerings there long before I was born, her voice threading through the morning mist like smoke.

Now, they wanted to rip it apart. For nickel. For gold. For whatever shiny thing they thought had more value than a place that carried the heartbeat of our bloodline.

River's jaw flexed. His knuckles went white on the steering wheel.

"They don't get it," he said. "They don't understand that the land doesn't belong to us—we belong to it."

I didn't answer. I didn't need to. He already knew.

The parking lot was full when we pulled up to the hall—trucks lined up like sentinels, old sedans, rust-eaten vans. Inside, the air was heavy. Not hot, but thick—with anticipation, with quiet anger, with the knowing silence of people who'd come prepared for a decision that had already been made without them.

Then I saw Billy.

He was near the front of the hall, standing like he owned it.

Worse—like he was saving it.

The only man in the room wearing a suit.

Not just any suit—*Chanel.* Tailored, slick, city-sleek.

A wolf in designer wool.

His truck was parked outside, buffed to a mirror finish, chrome rims catching the light like teeth. His hair was slicked back, not a strand out of place. Billy had always known how to perform and look like what the world wanted.

He looked like someone who had already shaken hands with city men in corner offices who'd never set foot on our land but still felt entitled to cut it open.

He was the new bright thing. The corporate Indian. The modern "success story."

Backroom meetings, a six-figure salary, bourbon neat in a Coal Harbour hotel lounge, and a polished LinkedIn page full of mining investments and "economic reconciliation."

He was everything River refused to become.

We took seats near the back. Close enough to see Grampa Oliver's face—lined like a map, still as stone, unreadable. His presence alone kept the room grounded, but even he couldn't hold back the coming tide.

Billy cleared his throat and stepped forward.

"Times are changing," he began, his voice smooth and rehearsed. "We can't stop progress. We need jobs, and the mine will bring that."

A murmur moved through the room—some in agreement, some in protest, most just tight-lipped and tired.

I felt River shift beside me, body going still. Not calm—coiled.

"This land has given us everything," River said, his voice low, like a warning from under the earth. "And you want to sell it?"

Billy didn't miss a beat. He had answers ready, laminated, and locked.

"I want to use it," he said. "For something that benefits us."

Us.

That word slapped harder than a backhand.

Because we both knew who Billy meant by *us*—and who he didn't.

I exhaled slowly. My hands were clenched under the table, nails digging into my palms.

Billy had always been slick, even as a kid. He knew how to charm people, when to smile, when to stay quiet when to nod solemnly while plotting his next move. River and I were blunt-force—loud, raw, heart-on-sleeve. But Billy? Billy played the long game.

Where we stayed on the land, Billy left. He went to UBC and then law school. I got recruited into consulting. Built a life out of numbers and development plans and words like "stakeholder engagement." He had learned to talk like them, dress like them, move through their boardrooms like he belonged.

He used to be the cousin who snuck out of ceremonies early, who'd roll his eyes when the old ones spoke in the language, who once asked Grampa why we still did "that old stuff."

I remember the day he said it, how Grampa looked at him—quiet, broken-hearted—but never said a word.

Maybe that was the day Billy started walking away from us. Or maybe it was earlier. Maybe he was always on his way out.

Now, here he was. Full circle. Come back not to help—but to finish what the colonizers started.

Billy believed what he was saying. That was the worst part.

He believed the mine would help. That would make things better. Selling pieces of our soul could be rebranded as an opportunity.

I glanced at Grampa. His face didn't move.

But his eyes—those deep, ageless eyes—watched Billy like he was watching a spirit that had already lost its way.

And maybe that was the truth of it.

Billy hadn't betrayed us overnight. He had eroded.

Slow. Like acid on stone.

And now we had to decide:

Should we continue to try to bring him back?

Or do we let him go—and fight him like we'd fight anyone else trying to take what wasn't theirs?

CHAPTER 4

Reckoning

After the meeting, Billy came back to the farm.

He always did that, showing up as if he still had a right to. Like proximity could make up for absence, his truck in the driveway meant something more than it did.

I spotted him near the edge of the gravel lot, standing by the old cedar post fence, still in that goddamn suit. Its crisp lines didn't belong here, not in this dust, not under this sky, not against the backdrop of waving hay and distant, glinting cow troughs. He looked like he was waiting for a film crew to show up and take headshots for a magazine piece on *Indigenous Innovation and Resource Futures*.

His eyes weren't on the land. Not really. He was looking past it. Through it. As if the fields were already flattened and parceled off, he could already see dollar signs showing where Grandmother used to lay her tobacco.

I walked up, boots crunching hard against the gravel, not trying to be quiet. I wasn't going to sneak up on him like a ghost.

At 5'5", I barely hit his shoulder. But I came in swinging.

"What the fuck do you think you're doing?"

He turned slowly, as if already tired of having this conversation. He was preparing to outsmart me with some hollow TED Talk rhetoric.

But I didn't give him a chance.

"You *know* Eagle Ridge is sacred," I spat, jabbing my finger into the cold fabric of his suit jacket. "You know it's not yours to sell. It never was. There will be a reckoning, Billy. Here—and from the spirit realm."

For a second—just a flicker—something moved behind his eyes. Guilt. Shame. Maybe even fear.

But just as quickly, it was gone. Smoothed out, replaced by that mask he wore like armor. Polished. Corporate. Untouchable.

"Nea," he said, using the short form of my name as if it was still his to use.

Wusnea. Named after the lichen that grows only where the air is pure. Mom said the spirits picked it for me, and I was meant to be medicine for broken things.

But Billy said it like it was a joke.

"Stop with you and Mom's woo-woo bullshit," he scoffed, dismissive—that voice—oily and rehearsed—grated against everything inside me. "The only thing coming for us is money. Doesn't Dad want a decent tractor and a truck that doesn't break down every week? Even his rez buddies laugh at it."

That last line landed like a gut punch. Not because it was true—but because it wasn't.

Daddio loved that truck. Said it had spirit. It always got him where he needed to be, even if it complained. When we were kids, he'd told us the truck knew the land better than half the people on it and that it would die only when the land did.

He'd laughed then. But now, I could hear the echo of that laughter in the back of my mind, cracking like dry leaves.

Behind me, I felt Mom approach. Quiet as ever. She didn't speak. She didn't touch my arm. She didn't try to stop me.

But I could hear her crying.

Soft. Silent. The kind of tears that didn't demand attention—only respect.

She stood there behind me like a pillar. Crying but unmoving. Supporting me was the only way she knew how—by showing up and standing still.

Billy saw her. He saw what it did to her, standing there hearing her oldest son talk about his father like that.

And he kept going anyway.

That was the part that burned.

I turned away. My blood was roaring in my ears, and I needed to move, or I was going to do something I'd regret. I took a step—then turned back.

"You're an idiot if you think some goddamn truck can fill a man's soul," I said.

And then quieter:

"I mean, I guess if you don't have one."

That landed.

Billy's jaw tightened, the vein in his temple ticking like a clock about to break. His fists balled at his sides. He stepped toward me.

I didn't flinch.

He used to be the brother who held my hand when the nightmares came. The one who carried me back from the riverbank when I cut my foot on a sharp stone. But that boy was long gone.

Before he could reach me, River stepped in.

He moved like a shadow—silent but immovable, his body cutting a clean line between us. His shoulders squared. His face was calm, but his eyes were something else. There was black in them. Not the color—*the feeling*. The kind that swells in the seconds before a storm breaks.

"Billy," River said, voice low. Controlled. The kind of quiet that made grown men flinch.

"It's time for you to leave."

A truck rumbled up the driveway, gravel spitting under tires, engine knocking in that familiar way. Daddio's old '72 Ford. Faded blue with rust along the wheel wells. Tisha stood alert in the truck bed, ears perked, her blue eyes locked onto Billy like she already knew.

She always could sense the tension. Once, she'd chased a drunk off the property just from hearing him raise his voice to Mom. That dog was more spirit than animal, and she was on edge now.

Billy didn't say another word.

His fists stayed clenched for a heartbeat longer. Then he exhaled, forced his posture straight, and adjusted the sleeves of his settler-approved suit. He brushed imaginary dust from his shoulder like he was flicking off the past.

River didn't move until Billy walked past him.

As he climbed into his shiny truck and reversed down the long gravel lane, I watched the red glow of his taillights disappear over the rise.

There was no victory in it. No satisfaction.

Just dust.

And the slow, quiet understanding settling over me like a fog:

He's long gone.

CHAPTER 5

The Wild Ones

In small-town BC, the truck you drove defined you.

It asked people if they were worth noticing, respecting, or stepping around. Lifted Chevys meant money. Rusted-out Toyotas meant stubborn pride. Fords, especially rebuilt ones with custom chrome and cherry engines, meant you had a soul—and time on your hands.

It was 1993—senior year.

I pulled into the school lot behind the wheel of River's perfectly rebuilt '79 Ford F150, which he spent three summers restoring with Grampa after the original engine died out near Lytton. That truck purred like a cat that knew its worth. Smooth, low growl. All presence, no need to shout. The chrome caught the morning sun like it had something to prove.

Heads turned.

Not just for the truck.

For me.

I was hot—and I *knew* it. That wasn't arrogance. That was survival. In a town like ours, where most girls either faded or fought to be seen, knowing you were, the fire was its armor.

I didn't need much. No contour, lip liner, or Aqua Net bangs that scraped the sky like the other girls in class. Just sun-browned skin from working hay season, wind-burnt cheeks, and eyes that didn't flinch when boys got stupid. I wore my Guess jean skirt, a white tee tied at the waist, and my worn brown cowboy boots, which Daddio bought me when I turned sixteen. Simple. Clean. The perfect tension between prairie-girl and something feral.

Then I heard it.

That low, slow rumble made your heart drop, and your breath catch.

Kai.

His dad's Harley rolled into the lot like thunder disguised as metal. It wasn't just a bike—it was a damn declaration. He didn't even try to come in quiet. Never did. That was part of the myth. He wanted people to *feel* him before they saw him.

And when they *did* see him?

Every head turned. Like a scene out of a movie, only it was real—and it was ours.

Six-foot-three of unapologetic wild. Sun-bleached hair that curled at the ends. Green eyes like pine needles after rain—sharp but half-lidded, like he was always barely awake or dreaming. Tanned arms gripped the handlebars with confidence you couldn't teach. Kai didn't strut. He didn't need to.

He didn't take off his helmet right away.

He waited.

Because he knew, I knew the whole parking lot was watching. I knew they wanted to look and didn't want to get caught looking. I knew what it meant to let anticipation do the heavy lifting.

And when he finally *did* lift the helmet from his head—casually, slowly, like he had all the time in the world—it was like someone turned gravity up.

The collective sigh from the girls in the lot was *audible*. Even the guys glanced twice.

I rolled my eyes, biting down the grin threatening to give me away.

He was mine. And they *hated* it.

Not because I was prettier. Not even because I had him. But because I *matched* him. We were the first white couple and interracial First Nations in this small town. I *chose* him the same way he chose me, and in a place where girls were supposed to take what they were given, that made us dangerous.

Kai swung off the bike smoothly, his long torso twisting as he landed. His tank top shifted, giving the world a flash of abs tight from working on engines and splitting cedar for older man Trotier up the hill. But it was the tattoo that got them.

My wolf.

Seméc.

Not just any wolf—*my* design, drawn on a napkin at the diner the night we first kissed behind the grain elevator and inked on his right shoulder three months later during a summer storm that flooded the back roads and left us stranded at my aunt's trailer for two straight days.

That wolf meant something. To us. To *me*.

He walked toward the truck—slow, deliberate steps on gravel—while the whole school watched like a goddamn soap opera was playing out live.

He didn't say anything.

I didn't have to.

He opened the door, leaned in, and gave me that *look*.

The one that made my stomach lurch and my knees weak. The one that said, *I see you. All of you. And I'm not going anywhere.*

He kissed me. Right there in front of everyone. Deep. Unapologetic. Like time had stopped, as the world had narrowed to the heat of his hands and the wild thrum of my heart in my chest.

Half the school gasped.

The other half wanted to die.

And me?

It was the best part of my morning.

But underneath all that heat and reckless wanting was something else. A knowing. That this thing between us—it wasn't made for quiet days. It wasn't built to last. We were fire meeting gasoline. Stars colliding mid-sky.

And in the back of my mind, I think I already knew—

Wild things never stay caged for long.

CHAPTER 6

War Paint

I didn't pick fights. But I didn't walk away from them, either. I never heard from anyone who tried to bully or insult me. I always figured it better to go down fighting than take that shit.

But the truth is—once you grow up under the constant weight of being *other*, you learn that silence doesn't protect you. It never did. It only taught them that you could be ignored and be belittled. That you could be treated like you were invisible.

And I was never invisible.

After PE, I was in the locker room, pulling on my boots. The leather cracked with the sound of old work and hard days. I'd spent most of my childhood on the ranch, learning to use tools before I could spell my name right, running with the cattle, and cleaning the barn. That's where I belonged. My boots were part of my skin. The smell of leather and dust was something I inhaled like air.

Then I heard it.

"Skinny Indian bitch."

It wasn't meant for me to hear. But I did.

Sherin's voice cut through the hum of the locker room, laced with that signature venom. It was meant to sting, like always. Like all the other slurs and name-calling I'd endured from her over the years. But it was worse this time. This time, it had an audience. Her flock of plastic, empty girls—her cheerleaders, her followers. They nodded along, wearing their collective bravado like a veil. They followed her lead because they didn't have anything else, and they sure as hell didn't have the guts to question her.

I didn't have to turn to know it was her. I didn't have to look at the bleach-blonde hair or the overdone lipstick. I knew it was her by the poison in her words. The same words she'd used since elementary school, always aimed at me.

I stood up, feeling the old anger stir, the heat of every insult, every sneer I'd ever gotten since the first day I set foot in that school. Every time, I'd been pushed aside. Every time, I'd been told I wasn't enough because I didn't fit their mold.

But this wasn't just about Sherin. It was about all of them. All the people who thought I should shrink, all the people who thought they had the right to define me.

I turned slowly, my eyes narrowing. Sherin had been leaning against a locker, her arms crossed, a smirk on her face like she had already won. But I wasn't the scared little girl who let those words roll off anymore.

No, I had learned how to wear my anger-like armor.

I took one step toward her, feeling the weight of the room shift. I could feel the eyes on me, every person holding their breath, knowing something was about to happen. They probably thought they knew how this would go—some cliche push and shove, maybe a few harsh words, and then it'd all fizzle out like it always did in this high school circus.

But they were wrong.

I stepped onto the bench between us in one fluid motion, my boots making a sharp sound as they landed. The room went silent—everyone in that locker room was waiting.

And then, I jumped.

Before Sherin could register what was happening, I was over the bench, landing in front of her and shoving her back into the lockers with enough force to rattle them. Her breath left her in a sharp gasp as she slammed against the cold metal.

She froze. And for a split second, I saw it. The vulnerability in her eyes. The fear. The realization that she had no idea who she was dealing with.

The air in the room was thick—a taut silence. I could hear a clock ticking somewhere distant, but it didn't matter. At that moment, everything else disappeared.

I leaned in, my face inches from hers. I wasn't screaming. I wasn't even raising my voice. I was quiet and controlled. But there was something in my tone that cut through the noise. Something that told her—and everyone watching—that I was done.

"You want to fight?" I asked my voice a razor's edge, low and dangerous. "I'd rather be a skinny Indian bitch than a wide load like you."

The words landed. Hard. It wasn't just about the insult—it was about everything she'd ever thrown at me. Every time, she tried to make me small. Every time she tried to make me feel like I didn't belong.

Sherin's face drained of color. All that self-assurance, that fake bravado, slipped away like water off the stone. She blinked, eyes wide, but she didn't say a word.

And that was the best part.

Because when it came down to it, she didn't have anything that could touch me anymore. Not the words, not the sneers, not the judgment.

I was finished letting them make me feel less than I was.

I stood there, steady as a mountain, watching her crumble in my silence. I didn't need to do anything more. Her friends stood behind her, unsure of their place and uncertain how to proceed. No one said shit after that.

And that was the point.

CHAPTER 7

The Bonfire Party

The gravel pits outside Kamloops weren't exactly a party destination, but they might as well have been a nightclub for us.

This place—surrounded by trees and a sky full of stars—was where we came to let off steam, to escape the rules that always felt like they were hanging over our heads—the smell of burning wood mixed with beer's cheap, bitter scent.

The night air was heavy with the sounds of trucks revving, voices raised in drunken laughter, and the beats of classic rock and country mixing like an unholy cocktail. The Hip, Garth Brooks, and Metallica shared equal time in the speakers, turning the place into a neon-lit chaos of raw energy.

Blough at High Dough blasted through the speakers, and I could feel the vibrations down to my bones.

I stood near the fire, the warmth of it fighting off the chill of the early fall night, cider bottle in hand.

My boots were planted firm in the dirt, and my short Guess skirt barely brushed the tops of my thighs. I wasn't drunk enough to forget where I was, to lose track of everything around me, but just drunk enough not to care what anyone thought.

Not that I cared much about that anymore.

Across the clearing, Kai was leaning against his dad's Harley. The bike was like an extension of him—sleek, powerful, and dangerous. He wasn't even trying to fit in with the crowd.

His arms were folded across his chest, one foot propped up on the kickstand, that lazy, cocky grin plastered on his face. He was talking to the guys, but I knew that look. He wasn't there with them. He was waiting for something. Or, more accurately, someone.

Me.

KAI

Every girl at this party had been looking at me all night.

I knew it. But I didn't give a shit. Not because I didn't care about attention—I was used to it, even enjoyed it most of the time. But tonight? Tonight was different.

Because I was only looking at her.

Wusnea.

Her presence had this way of making everything else fade into the background. Every time I saw her, it hit me in the gut.

And I wasn't sure what was stronger—this wild mix of love, lust, pride, or the possessiveness that came with knowing that I couldn't get enough of her, that I didn't want anyone else to have her.

Sherin had been circling all night, flipping her hair, laughing too loud, trying to catch my eye. Half the girls here had been doing the same, but they were static—background noise.

Because Wusnea had walked back into my life like she owned it. And maybe she did.

The firelight danced in her hair, turning it into liquid copper, and I could feel her heat even from across the fire. She was standing near the flames, cider in hand, that same mix of strength and grace I'd always admired in her.

The way she stood there—unbothered, unashamed—told me everything I needed to know. This wasn't some shy, uncertain girl who needed validation. She had found her place in the world, and I couldn't help but feel like I had always been meant to be part of it.

She caught me staring. I didn't blush. She didn't look away. She tilted her head slightly, took a slow sip of cider, and smirked.

Jesus Christ.

I didn't even think twice. I excused myself from whatever conversation I'd been in, pushing through the crowd, heading straight for her. Every step felt like pulling me closer to something I didn't know I needed until I had it.

NEA

I smirked when he walked up. I didn't even need to hear what he had to say next. His eyes were already making promises he didn't need to speak aloud.

He reached for the bottle in my hand, tilting it back, taking a slow drink, not even bothering to say "hi" or "what's up." Kai didn't do small talk. Not with me. We had our language, a rhythm built from years of shared history and unsaid things.

"Yeah," he said, wiping his mouth with the back of his hand. "I'd rather be with you."

I didn't have time to respond before he grabbed me, pulling me against him in one smooth motion. And then his lips were on mine—hot, reckless, and possessive.

He kissed me like he meant it like he hadn't missed a moment when I'd been gone. His fingers slid under the hem of my shirt, the warmth of his touch scorching against my skin.

The fire behind us was nothing compared to the heat between us.

I barely heard the cheers and whistles from the guys around us. It wasn't just a kiss. It was a declaration. And it was ours. Nothing else mattered at that moment.

Except for her.

Across the fire, Sherin was watching. She wasn't talking shit—not tonight. But I could see it in how she clenched her drink, her nails dug into the red Solo cup, and her mouth turned into a tight, bitter line.

She had had her chance with Kai. She had wanted him for years. But now? Now, he was mine. And I didn't need to gloat. I didn't need to smirk. Because the way Kai looked at me—like he owned me, like I owned him—said it all.

Let her seethe. Nea took a deep breath and centered herself as her mom had taught her. She realized she needed to block and eliminate this negative energy once and for all. She closed her eyes and wrapped herself in golden white light, impenetrable and unseen by anyone who couldn't *see* beyond what their eyes could see. In that instant, she could see the black tendrils of envy reaching out from Sherin. In one swift motion, she protected herself and asked her seméc, the wolf, to take this black energy to the sacred fire. It was done, and she would never be bothered by her again.

There were other people around, but the real tension hit me when I saw the familiar faces near the edge of the clearing. The NorKam boys—Baron Whitmore, Kyle Mason, Devin Something-Or-Other—guys I used to hang out with back when I lived in Kamloops. They were all part of the circle I ran with back when I'd been a kid in this town.

Back then, they had treated me like one of their own. I'd been one of the boys. We'd laughed together. Partied together. But now?

Now, I wasn't sure where I stood with them anymore.

They were watching Kai.

I frowned, instinctively moving closer to him, feeling that familiar feeling crawl up my spine. The unease. The way the air shifted when the past and present collided.

Kai caught the movement, his head turning just enough to glance at them. His face didn't change, but I could feel the shift in his energy. He knew something I didn't.

He knew what was coming.

I didn't.

Not yet.

CHAPTER 8

The NorKam Boys

The thing about high school friendships was that they were tight—until they weren't.

I used to be one of the NorKam crew, a part of their circle that had felt more like family than friends. I'd arrived in Kamloops in Grade 6, when my mom packed us up and left my dad behind. He'd been drunk too much, and things were ugly. Kamloops was where people kept their heads down, but the boys from the Kamloops Indian Band, we called KIB, made it feel like home. I had cousins on that rez, too, so it was natural that I ended up hanging out with them. They became my city brothers.

Baron, Kyle, Devin—hell, we were inseparable. We stuck together, protecting each other like a pack. It was something I had never expected to find, but I had. For all the differences in our backgrounds, we were all united in the sense of being outsiders in our ways. My mom worked long hours at the friendship centre, and I spent hours running the streets of Kamloops, picking up the pieces of my broken home.

I had always felt a bit jagged in the world, growing up partly in the city and on the rez and never quite belonging fully in either, but with them, I didn't feel like that. It was easy. We had a rhythm, and I was part of it.

But things changed when we moved back to Barriere in Grade 8. Sure, I spent the next few years driving back and forth to school in Kamloops, but it was never the same. Barriere was a small town, and the racism there wasn't subtle. It was there, lingering like a dark cloud. Kamloops felt different, slightly more progressive but racism still ran deep. The faces were a mix of cultures, and I didn't stick out as much. I could breathe.

When I was 16, everything started to shift. I bumped into Kai at a party in Barriere—the same place I'd known him since kindergarten. He'd always been trouble, always had that tough guy aura. I remembered how, in Grade 3, he tried to bully me by ramming me with his mountain bike. That was until I grabbed a stick and knocked him off the bike. We were cool after that, though. No hard feelings. But now? I couldn't ignore the heat between us, the way he'd pursued me relentlessly.

When the summer after Grade 11 hit, I returned to senior year at Barriere High. Things had changed. The dynamics had shifted, especially when Kai and I started spending more time together. We got closer, and the old crew from Kamloops? They had their opinions, and things got complicated fast.

"Nea, what the hell—"

Baron's voice cut through the noise of the party like a knife. I could hear his footsteps crunching over the gravel before I saw him. There he was, a beer in hand, his muscles bulging through his plain T-shirt. His eyes flicked between Kai and me, a mix of confusion and something else. Anger, maybe?

He looked good—like the Rez hockey player he was, solid and built to withstand whatever life threw his way. But with me? I thought we were just friends. He was like a brother to me.

Turns out, I had been wrong.

"I was wondering when you were gonna come say hi," I said, trying to keep my voice steady as I took a sip of cider, watching him carefully.

"Yeah, well," Baron muttered, jaw tightening, "didn't think I needed an introduction."

I felt Kai tense beside me, his body rigid, though he didn't say anything. But I could feel the heat rolling off him—the anger simmering beneath the surface. The kind of anger that said something bigger was at play.

Baron's eyes narrowed, and behind him, Kyle and Devin appeared. They looked like they had an agenda, their expressions hard, sizing Kai up like they were measuring how fast they could take him down. Their glances didn't land on me—they weren't looking at me. Not really. They were looking at him.

"I thought you were staying in Barriere," Baron said, his tone flat, like he was trying to reveal the truth in some roundabout way.

"I am back at the rez," I said, my heart pounding in my chest. I shrugged, playing it cool and pretending it didn't hurt. "Just back to hang with the old crew tonight."

The way Baron's gaze flicked to Kai again, the contempt barely concealed in his voice, made me feel like I had something to prove. "With him?"

That tone. It made my stomach twist. Like Kai was some fucking stray I'd just picked up off the side of the road.

Kai's smirk was colder, sharper than usual, and I felt the tension tighten in the air like a wire ready to snap.

Baron's jaw clenched. "You don't belong with this guy," he said softly, his voice almost… pleading. "He's not one of us."

The words hit harder than they should have. I blinked, fighting back the lump in my throat.

"'One of us?'" I repeated, trying to keep my voice steady. "What the hell does that even mean?"

Baron stood his ground, his face hardening. "You know what it means."

Yeah, I did. He wasn't native.

It meant they had already made up their minds. Kai wasn't part of their world. And because I had chosen him? I wasn't either.

I stepped forward, feeling Kai's body stiffen beside me, ready to step in at any moment. He muttered under his breath, his eyes narrowing.

"Get her outta here," he growled, low and dangerous.

Kyle laughed, but it wasn't a friendly sound. "That's cute," he sneered. "You think you're giving orders?"

And that was it. The energy shift was instant. Tension crackled in the air like dry wood about to catch fire.

Before I could react, Kyle swung at Kai, a move so fast I barely had time to blink. Kai dodged it; he'd been boxing with his dad since he learned how to walk, his movements like water flowing with the precision and speed of someone who knew how to fight. He returned with a right hook so fast that Kyle's head snapped to the side.

And then the chaos broke loose.

Baron lunged, his fists swinging, but Kai didn't drop. He absorbed the hit to his ribs with a grunt, partially blocking with his arms, then countered, hitting Devin square in the jaw. A second later, Kyle was back at him, and that's when the numbers were against Kai. Three against one. The boys from NorKam had no idea how far he was willing to go.

I screamed at them to stop, but no one listened. They were too deep in the moment, too lost in their rage and whatever they thought they had to prove.

But Kai wasn't just fast. He was faster than they expected. He ducked, swung, and took two of them down. One hit the ground, out cold.

"Nea, get to the truck!" Kai shouted over the noise.

I froze, then turned on my heels fast, having grown up around violence on the rez my whole life. Nothing phased me.

Kyle recovered, and before I could react, he lunged for me, grabbing my wrist with a force that made my heart skip.

That was the moment Kai lost it.

With one raw, primal motion, he ripped Kyle off me and slammed him into the side of a truck so hard the metal caved in, and for a split second, I was sure he'd broken something.

We were running fast to the truck before things got any worse. My heart pounded in my chest, but I didn't look back. The shouts from the NorKam boys faded into the night, the sound of tires spinning gravel filling the silence.

Kai's knuckles were split, blood dripping down his jeans, but he didn't care. He kept his focus straight ahead. I looked at him, my heart still racing, and he caught my gaze. His face softened, exhaustion lining his features, but something was in his eyes. Something that said we were both hanging by a thread.

"You okay?" he asked, his voice softer now, almost... tender.

I let out the breath I'd been holding. I was fine. The pressure burst, and we laughed, not believing the whole situation.

"Yeah. Oh my god, like, what the hell!"

Kai exhaled, shaking out his hands, his shoulders sagging slightly. "Guess we're not welcome on this rez anymore."

But that was the cost of choosing him.

And I couldn't help but wonder—if this was how things would be now, how far would we be willing to go to fight for what we had?

I didn't know the answer yet. But I was starting to think I wasn't ready to give up. Not on him. Not on us.

CHAPTER 9

The Calm Before the Storm

After the fight, we had to get Kai's dad's Harley back to Barriere. But even before we got to that, the night was already over. The adrenaline that had kept us running in those moments after the chaos had begun to wear off and reality had set in.

The NorKam boys had gotten their hands on the bike. They'd trashed it—kicked the gas tank in, ripped a mirror clean off, left deep scratches down the side, as though it wasn't just a piece of machinery but a symbol—a symbol they wanted to destroy.

Kai was pissed—not just because it was his dad's bike, but because he knew what was waiting for him when he got home. The storm that would rise from the aftermath of this.

I knew it, too. And there was shit I could do about it. The NorKam boys had drawn a line in the sand, and now it was clear—there was no going back.

The next morning, he showed up at the farm.

I knew the damage wasn't just physical from seeing him. His lip was split. His eye was swollen and half-shut, and bruises were already creeping up under his shirt collar, hinting at the battle he'd lost. The bike was bad, sure. But the real pain? That was the shit he wasn't showing. The emotional wreckage. The fact that Kai had never really been a part of anything. Not really. Not like this. Not like family.

He didn't say anything that morning. Not a word. He just walked into the kitchen, as if it were the most natural thing in the world, sat at the table, and started eating pancakes. Like he lived here. Like he'd always been a part of this family.

And that was it. He didn't go back home. Not to the wrecked bike.

At first, it was just a few nights on the couch. Kai had never had a home that he could settle into. His life had always been in flux—always moving, always running. And yet, here he was.

Then it turned into a week. Then, before I knew it, his boots were lined up next to River's by the door. And it wasn't just the boots. It was the quiet things. The way he'd sit at dinner and laugh at River's dumb jokes. He'd grin at Mom when she asked if he wanted seconds and give the same look he used to when he was at my place for a sleepover as a kid—genuine, unforced.

Mom never said a word. She didn't need to. She just set an extra plate at the table like it had always been there. She'd always had a way of making space for people. And now, somehow, it wasn't just me who felt at home. It was Kai, too.

Daddio didn't hesitate either. He put Kai to work right away. He showed him how to fix the tractor, mend the fencing, and care for the land—things I hadn't thought twice about. When you've spent your whole life on the farm, the way of life becomes second nature. But for Kai, it was new—a challenge.

River, though? River loved it. He loved having another guy around. It felt like they were cut from the same cloth—rough around the edges but able to throw jokes around like they were second nature. Working side by side, elbows bumping, teasing each other, throwing hands up in the air, shadow boxing over the engine rumble—Kai became a fixture in River's world just as much as he became one in mine.

I would sit for hours watching Kai and River sparring in our backyard, a punching bag set up hanging from one of the pine trees. They had an assortment of weapons, including nunchucks, and would spar with bo staffs as they started training in MMA, too. I picked up some, too, and trained for fun. Our lawn was the size of a football field. My Dad's pride and joy: when he wasn't on the tractor in the fields, he was on his rider's lawnmower, which I think was his secret other love aside from the tractor, he would be chewing on a blade of grass mowing around and round.

I could see the changes in Kai as the days went on. But it wasn't just the physical work that changed him. It was the way the farm worked on him.

He had been rough, stubborn, always running hot with an edge. But over the next few weeks, I started to see the Kai I hadn't known existed. His rough edges softened—not wholly, but enough to see that there was more to him than the hardened shell he'd worn for years. The anger, the defensiveness started to fade just a little.

He started laughing more, too. I joked with River, teasing Daddio when he'd try to teach him something, cracking-wise about how I talked while trying to explain something for the millionth time. The sarcasm and bravado didn't disappear, but it became something familiar. Something that felt like it belonged here.

And I realized as I watched him sitting there, laughing with River, that maybe this place had done what no one else could. Perhaps it had cracked open something inside of him. Maybe this farm—the simplicity of it, honesty, and the work it demanded—had given him the one thing he'd never had: stability.

And for the first time in my life, I felt like I had it, too.

But I wasn't stupid. I knew a storm was coming somewhere.

And it wasn't the NorKam boys this time.

It was Kai.

I never thought I'd see him with a schoolbook in his lap, but one afternoon, there he was. On my bed, sprawled out on his stomach, half-asleep over a history textbook. The guy who had never given a damn about the school, who always seemed to run from anything that tied him down—there he was, his eyes barely open, his mind still on the engine he'd been working on earlier.

"You're drooling," I teased, leaning against the doorframe, my arms crossed.

His eyes cracked open just enough for a single brow to lift in that familiar, lazy way. "I'd be drooling a lot more if you weren't making me read about dead white guys all night."

I laughed, stepping into the room and tossing a pillow at him. "Well, you wanna graduate or not?"

He groaned, rolling over onto his back and staring up at me like I was the one torturing him. "I dunno, Nea. Perhaps I should consider working full-time for my dad. Get away from all this"—he waved a hand vaguely at the book—"this shit."

"Kai," I said firmly, the softness in my voice slipping away.

He sighed, rubbing a hand through his hair. "Yeah, yeah, I know. You don't have to keep telling me."

But I could see it in his eyes. The pull between the life he had known—the one he was comfortable with—and the one offered to him here, with me, Mom and Daddio, with River. The life that made him show up every day, even when he didn't want to. The life that held promises he hadn't figured out yet.

I knew school wasn't his thing. He had that restless energy that didn't sit still for long and was better suited to engines and tools than classrooms. But I also knew he was smart. I knew he could be more than what everyone had always written him off as.

I leaned over, resting my chin on his shoulder, and whispered, "Come on. One more chapter, then I'll make you something to eat."

He turned his head slowly, looking at me with that intense gaze that had once made me nervous, but now, I could almost feel it from the inside. "You bribing me?" he asked, a sly smirk curling on his lips.

I smirked right back, but I felt the warmth in my chest. "Maybe."

Kai exhaled through his nose, and a slow, genuine smile crept onto his face. "Fine. One more chapter."

And maybe I had him wrapped around my finger.

The days stretched into weeks, and the farm became his safe place. A place where he didn't have to hide who he was. Where he didn't have to prove anything to anyone, he didn't have to keep fighting, keep defending himself. Here, he could just be. And little by little, I watched him change.

He wasn't perfect. He still had that raw edge to him. The anger simmered beneath the surface, but it wasn't all-consuming anymore. There were cracks in the wall. Cracks that I could see made me wonder if we could make it, maybe, we could make it.

And for a while, it felt like maybe this was forever. Like maybe I'd won. Maybe, just maybe, we could be okay.

But I knew better than to let myself believe in forever. I knew the storm would come for us. And when it did, we'd have to face it together.

I just wasn't sure we were ready.

CHAPTER 10

The Promise

The ring was simple.

A small silver band, not flashy or elaborate, but in my hand, it felt impossibly heavy. It was the kind of thing you'd find in a fancy jewelry store, polished to perfection, gleaming under bright lights. I wondered what mischief he got up to to afford it. This ring was the promise that could change everything—and maybe, just maybe, I was too young to fully understand what it meant.

Kai sat beside me in his truck, parked in our usual spot near the river. The moon spilled soft silver light over the water, turning the surface into a sheet of glimmering glass, rippling with the slightest breeze. The quiet hum of the world around us only made everything feel more real like time was holding its breath for the decision I was about to make.

His eyes were on me, the usual cocky confidence now replaced by something else—vulnerability, maybe? Nervousness. Seeing him so exposed was rare, but I could tell this moment meant something to him.

"I know we're young," he said, his voice quieter than usual. "I know it's fast. But Nea… I love you. I want this. I want you. I want to give you this promise."

I swallowed hard, staring down at the band in my palm. There it was—the question looming between us, unsaid for so long. Could I do this? Could I say yes to forever at seventeen, when the world was still so big and full of possibilities I hadn't even begun to touch yet?

I loved him. There was no doubt about that. I loved him with everything I had, in a way I had never loved anyone before. But future marriage? A promise like this, at this age? I felt it in my gut, a twisting, gnawing sensation that told me there was no going back once I said yes.

I had plans. I had a future. It wasn't just about me anymore. It was about us. And as much as I wanted to believe in forever, something in my chest told me that forever was much more complicated than it seemed.

Kai watched me carefully, the tension in his jaw betraying the hope—and the fear—that rode on my answer. I wasn't sure I could give him what he wanted. Not yet. But I also didn't want to break him.

For a long moment, I said nothing, my thumb running over the smooth edges of the ring, my heart pounding faster than I cared to admit. The silence stretched between us, the weight of the decision growing heavier by the second.

Finally, I forced a smile, slipping the ring onto my finger, feeling the cold metal settle against my skin like a quiet commitment, an unspoken promise of something I wasn't entirely sure I could keep.

"It's beautiful," I said softly, looking up at him with the best smile I could manage, even as my heart swirled uncertainly.

His body seemed to relax, and I saw the relief flood into his green eyes. The intensity there shifted from desperation to something softer, something more tender. "So… is that a yes?"

I bit my lip, staring at the ring again, turning it between my fingers. "It is; I'm hopeful for our future, although I think we're a bit young.'"

Kai's jaw tightened slightly at my words, a flicker of disappointment crossing his face. But it didn't last long. He nodded, slow and steady, like he understood the weight of my hesitation. Like he knew I needed time.

"For now," he murmured, reaching out with a hand that shook slightly, his thumb tracing the curve of my cheek as if grounding himself in the touch.

His eyes held something deeper than love, something I wasn't sure I was ready to understand. Something raw, something dangerous. And maybe that was the part of him that had always scared me—the part capable of loving with such intensity and fierceness that it could consume everything in its path if you weren't careful.

But at that moment, with his tender touch and intense gaze, I didn't want to think about the consequences. I didn't want to analyze it.

I just wanted to be with him.

When he kissed me, all the noise in my head quieted. The world—our pasts, futures, doubts, and fears—faded away. It was just him and me, the feeling of his lips on mine, the warmth of his breath against my skin, and how he held me like he never wanted to let go.

In that kiss, I forgot everything else.

And maybe that was the most dangerous part of it all.

Kai had always been a storm in my life. Even back in Barriere, when we were just kids, something about him made you either want to run for cover or be swept up. His reckless energy, unpredictability, and how he challenged everything I thought I knew about myself. He had always been an undeniable force, even when we were too young to grasp what it meant fully.

I had watched him fight and fall apart, and I'd seen him start to rebuild himself in ways he hadn't thought possible. He was like the river next to us—wild, untamed, unpredictable, but still there, carving its path, no matter how rough the terrain. I was starting to see him not just as the guy whose past had broken, but as someone learning to be whole, piece by piece.

But I also knew that sometimes, you could love someone so much, it could swallow you whole. I had seen how he loved me and how his eyes darkened when he thought about the future. It was intense. It was fierce. And sometimes, it was too much for me to handle.

I wasn't sure if I was ready for that kind of love. The kind that came with no guarantees, no promises that it wouldn't break me.

But what I did know—what I could feel in the pit of my stomach—was that I couldn't walk away from him. Not now, not after everything. Not after all we had been through.

So, I said yes. And in that moment, with the river winding quietly beside us, and the world sleeping in the moonlight, I let myself believe that maybe we could be enough for each other. Maybe this was the promise we both needed, even if we weren't sure what it meant.

Maybe, for once, we could be something real.

But I couldn't ignore the feeling deep in my gut—the one that whispered that all promises came with consequences.

CHAPTER 11

The Heat Before the Fall

We didn't make it home that night.

Instead, we found ourselves in the back of his truck, blankets tangled around us, the rhythmic rush of the river beside us. His Dad had given him his old grey Pathfinder the year before and we spent much time in that truck. The air was thick with the scent of wet earth, the distant hum of crickets and frogs and the occasional rustle of leaves in the wind. It was one of those perfect summer nights that make you forget about everything else—about the world outside, about the questions you're too scared to ask.

But for us, it wasn't just about the night.

It was about what was happening between us.

Kai had always been hungry for me, his touch like a fire, a heat that seemed to come from a place deeper than desire. But tonight, it was different. It was desperate. Like he was trying to hold onto something slipping away. Like he was afraid of losing me, afraid of something neither of us could name but both of us could feel.

His hands were rough but gentle as they slid under my shirt, tracing fire lines across my skin. He kissed my neck and the tender flesh of my shoulders. There was something in the way he touched me, like he was trying to memorize every inch of me, like he needed to prove that I was real, that I was his.

"Tell me you're mine," he murmured against my throat, his voice hoarse, almost pleading.

I could feel his raw need, tremble in his fingers, the intensity of his gaze. I had never seen him like this—vulnerable, desperate, full of something I wasn't sure how to respond to.

"I'm yours," I whispered, my voice unsteady, as much a promise to him as a plea to myself. I needed to believe it, too.

His breath hitched, like he needed to hear it as much as I needed to say it. In that moment, I realized how much of him was tied to me, how much he had wrapped himself around me, and how much of me was already tangled in his life.

Fingers tangled in hair, lips grazing sensitive skin, bodies pressed so close it felt like we could become one person—like there was no me without him, no him without me.

He kissed me like he was trying to carve his name into my bones, like he needed to leave something permanent, something that couldn't be erased. And I let him. Because at that moment—he was everything.

He was all I had ever wanted.

I felt it in every breath, touch, and kiss that felt like it could burn us alive. We had been inseparable for weeks. Our days filled with love and passion, heated arguments ended in clothes strewn across the floor and limbs tangled in sweaty sheets. It was intense, unstoppable. The kind of love you never question because it feels unbreakable, like it was meant to be.

But nothing is ever unbreakable.

The world felt perfect as we lay there, bodies tangled in blankets. It felt like the promise of something lasting. But deep inside, I knew the truth. Life wasn't so kind to love, not to the kind that burned this hot.

I had learned that much already.

And then everything changed.

His Dad got sick.

It happened fast. Too fast. Like a storm rolling in, dark and violent. One day, his dad was just fine—drinking beers in his garage, cracking jokes, acting like he always did. And the next? He couldn't get out of bed without gasping for air. He'd been to the doctor, gotten the tests. They hadn't found anything at first, but then… it was too late.

I watched it happen, watched Kai's world tilt on its axis.

It was like the ground disappeared beneath him. His anger started to twist into something darker, something more reckless. The boy who used to laugh at everything, tease me in the middle of an argument and then pull me close with a grin, was disappearing, piece by piece.

Now he was restless. He couldn't stay still. He couldn't sleep. He couldn't focus.

And slowly, he started to slip away from me.

It was subtle at first. A quiet distance that I couldn't quite put my finger on. He'd get in the truck and drive off without a word, the engine rumbling in the quiet night, and I'd wait for him to return.

When he did, he'd be different. Tired. Hollow. And sometimes, when he looked at me, there was this emptiness in his eyes. Like he wasn't seeing me anymore.

I was used to Kai being tough, but this was different. This wasn't something he could fight off with his fists or with his usual cocky grin. This was something deeper that had gotten under his skin and wouldn't let go. And the worst part was, I didn't know how to fix it.

I didn't know how to fix him.

I knew what he needed. He needed space. He needed time to deal with everything happening with his dad, with the world falling apart. But at the same time, I didn't want to lose him. I didn't want him to pull away and leave me with nothing but the memory of the boy who used to hold me like I was the only thing that mattered.

We had talked about it once, when I tried to ask him what was happening. He had pulled away, his jaw clenched tight, his voice cold. "I can't do this right now, Nea. You wouldn't understand."

I had understood more than he knew.

But I couldn't make him see that.

And so, I watched him go. Slowly, quietly. The boy I loved slipping through my fingers, piece by piece. All I had left was the memory of his kiss, the way he held me like I was the centre of his world, and the sound of his voice when he said, "I'm yours."

He didn't feel like mine anymore. If anything, he was starting to feel like a ghost.

And I was starting to realize—sometimes, even the hottest fires burn out. Sometimes, all the passion in the world can't save you when everything starts to fall apart.

And everything was starting to fall apart.

CHAPTER 12

Prom Night

P rom night. It was a night that everyone talked about for months—so many whispered promises of magic, memories, and love. And yet, for all the anticipation, there was a tension in the air, a sense of something lingering between us, unspoken. It should have been a celebration night, wrapping up everything we had worked for and looking ahead to the future. Still, in the pit of my stomach, I knew this night would be different. The weight of decisions yet to be made, of things I wasn't ready to face, hovered over me like an uninvited guest.

I had never been one for extravagant dresses. But this night? Mom had insisted. We drove the three hours to Vancouver, the city sprawling beneath us in long stretches of glass towers and neon-lit streets as we crossed the Port Mann bridge on our way downtown. The air was thick with the smell of rain, salt, and asphalt—so foreign to me after the crisp mountain air of home. It felt like a different world.

Mom had saved up for this moment and insisted I find something beautiful, something unforgettable. She'd dragged me through a dozen stores, watching me roll my eyes at fluffy pink tulle and sequin-covered bodices before I finally found it. A red satin dress. Strapless, with a sweetheart neckline that dipped just enough to make me feel dangerous yet undeniably feminine. The dress clung to my body, pooling at my feet like liquid fire, sleek and sensual. It was unlike anything I'd ever worn—sexy, grown-up, a woman's dress, no longer a girl.

When I stepped out of the dressing room, Mom's eyes welled up with tears. She didn't speak at first, just pressed her hand to her chest, eyes wide. "Wusnea, you look…" She paused, choked up. "You look like a goddess."

That was it. The dress was mine, and I knew it. The love and pride in her voice and her eyes was enough. It was everything.

The week before prom passed in a blur—final exams, whispered gossip in the halls, and the constant anticipation of the night soon to come. The dress hung in my closet, wrapped carefully in plastic, waiting. Kai had barely let me breathe about it, pestering me for details, for clues, but I refused to share. He would see it when the time was right.

The night arrived, and as I stood before the mirror, I almost didn't recognize the girl staring back at me. My skin glowed, my long hair curled in glossy waves over my shoulders. The red satin sculpted every curve of my slender body, and I felt powerful. Confident. For the first time in what felt like forever, I felt like I was exactly who I was supposed to be.

I heard the rumble of Kai's truck pull up the drive, headlights cutting through the dusk. I took a deep breath, then stepped outside.

There he was. Tall, broad in his black suit, tie loose around his throat, like he already wanted to rip it off. When his eyes found me, he froze, jaw slack. I couldn't help but smile.

"H—holy shit," he stammered, eyes wide. "You look... damn, Nea."

I smirked, my pulse quickening. "Good?"

"Good?" He shook his head, then let out a low whistle. "Good doesn't even begin to cover it."

He reached for my hand, kissing my knuckles, his lips warm against my skin. "You ready for this?" he asked, his voice soft, as if asking for permission.

I nodded, my heart pounding in my chest. "Let's go."

The gym had been transformed for prom—fairy lights twinkled in every corner, and silk-draped tables lined the walls, casting a soft glow. The music swelled around us, a slow country song that swirled through the air like a shared secret. Couples filled the dance floor, their bodies swaying together, moving in sync as if they'd been dancing their whole lives. Kai and I wove through the crowd, hands linked tightly together. The eyes of the school were on us, but tonight, it didn't bother me. Tonight, I felt powerful, like I was the one turning heads.

We danced slowly, close. My arms wrapped around his neck, my cheek pressed against his, his hands tracing slow, deliberate circles on my waist. In that moment, everything else—the weight of everything—seemed to fade away. The mine. The fights. The unspoken fears about the future. It was just us. Just this.

"I'm gonna remember this," Kai murmured, his lips grazing my ear. "You, in that dress. Forever."

I smiled, warmth flooding me as his words settled over me like a blanket. "Me too."

The night stretched in a golden blur, the music swelling and dipping, punctuated by laughter and stolen kisses in the shadows of the dance floor. The promise of something endless hung in the air, an unspoken vow in how Kai held me and I leaned into him. It was everything I had ever dreamed of and more.

But deep down, a quiet part of me couldn't shake the thought that maybe it wasn't forever. Not yet.

I loved him. God, I loved him more than I had ever thought possible. But the thought of being bound to him—of making that decision, of locking myself into a future I wasn't sure I was ready for—felt suffocating.

And that's when it happened.

Later in the evening, Kai pulled me aside, away from the music and the crowd. His eyes were serious, his voice lower than usual, full of emotion. "Nea," he began, and I could see the hesitation in his eyes. "I want more. I'm ready for more. I'm ready for us. I want this to be… forever."

My heart raced, my mind swirled with emotion. I knew what was coming, and yet I wasn't prepared. Kai dropped to one knee, and the world seemed to stop. The music faded into a muffled hum in the background, my pulse hammering in my ears.

"Will you marry me, Nea?" His voice cracked, a rawness there I hadn't heard before.

I stared at him, my heart twisting. It was everything I had ever dreamed of. It should have been everything I wanted. And yet, in that moment, something inside me recoiled. The weight of the future crashed on me, the pressure of a commitment that felt like it would change everything.

I wasn't ready.

"Let's talk about this later," I whispered, my voice barely above a breath, trying to mask the panic swirling in my chest.

Kai's smile faltered, his brow furrowing as he stood. "Nea, I—"

"I'm sorry," I interrupted softly, my throat tight. "I just… I need time."

He nodded, his face falling ever so slightly, but he understood. His shoulders slumped, and for a moment, the energy around us felt heavier and colder.

"I get it," he said quietly. "We'll talk. Later."

But as we rejoined the others, a knot formed in my stomach. I had left something unsaid, something that felt critical, something that hung between us like an invisible thread. The night that should have been perfect was now marked by uncertainty, by an unanswered question that I couldn't escape.

CHAPTER 13

Graduation

Graduation day was like a storm cloud on the horizon—dark, looming, but somehow inevitable. The sun shone brightly, a perfect spring day that made the world seem full of promise. And yet, as I stood in front of the mirror, adjusting my cap and gown, I felt a heaviness settle in my chest. I had worked so hard to get here, to cross this finish line, but an undercurrent of something else tempered the excitement of the moment. Something I couldn't quite put my finger on.

Kai was standing beside me, as always. He looked at me with that soft smile he always gave when he was proud of me—his green eyes sparkling with that familiar warmth. But there was something different in how he held himself, an almost imperceptible distance, as though he knew the same thing I did. Things were changing. We were changing.

I couldn't ignore the feeling that this was the end of something, not just the end of high school but the end of a version of me shaped by all the memories and experiences I'd shared with him. I was no longer the naive girl I had been when I first entered this school. I'd learned so much over the past few years—about love, loss, betrayal, and growth—and I had become a different person with each lesson. Stronger. More independent. I am more aware of my own needs.

The idea of staying with Kai forever—of locking myself into something that had once seemed so clear-cut—wasn't as simple as before. It wasn't just about him anymore. It was about me. About what I wanted for my future, about the direction I was heading. And my direction didn't seem to align with his anymore. Or maybe it was that I had outgrown what we once were.

As I walked across the stage to receive my diploma, I tried to shake off the feeling, my heart pounding and thoughts tangled. The applause from the crowd was distant in my ears as I met Kai's eyes in the stands. His proud smile should have filled me with joy, but I felt a strange, bittersweet pang in my chest. Something was missing. Something had shifted between us, and neither had the words to articulate it.

I stepped off the stage, my legs shaky beneath me, and as I found Kai in the crowd, the look he gave me said it all. He was proud of me, but there was also an unspoken sadness in his gaze. We both knew this wasn't just a graduation. This marked the beginning of a new chapter, and we had no idea what it would hold.

After the ceremony, we found a quiet spot by the bleachers, away from the buzz of excited families and friends. In the silence between us, it was there that the conversation I had been avoiding finally happened. Kai took a deep breath, running his hand through his hair, his eyes darting away from mine as though searching for the right words.

"I think we need to talk about the future," he said, his voice steady but laced with an undertone of nervousness. "After everything we've been through, I still want us to move forward together. I want to take the next step, whatever that looks like. I still want you, Nea."

My heart twisted at his words. I loved him. God, I did. But at that moment, I couldn't bring myself to say the words he was desperately waiting for. I wasn't sure what I wanted anymore. I wasn't sure that "forever" was what I needed.

"I don't know," I murmured, my throat tight as I forced the words out. "I'm unsure if we're on the same path anymore, Kai. You're heading to the oil patch, and I'm… I don't even know what I'm doing yet maybe just going to college in Kamloops. I just feel like everything is changing. I'm changing."

Kai's face faltered, his lips pressing into a thin line as he looked at me, really looked at me, for the first time in a long time. His hands clenched at his sides, the same nervous energy I had felt earlier radiating off of him.

"I get it," he said quietly, his voice heavy with something I couldn't quite name. "I just… I don't want to lose you. But I can't hold onto something that's slipping away, Nea. I can't."

The pain in his eyes mirrored my own, and in that moment, I realized how much we had both changed. How much we had grown apart, even though we hadn't intended to. We were no longer the same people who had fallen in love in the quiet spaces of our little town, on the farm, in the back of his truck. We had grown into different versions of ourselves, which weren't always compatible.

"I don't want to lose you either," I said, my voice shaking as I touched his arm. "But I can't promise anything right now. Not when I don't know what I want. Not when I'm still figuring things out. I'll still see you when your back home, I'm not leaving."

There was a long silence between us, the weight of our unspoken words settling in the shared space. Kai nodded slowly, his lips twitching as if he wanted to say more but couldn't. Instead, he pulled me into a tight hug, holding me close, his warmth grounding me in a way that made me want to hold on forever.

"I just want you to be happy," he whispered, his voice muffled against my hair. "I'll figure it out, Nea. I always do."

I closed my eyes, taking a deep breath, trying to steady the whirlwind of emotions inside me. I loved him, but I wasn't sure what kind of future we could have if we couldn't find our way back to each other.

As we pulled apart, I looked up at him, seeing the same uncertainty mirrored in his eyes. "Maybe we just need some time," I said softly. "Time to figure things out."

Kai didn't argue. He nodded, his hand brushing against mine in a gesture that felt both familiar and strange. "Yeah. Time."

As we stood there, surrounded by the noise of the world moving around us, I couldn't help but feel like the world was on the verge of shifting again. And this time, I wasn't sure where it would take me.

CHAPTER 14

The Mine & The Fight for Eagle Ridge

The first time I stood at the top of Eagle Ridge, I felt it in my bones. There was something raw and ancient about that place, something that made the hairs on the back of my neck stand up. This land wasn't just land—it was breathing. The wind moved through the cedar trees like a whisper from the ancestors, carrying ancient voices on the breeze, reminding me of the people who had walked this earth before us. The river below sang a song older than any of us, its rhythm the land's heartbeat.

But now? Now, they wanted to tear it apart.

I could feel it coming. The tension. The quiet invasion. QwikGold Corp., a mining company with more money than morals, had been sniffing around our land for years. But now, they weren't just sniffing. They were moving in, getting closer. And every step they took brought them closer to something I couldn't allow them to have.

The land was sacred. It wasn't just dirt and rock. It was our history, our identity. The stories of our people were woven into the soil and passed down through generations. The thought of that land being destroyed, of the river being poisoned, of the sacred mountains being gutted made my stomach churn with rage.

And the worst part? My damn brother, Billy, was in on it. He was sitting there, shaking hands with the men planning to rip our home apart. Seeing him do this was like a knife twisting in my gut. Billy had always been the one to bend under pressure. The one who wanted to fit in with the world that didn't care about our people. But this? This was a betrayal I couldn't swallow.

Another community meeting and charade. The so-called representatives of QwikGold stood before us, their pressed suits glistening under the harsh fluorescent lights, spewing their empty promises about 'economic growth' and 'opportunity.' The words sounded like music to the ears of anyone desperate enough to listen, but I knew the truth. They were here to steal what wasn't theirs. They were here to destroy everything we had fought to protect for generations.

"Economic growth?" I spat under my breath, sitting in the back of the room, arms crossed. "Economic growth doesn't look like a poisoned river or dead mountains."

The men in suits didn't see it. They couldn't see it. They saw nothing but dollar signs. They saw nothing but profits. And Billy? Billy saw his future. A future filled with money. A future that was slipping away from our people. A future was built on our ancestors' backs, and he was willing to sell them out for a fat paycheck.

After the meeting, I couldn't hold back anymore. My heart was racing, adrenaline pounding in my veins as I spotted Billy standing outside, talking to one of the investors, smiling like he'd just signed his life away. I stormed up to him, my chest tight, my words sharp as I pulled him aside.

"You're seriously siding with them?" I hissed, the anger in my voice raw.

Billy sighed, rubbing the bridge of his nose, trying to avoid my gaze. "Nea, don't start."

"Oh, I'm just getting warmed up," I snapped, my fists clenching at my sides. "You're gonna destroy everything our people fought for. All of it—gone, for what? A few hundred thousand bucks? You think that's worth it?"

His jaw tightened, but he wouldn't meet my eyes. He knew he was wrong. He had to know. But the greed, the ambition—he was lost in it. He didn't see what was in front of him, didn't see the destruction that would follow.

"Look, you don't get it—" he began, but I wasn't.

"I don't get it?" I interrupted, my voice rising. "I grew up here, Billy! This is my home! Our home! Do you think white men's money makes up for what they'll take from us? What they'll take from our kids? From our grandchildren?"

Billy opened his mouth, but no words came out. His silence was all I needed to hear. He wasn't sorry. He wasn't ashamed. He had sold his soul to the highest bidder, and I could see it in how he stood there, posture slouched, defeated before the world even had a chance to break him.

I shook my head in disgust, the words burning in my throat. "You sold your soul, Billy."

I watched him flinch, the guilt hitting him in the chest. But it was too late. The betrayal was done. He couldn't take it back. Not now.

And in that moment, I swore to myself—no matter the cost—I would fight for this land. I would fight for everything we had lost and were about to lose. I couldn't let them destroy it, couldn't let them take it from us. Not without a fight. Even if that fight meant going up against my brother.

It wasn't just about the land. It was about honor. It was about remembering our ancestors who had walked this land with pride. It was about our people, culture, and everything that made us who we were. I had no choice.

The company was already encroaching. I had seen the surveyors near the ridge, their flags marking out boundaries, their equipment sitting like vultures in the distance, waiting for permission to tear it down. And Billy? He was too busy counting his money to see the destruction he was helping bring about.

I turned my back on him, feeling the weight of everything crash down on me. The fight was beginning, and I was ready. I had no idea how long it would take or how much it would cost me, but I knew one thing: I would stand between QwikGold and Eagle Ridge, no matter what. I would fight for the land. I would fight for my people. And if it meant fighting my blood, then so be it.

Billy wasn't the only one who had to choose a side. This was my fight, and I wouldn't let anyone forget it.

CHAPTER 15

The First Kevin Fight

The Whispered Warnings

It started in the weight room at the gym.

"He's on something," a guy told River. *"You seen him lately? He's fucking huge. No way he got like that naturally."*

SteroIds.

Then, at a house party, I overheard a couple of girls whispering to each other.

"Kai was wired last night. Like, wired wired."

"Yeah, I heard he's been doing coke."

"I believe it. He's not just drinking anymore; you can see it in his eyes. Dude's losing it."

I didn't want to believe it.

Kai had always been reckless, but drugs? That wasn't him.

At least, it didn't used to be.

However, I then began watching more closely.

The weight gain. The mood swings. The way his hands clenched into fists for no reason. The hollow look in his eyes when he wasn't drinking.

The explosive anger.

And I realized…

Maybe the Kai I knew wasn't there anymore.

Maybe he had been gone for a long time.

The Death That Broke Kai

His father was dying.

The man who had beaten him. Broken him and made him feel small. The same man he had spent his entire life trying to make proud.

I had seen the shift in Kai when his dad first got sick.

The way he carried the weight of it like a stone in his chest. The anger. The denial. The desperation to pretend everything was normal.

But cancer doesn't give you the luxury of denial.

It takes its time. It devours piece by piece.

And Kai had to watch it all.

Every ounce of strength that had once made his father invincible was stripped away. The strong, angry, cruel man who had ruled Kai's life was reduced to something fragile, something helpless.

Kai didn't know how to handle it.

So he didn't.

Instead, he numbed himself in the only ways he knew how.

Kai was burning himself down to the ground.

Every night, he was in some bar. Some girl's bed. Some fight.

He was reckless. Unhinged.

And the worst part?

He didn't care.

The drinking was one thing. The fighting was another. But the women—there were so many.

I lost count.

Friends of mine. Strangers. Girls from our high school. Girls from the rez. Girls from the city.

He fucked them all.

And if he thought for even one second, it would hurt me?

He made damn sure I knew about it.

It was never about love. It was never even about sex.

It was about power. Control.

Kai couldn't control losing me.

He couldn't control losing his father.

So he tried to control the only thing he could—his pain.

He tried to bury it in warm bodies and cheap beer.

But no matter how much he drank, no matter how many women he touched, it didn't work.

He was still angry.

Still empty.

Still broken.

Kai wasn't the same guy I'd known; the reckless energy that had always lurked beneath the surface was now bursting out of him in waves.

It was like everything was too much for him to handle—too much pressure, too many feelings, too much of the past that never seemed to leave him alone.

He'd always been restless, always had that fire in him. But now? Now, it felt different. Unpredictable. Dark. Like he was looking for something he couldn't name to fill the hole growing inside him for months.

And the alcohol? It only made it worse. His temper was shorter, his words sharper. We'd fought more times in the last couple of weeks than in the past year and a half combined.

But no matter what, I kept hoping that he'd come back to me, the guy who'd laughed and joked, who made me feel safe in his arms. But I was starting to wonder if I'd ever get him back.

And then came Kevin.

It was supposed to be a simple party, one of those nights where we got together with people we'd known forever, swapped stories, laughed at bad jokes, and drank too much.

Kamloops was a town that never felt like home, not like the farm, but it was fine; it was familiar. And Kevin was someone I'd known for years—he'd been in Barriere since we were kids.

He was always friendly and easy to talk to, and tonight, I found myself chatting with him over a drink like it was nothing more than catching up with an old friend.

I hadn't even thought about it when I smiled at Kevin; I hadn't thought about the way it might look. But I guess Kai had. Because the moment he saw it, the shift in him was instant. He was home from his stitch in the oil patch for the week.

"What the fuck was that?" Kai's voice was low, almost a growl.

I turned, frowning, but his glare was already burning into me. "What?"

His jaw was clenched so tight I could see the muscle ticking in his cheek, the way his body tensed like a coiled spring, ready to snap.

"Don't play dumb, Nea." His hands curled into fists, the tension in his arms visible even from a distance. "You think I didn't see you?"

I blinked, confused. "Kai, I talked to Kevin for two minutes. That's it."

His eyes narrowed, darkening with something I didn't recognize. "Yeah? You think I'm fucking stupid?" His voice was a dangerous mix of hurt and rage, and it hit me like a slap.

I hated it. The way he was twisting something so simple into something ugly, the way he was looking at me—not like I was his girl, but like I was a threat. Something to break, something to control. And the worst part? I was becoming so tired of it.

"Kai, you're drunk," I said, trying to keep my voice calm, but the pounding in my chest was almost deafening. I didn't know what was happening, but it was clear that Kai wasn't thinking straight.

And then, just like that, he stepped closer, and his fist slammed into the wall beside my head with enough force to rattle the pictures on the wall. The sound was deafening, and my heart skipped in my chest. I flinched, my body frozen in place, the hairs on the back of my neck standing up.

He'd never hit me before.

But for the first time, I wasn't sure if he would stop himself.

I swallowed hard, trying to push past the shock and the fear. "I'm leaving," I said, my voice trembling. The words felt too small, too weak for the situation.

I wasn't just leaving the party—I was leaving Kai, leaving this version of him that felt so foreign.

I turned toward the door, desperate to escape the suffocating heat of the room. Still, before I could make it, I felt his hand wrap around my arm hard, pulling me back, yanking my side and shoulder painfully. His fingers bruised my side, and the sharpness of it made me wince. And this wasn't the first time; I just had enough.

"Nea—" Kai's voice cracked, a mix of anger and something else. Hurt? Regret? I didn't know anymore.

I didn't think. My hand moved before my brain could process what I was doing, and the slap echoed through the room like a gunshot, sharp and clean. I saw the shock in his eyes, the way his face flinched as though I'd struck him physically. For a moment, neither of us moved.

He stared at me, stunned as if he couldn't believe what had happened. And then, the distance between us that had been creeping in for weeks felt like an entire chasm. He took a step back, the surprise in his eyes giving way to something darker, something unfamiliar.

And then, I ran.

I didn't know where to go, but I had to leave. I needed to breathe. I needed to put space between me and the whirlwind of emotions that had just torn through the air. I couldn't think, couldn't process what had just happened.

But one thing was clear: things had changed. The guy I'd loved—trusted—was slipping away, and I didn't know if I could hold on long enough to pull him back.

The laughter and music felt like an alien world as I walked through the party to the door. I couldn't focus on anything but the pounding in my chest and the sick feeling twisting in my stomach. I didn't know what Kai and I were anymore. I didn't know if I could save him. Or if I could save myself from whatever was happening to us.

And I couldn't shake the feeling that this was only the beginning. It was the beginning of something bigger, something darker, and I wasn't sure either of us was ready for it.

CHAPTER 16

Kai The Downward Spiral

Kai tried to apologize. He tried, over and over again, like words could glue us back together. But every time he said, *I'm sorry*, my chest tightened with something that wasn't forgiveness. It wasn't even anger. It was a kind of emptiness that settled into my bones, a feeling I hadn't had when we first met. The easy, confident, passionate love we shared had frayed at the edges until all that remained was a thin thread, too fragile to hold onto. He would look at me, his eyes filled with regret, his hands reaching for mine, but it was never enough. And it would never be enough.

Because something had broken inside of me.

When he grabbed me that night in the bar, I'd felt it more clearly than I ever had before: the final shift in the balance between us. The love, fire, and passion that had once been so consuming and absolute was no longer a certainty. It was a shadow—a distortion of what we used to have. The arguments, the fights, the alcohol-soaked nights that had turned from passionate to toxic had already begun to crack the foundation of everything. And I couldn't keep pretending it would be okay. I waited anxiously for the next bout of anger, a push against the wall, shaking me so hard I thought my teeth would fall out for disagreeing with him. It had gotten to the point when he reached out I braced not sure what was next.

"I love you," he would say, and I would nod, because what else was there to say? *I love you*—but not enough anymore. Not enough to stay, not enough to put myself through this pain again.

The Bar Fight

The night had been an escape—a brief reprieve from the weight of everything. I had started college in Kamloops, unsure of what I was studying. Still, I was taking everything that interested me in the social sciences. College life was overwhelming—new faces, new experiences, new expectations. The pressure was suffocating sometimes, but I felt lighter with friends beside me, old and new. The loud beats of the club pulsed through my body, and the neon lights bounced off the sweaty, smiling faces around us. I wasn't thinking about Kai. Not really. For the first time in what felt like forever, I was just... me.

Kevin was different. There was a calm in him that I couldn't quite explain. We hadn't talked about *us*, not really. But there was something easy between us. He wasn't complicated. He didn't drink to escape the ghosts of his past or shout until his voice cracked. He didn't push people away with the same ferocity that Kai did. And I never had to worry that I was safe with Kevin. It was like breathing in and out with Kevin, steady and sure.

The shot he bought me was warm against my throat, the bitterness of it softened by the humor in his eyes as we toasted to nothing in particular.

"To escape the past," I joked, my voice light.

"To the future," Kevin added, a grin tugging at the corner of his mouth.

The warmth of the liquor spread through my chest, momentarily making everything else fade into the background. But the moment didn't last.

I felt it before I saw it—that sick, heavy feeling in the pit of my stomach. The hairs on the back of my neck stood up. And then, there he was. Kai.

I didn't need to look up; I could feel the shift in the air like the temperature had dropped ten degrees, like a storm cloud had moved into the room. I didn't want to look. I didn't want to deal with him tonight, not like this.

But when his eyes locked onto mine, the world narrowed to the two of us. His gaze flicked briefly to Kevin, and the tension in his shoulders spoke volumes. His jaw clenched, hands balled into fists at his sides.

I exhaled, already bracing myself.

"Ignore him," Kevin whispered, trying to keep his voice low.

I nodded, but it didn't matter. Kai was already walking toward us, cutting through the crowd like a predator zeroing in on its prey. Tall, green eyes flashing in a tank top and jeans, his Harley boots and arms were massive, twice the size I remembered, and flexed. He looked angry.

"What the fuck is this?" Kai's voice was slurred, thick with booze, his eyes glassy and something darker I couldn't name.

I tried to stay calm and tried to keep my voice steady. "Not tonight, Kai."

"Not tonight?" he repeated, mocking me like he couldn't believe it. "You mean, not ever again, right? That's the game now? You erase me and move on like I never existed?"

I winced at his words, and the hurt in them twisted something inside me. But I had no words left.

Kevin turned to face him, his face hardening. "Back off, man."

Kai's sneer was savage. "Oh, I see how it is. You think you're her fucking hero now?" His voice was bitter, venomous. "You're nothing, bro. She's just using you to get over me."

Kevin's muscles tensed, and I could feel the shift in him—he was ready to defend me, prepared to do what needed to be done, but I wasn't sure I wanted that. I wasn't sure I wanted him to fight. Kevin, the starting lacrosse player at the university, was a head shorter than Kai but just as big and muscular. He had dirty blonde hair and hazel eyes with green and yellow hues. The two looked like cousins, but their anger was like a storm.

"Fuck you," Kevin said, his voice a low growl.

And just like that, everything broke.

Kai lunged, fists flying in a blur of aggression. The sound of flesh hitting flesh was loud and violent. People screamed. Chairs scraped across the floor as the chaos spilled out. The bouncers were too slow to react, and before I knew it, the bar had turned into a battleground.

I didn't know who landed the first punch, but it didn't matter. It wasn't about Kevin anymore. It was about something primal. Something deep inside of Kai that was clawing its way out.

Kai wasn't fighting to win. He was fighting to destroy.

And that's when I saw it. His eyes locked on mine, and the rage there—the hate, the desperation—was something I hadn't seen before. It wasn't just about me being with someone else. It was something deeper, something consuming him. And the look in his eyes… was like he was accusing me. *You did this to me.*

Before I could react, Kai was on me.

His hands were around my throat.

The pressure was immediate. Intense. His fingers dug into my skin like claws, and I couldn't breathe. I gasped, my lungs desperately searching for air but nothing. The world around me blurred, and I couldn't think or move. His hands tightened, squeezing the life out of me.

The lights in the bar flickered, and the sounds of shouts and chaos became muffled and distant. The last thing I remembered before everything went black was the frantic sirens blaring from outside, the bouncers running over, and the last shred of oxygen leaving my lungs.

I couldn't escape. I couldn't get away from him.

And when the darkness finally took me, I couldn't tell if it was an end or just the beginning of something worse.

CHAPTER 17

The Fallout

"When I woke up in that hospital bed, I knew my life was split into two timelines—before the bar fight and after. Before, I had clung to Kai, to love, to the idea that we could fix each other. After, I understood that some things are dead inside me. That love wasn't enough to save someone who didn't want to be saved."

The sterile antiseptic smell filled my lungs before I even opened my eyes. It was suffocating, a cold reminder of the hospital's clinical environment. The beep of a heart monitor punctuated the stillness, steady and rhythmic, like a reminder that I was still alive.

I blinked against the harsh fluorescent light above me, feeling my head throb in sharp pulses with each blink. My throat burned, each swallow sending a wave of pain across my body. Then, it all rushed back to me in an overwhelming flood.

Kai. The bar. His hands. Around my throat. The pressure. The fear. The panic.

I shot up in bed, gasping, a sharp, strangled cry escaping from my bruised throat. The pain in my skull hit me like a truck, and I slumped back down, my hand clutching my head as I fought to breathe. My eyes were blood red from the oxygen that couldn't reach my lungs.

A warm, steady hand pressed gently to my arm.

"Nea, it's okay, you're safe."

I turned toward the voice. River.

He was sitting next to me, his posture tense, his face a mask of fury, and something deeper—something unfamiliar to me. His knuckles were raw and scraped, like he had been hitting something—no, someone. And I wasn't sure if I was relieved or terrified.

I blinked again, clearing the fog in my mind, my throat dry and aching. "Where—?" I whispered, my voice hoarse.

"They took him." River's voice was tight, a low growl beneath the calm. "The cops arrested him outside the club. He's in jail."

My chest tightened at the thought. I wanted to say something—wanted to cry, scream, or even laugh, because it all felt so surreal—but the words wouldn't come.

"Arrested?" I croaked, my voice rasping. I tried to swallow, but the motion felt like I was scraping against glass.

"Aggravated assault," River continued, his eyes dark with fury, "and probably attempted murder."

Attempted murder.

I couldn't wrap my head around it. It was like my body had frozen in place, every part of me numb to the reality of it. *Kai*. My *Kai*.

I swallowed, trying to process the words, but they tasted like ash in my mouth. A bitter realization settled in my chest.

"Mom's here," River added, his voice softening. He looked at me, his eyes full of that protective instinct that had always been there. "She's been outside talking to the doctors. You scared the shit out of her."

Before I could respond, the curtain around my bed shifted, and I saw her.

Mom.

She stepped inside slowly, her face pale, her eyes red-rimmed from crying.

"Oh, my girl," she whispered, rushing to my side.

She held me, her hands trembling slightly as she smoothed my hair away from my face, her touch gentle, as though trying to calm both of us.

"You're safe now," she murmured, her voice shaking, her relief palpable.

For the first time in what felt like years, I believed her. The weight of the world lifted just slightly. She was right. I was safe for now.

The Police Arrive – The Reality Sets In

A knock at the door broke the moment.

Mom looked up, wiping her face quickly, her fingers swiping away the remnants of tears. Two officers stepped inside. The female officer's face was full of sympathy, but it was a sympathy that I couldn't fully process at that moment. Not when everything felt like a dream, a nightmare I wasn't sure I could wake up from.

"Nea," the officer said gently. "I'm so sorry this happened to you. We need to ask you some questions about last night. Are you up for that?"

I nodded. My body felt like it was operating on autopilot. I didn't know if I could honestly face the words that would come out of my mouth, but I nodded anyway because what else could I do?

The male officer pulled out a notepad, his expression hardening as he prepared to get to the heart of the matter.

"Your attacker, Kai Walker, has been arrested. He's in custody now."

Hearing his name was like being hit with a tidal wave. It wasn't just a name anymore. It wasn't just a person I loved, who once made me feel safe, or even the boy who had haunted my dreams with anger and desperation. Now, it was a *criminal*—a man in handcuffs.

And everything that we had, everything we once were, had shattered into a thousand irreparable pieces.

I squeezed my eyes shut. I couldn't breathe. I felt the room closing in on me, the walls pressing in as I fought against the gravity of it.

Kai.

The boy I had loved. The boy who had kissed me with such passion, such hope. Who had held me through my hardest times? Who had promised me forever?

The boy who had nearly killed me.

"We need you to tell us everything you remember," the officer continued, breaking through my haze of shock.

Everything.

The memories crashed into me. I remembered his eyes—dark and full of something I had never seen before. I remembered the way his hands wrapped around my throat, the pressure, the suffocating grip. I remembered the moment when I realized he was going to kill me. And I remembered the cold, dead certainty that had settled in my gut.

I started to shake. My chest heaved as my breath quickened, and a wave of dizziness hit me like a freight train.

Mom squeezed my hand, her voice soft yet firm. "Baby, just nod if you need a minute."

I nodded, my lips trembling as I closed my eyes. I could feel her presence next to me, feel the weight of her support, but nothing could block out the horror of what had happened.

Everything I thought I knew about love, about safety—everything I thought I knew about *him*—had shattered in that club. I had spent years believing that Kai would be the one to pull me from the dark, that he would be my light. I had clung to him, believing that we could fix each other, that love would be enough to make everything right.

But I had been wrong.

I had loved a boy who was too broken, too far gone to save—a boy who almost took everything from me.

And I would never be the same again.

As the officers continued their questions, I realized that the girl I had been—before the bar fight, before the chaos and the pain—was gone. She was a version of myself that no longer existed. In her place was someone else. Someone hardened by violence. Someone who had seen the darkest parts of love and had learned that sometimes, love was not enough to save anyone.

And it was a lesson I would carry with me, always.

CHAPTER 18

The Fight That Changed Everything

Then: 18. Now: A woman who knows violence is never simple.

"The night Kai hit me was the night I lost him forever. But that night, I also lost a part of myself."

The girl I had been before that night—the girl who believed in love, healing, and the power of forgiveness—was gone. She had been replaced by someone else—a woman who knew better.

I had thought I could fix Kai, just like I thought I could fix myself. But we were too broken. We were two halves of something that could never be whole again. And it was no one's fault but our own.

Kai, a boy who had turned into a man too soon, was broken by a father who had never been there. A man who had been raised on rage and pain, forced to grow up in a world that expected him to shoulder burdens no child should ever have to bear. Then, the sudden death of his father was a pain he couldn't process. The worst part? I had been his lifeline. I had been the one to hold him, to believe in him, to think that maybe—just maybe—I could be the one to save him.

But when he thought he lost me, when he realized I was slipping away, he lost himself too.

That night set off a chain reaction. Kai spiraled further into his darkness, pulling me into it. The downward spiral was inevitable, and for the first time, I realized just how helpless I was to stop it.

I had left months before. I had no other choice.

But it wasn't just about leaving him. It was about leaving everything I thought I knew. Leaving the girl I was when I met him—the girl who believed in the possibility of redemption and thought love could heal anything. I had to leave that girl behind, because the reality was far more complicated than I ever expected.

And as I walked away, I didn't know where I was going, but I knew I could never return.

This wasn't just about Kai. It was about me. It was about the woman I had become, the woman who knew that violence wasn't simple, that love wasn't always the answer, and that sometimes, no matter how much you want to fix something, it's too broken to save.

I didn't just lose Kai that night. I lost myself, too. But in losing him, I finally found the strength to walk away.

CHAPTER 19

The First Night Home

The drive back to the farm was heavy with unspoken words. The air in the truck felt thick, like it was holding something back. Mom sat in the passenger seat, staring out the window, her silence carrying the weight of her worry. Dad wasn't there he had been working up North for the last couple weeks. River drove with a tight grip on the wheel, eyes flicking to the rearview mirror occasionally, but his expression was unreadable. His quiet presence in the backseat was both comforting and a reminder that even the ones closest to you can feel like distant strangers in moments like these.

I kept my gaze fixed on the blurred landscape outside the window. The trees, the familiar bend in the road, the fields stretching out on either side were all the same. But none of it felt like it belonged to me anymore. Everything that had felt so certain, so rooted in my bones, now felt foreign. I felt like I was driving through a place I knew once, but could no longer call home.

As we pulled into the long gravel driveway, I felt the weight in my chest that had been building for miles, pressing down harder now.

The feeling wasn't a physical weight, not something you could touch, but something that sat in your gut and made everything feel too tight, too small. It was the weight of memories, of ghosts that weren't literal but lived in every corner of this place.

Kai had been here. This was where it had all started, where we had spent so many nights together, our laughter mixing with the crackling of the fire pit. I could almost hear his voice in the quiet of the truck as it came to a stop in the driveway, feel the echo of his touch when I would find his hand reaching for mine in the dark, under the stars. The world we had built together was in every inch of this place.

But now... he was gone.

Kai wasn't a part of my life for the first time in almost two years. His absence settled over me like a thick fog, blocking everything I had once known. There was an emptiness, a void where once there had been something real that had felt like a future. Now, all I could feel was the bitter reality of what we had become—two people bound together by pain and love that had turned toxic.

Was I relieved or devastated? I didn't know anymore.

The confusion felt like an ocean, swallowing me whole. Part of me wanted to celebrate that I was finally free, that I had managed to break away from the storm of him, from the chaos that had haunted us. But another part of me mourned what we had lost, what I had lost. I couldn't even remember who I was before Kai, and that thought hollowed me out even further.

Mom's voice broke through my thoughts, gentle and tentative. "Are you hungry?" she asked as we stepped out of the truck. I could hear the hesitation in her voice, the way she was walking on eggshells, trying to gauge where my mind was, what I needed.

I shook my head, the motion small and automatic. "I just need to lie down," I muttered, unable to put anything more into words.

Her gaze softened, but she didn't push it. She knew better by now. She could see how I was unraveling and could feel it, too. Mom nodded, pressing her lips together like she was fighting the urge to say something.

River didn't ask questions. Instead, he reached out and pulled me into a one-armed hug, his strength always a steadying force. His embrace felt different now, though. His protective side, once a quiet part of his nature, had become something more pronounced as he'd seen me through all of this. I leaned into him, letting myself feel the comfort of someone who loved me without expectations, without a history of broken promises. After a moment, he let go, nodding toward the barn. Without a word, he headed off in that direction, his figure dissolving into the darkening evening.

I made my way up the stairs to my old room, the familiar creak of the floorboards beneath my feet the only sound that echoed in the quiet house. When I reached the door to my bedroom, I hesitated. This room, this space—it was supposed to be mine. It was supposed to be a place where I could find peace and rebuild after everything that had happened, a break from college to collect myself.

But when I stepped inside and shut the door behind me, it felt like walking into a stranger's life.

I stood there for a long moment, just breathing. The weight in my chest had turned into something unbearable. I hadn't let myself truly feel any of it until now. I had pushed through, kept moving forward, and tried to numb the pain with busyness and distractions. But now that I was home, I couldn't longer avoid it.

I sat on the edge of my bed and let everything hit me all at once. The heartbreak. The betrayal. The loss. It felt like an avalanche crashing down, burying me under its weight. How had I let myself get here? How had I become someone who let a boy break her, piece by piece, until there was nothing left but shattered remnants of the person I used to be?

I curled up on my bed, pulling the covers over me as though they could protect me from the overwhelming emotions. The darkness of the room mirrored the darkness in my heart. I stared at the ceiling, trying to find some thread of who I had been before Kai before this storm of love and pain had pulled me under.

But I couldn't. The girl I had been before was a memory now that seemed too far out of reach. I had changed in ways I wasn't sure how to process. The person who had loved Kai with all her heart—the girl who had believed in him, in them—was gone, replaced by someone who had learned the hard way that not all love was kind. Not all love was enough.

I wasn't sure who I was anymore.

But for the first time in a long while, I realized that maybe it was okay not to know. Perhaps this was the beginning of something new, even if it didn't feel like it. Perhaps this was the space I needed to rebuild—without his weight, without the ghosts of everything that had once been.

As I lay there in the dark, letting the quiet wash over me, I couldn't help but feel the faintest flicker of hope. Maybe there was still a chance for me to find myself again.

CHAPTER 20

The Sweat Lodge & The Fallout:

After Kai Gets Arrested

The weeks after the attack were a blur. A haze of whispers that wrapped themselves around me like chains. They were everywhere: in the grocery store, post office, and every corner of the small town of Barriere. No one said anything to my face, but I could hear it all. People spoke in hushed tones when I walked by, their eyes darting away as if I were a walking scandal, an untold story they had no intention of sharing.

The worst part wasn't the words themselves—the feeling of being swallowed whole by them. People had picked sides, as though my life was a game of blame. Half the town blamed me. The rumors ran wild.

"She always drank too much."

"She was always wild."

"She probably started the fight."

"He was such a good guy before her."

The words stung thick with racism. They always did, but it wasn't just the words. It was the weight they carried. I wasn't just the victim anymore; I was the villain. The bruises on my neck were nothing compared to the scars on my heart, carved by the very people who had once called me family.

And then there was the other half. The silent ones. The ones who knew the truth but were too afraid to speak. Too afraid to stand up and call out the injustice of it all. It was the most cowardly betrayal—seeing the pain and not doing anything about it. I used to think there was safety in silence, but now, I realized how damaging it could be.

Kai was still around sometimes between his stitches at the oil patch. Always lurking in the background, like a shadow I couldn't escape. Kevin and I saw him everywhere—in town, at the gas station, whizzing by on his Harley. There was no shame in him, no guilt. He'd look at me, his gaze as empty as the spaces between us, then turn away like we were nothing more than strangers. Like he hadn't nearly taken my life in that alley. There was a restraining order so he never stuck around anywhere I was luckily. I stayed in Kamloops after that, not needing more stress and drama.

The fury built inside me every time I saw him, but so did something else. A dull sadness, a deep ache that I didn't know how to name. Part of me wanted to scream at him, to shake him until the life he'd stolen from me came back. But the other part, the quieter part, just wanted him to disappear. For everything to stop, the world to stop spinning on its axis, so I could breathe again.

And then there was Kevin.

Kevin, my anchor. My lifeline in the chaos. He was the steady beat of my heart when everything else was drowning in noise. His presence grounded me, a calm amidst the emotions that threatened to tear me apart. He never judged me. Not for the things I did or the choices I made. He never looked at me as broken or damaged. He just... loved me.

He arm-wrestled my cousins at family parties, his muscles bulging with effortless strength as he laughed and joked with them. He never lost. Not once. He was everything Kai had never been: steady, unwavering, real.

I wanted to let him in. I wanted to give him all of me. But there was nothing left. Just jagged edges and empty spaces. I couldn't offer him the person I had once been. Not yet.

One night, we sat on the hood of his car after another party, the distant sound of laughter still lingering in the air. Cold and brilliant, the stars stretched above us like they could see everything. Kevin broke the silence, his voice casual but laced with something deeper.

"You know," he said, his eyes reflecting the glow of the moonlight, "I'd marry you tomorrow if you let me."

I turned to him, a smile tugging at my lips but not quite reaching my eyes. "You don't want to marry someone like me, Kev."

"Yeah?" He grinned, his expression genuine. "I think I do."

I laughed softly, shaking my head. "I'm too broken."

He stretched his arms behind his head, the muscles in his chest shifting as he settled back against the car. His voice was light, but his eyes never left mine. "Nah," he said with a small laugh, but something in his gaze told me he wasn't just saying words. "You're just waiting to remember who you are."

I didn't know who I was anymore. And maybe I didn't want to. Maybe I was afraid to face the girl I had been before. But Kevin was there, waiting. His love was the kind I didn't know how to accept, but I also didn't know how to walk away.

The Sweat Lodge

Grampa Oliver saw it before I did.

"Time to come home, girl," he said one evening, standing in my driveway, the smoke from his pipe curling around him like an old spirit, settling into the earth beneath his feet. I had heard the whispers of the Elders, and felt their quiet pull over the last few weeks. It was time.

I had been running from the grief, running from the pain, running from the broken pieces of myself. But now, it was time to face it. To heal.

So River and I went. Back to the land. Back to the ceremony. Back to the sweat lodge.

The lodge stood strong beside the *setétkwe*, the river where our great-grandmother had built it long before we were born. The land had always been a place of healing, of restoration. It was where the spirits spoke, where the medicine flowed like the river beside it.

Inside, the heat pressed in like a second skin, thick with the scent of sage and sweetgrass, the air heavy with ancient energy. The stones in the pit glowed a deep, red-hot hue, pulsing like living hearts. The warmth surrounded me, but instead of offering comfort, it made everything feel too much.

I closed my eyes, trying to focus and let the heat, the smoke, the medicine take me to the spirit world like it had so many times before. But there was nothing. No visions. No spirit voices. Just silence. The same silence that had haunted me since that night in the club, the night everything had fallen apart.

Grampa Oliver's voice came from the darkness, low and steady, singing the old songs, calling to the spirits. His words were like a prayer, a promise, but I couldn't hear them. Not anymore.

"You have to let it go," he said after a long silence. "All of it. Let the spirits take it."

I wanted to. God, I wanted to. But there was nothing. No release. No peace. I had always been able to sense it —the other realm—the connection. But now, it was just smoke—just heat.

A single tear slipped down my cheek, hot as the stones. I couldn't find the words to explain how broken I felt. How lost I had become.

"It'll come back," River whispered beside me, his voice quiet but filled with certainty.

But I wasn't sure it ever would. The spirits had always been my guide, my connection to everything that had come before me. But now, all I felt was emptiness. The darkness had taken everything. And I wasn't sure if I would ever find my way back.

CHAPTER 21

Spiraling

I didn't feel it at first. The loss. The grief. The way something inside me had cracked wide open, creating a chasm that nothing seemed capable of filling.

At first, it was just numbness. A kind of detachment that made the world seem distant, like I was watching everything happen through a thick pane of glass. I floated in the haze, just trying to get through each day. My mind was clouded, too heavy, too foggy to feel the actual weight of what had happened. It was as if I were on autopilot, going through the motions of life but not truly *living* it.

But the numbness didn't last.

And when it hit—when the storm of grief, anger, and betrayal broke loose—it was like the earth had crumbled beneath me. I felt it all at once, and it overwhelmed me. The pain tore through me, raw and jagged, a sudden, violent eruption from the depths of my chest. I had no place to put it, no way to escape it. The wave of loss hit with such force that I could hardly breathe beneath it.

I started drinking.

It started small, a sip occasionally, but it quickly escalated. I didn't drink to have fun. I didn't drink to fit in or party. I drank to survive the day. I drank to escape. Because when I was drunk, the world didn't seem quite so sharp. The edges softened, and the pain dulled. When I drank, I didn't have to feel the shame—the shame of what had happened to me, of what Kai had done. I didn't have to feel the anger that festered in my chest every time I thought of him, the betrayal that clung to my skin like a second layer.

Most of the time, I didn't think about how Kai had looked at me that night—how he had twisted the love we once shared into something ugly and dark. His eyes were full of rage and contempt, as if I was no longer the girl he had loved. As if we had never been anything at all.

But sometimes, I could still see it when I closed my eyes. The disgust on his face. The way he had thrown me away like I was nothing. A piece of trash discarded without a second thought. And I hated myself for it. I hated the fact that I had let him do that to me.

Everyone took sides. They always did. Our friends whispered behind my back, avoiding looking me in the eye when we passed each other. It was as though I was walking around with a scarlet letter branded on my chest, a reminder that I was the girl who her ex-boyfriend had strangled. The girl who had nearly died at his hands.

And then there was Kai.

Kai did precisely what I should have expected. He moved on fast. Faster than I could have imagined. He slept with every girl he could find—every single one—as if to prove a point. To show the world that he was fine. That I meant nothing. Like he was trying to erase me from the story of his life. Like I had never existed.

And maybe, for him, I hadn't.

But it didn't stop the way it tore at me. Watching him parade those girls around, hearing their names whispered in the same spaces where mine had once been. Seeing how his eyes would light up with them, how he would touch them the way he used to touch me. It felt like salt on an open wound.

Then came the worst part.

The day I walked into town and saw her.

She was standing outside the pub, laughing, talking to a group of friends. And I stopped dead in my tracks, my breath catching in my throat. She was... her. The girl who looked just like me. Same hair. Same build. Same frame. She was a mirror image of me, a perfect replica of who I had been before everything had fallen apart.

It was as if Kai had gone out and found my fucking twin.

I could feel the weight in my chest, the crushing pressure of something heavy and cold settling there. A mixture of rage, disbelief, and heartache. I wanted to scream and yell at the universe for being so cruel and making me walk into that moment. I wanted to rage against it all. To drink until I couldn't feel anything. I want to erase myself from the world just like Kai has tried to do with me.

But instead, I walked straight to Kevin.

I didn't know why. I didn't have an explanation. But at that moment, I needed something to anchor me. I needed someone to make the world stop spinning, if only for a moment. Kevin was always steady. He had always been the one to keep me grounded when I was lost in my chaos.

He was sitting on the porch when I arrived, his eyes lightening when he saw me. He stood up, a grin tugging at his lips, but it faltered when he saw my face. I didn't need to say anything. He could read me better than anyone.

Without a word, he stepped forward, and I let him. I let him pull me into his arms, let his warmth wrap around me like a shield. He didn't ask questions, didn't press me for answers. He just... held me.

And then, without thinking, I let him kiss me.

It wasn't a love confession. It wasn't a fairy-tale moment. It wasn't even about love, not really. It was a distraction. A way to feel something other than the pain that was consuming me. His lips were soft, but there was something desperate in how they met mine. It was as though he was trying to heal me with his care and lips.

But as his hands found their way to my back, pulling me closer, I realized I wasn't doing this for him. I wasn't doing it for *us*. I was doing it because I needed to feel alive. To feel wanted. Even if it was just for a fleeting moment.

Kevin didn't push. He didn't ask for more than I could give. He let me fall into him, and I let myself fall because it was easier than standing still and facing the truth of what had become of me and who I had become.

The kiss ended, but the weight in my chest didn't lift. I felt it still—more pressing than before, like a rock sitting on my lungs. The moment had passed, and all I had left was the raw, gaping wound that no amount of alcohol, no number of distractions, would ever heal.

But I wasn't alone for that fleeting moment when Kevin's arms were around me. And maybe that was enough.

CHAPTER 22

The Breaking Point

"Grief doesn't come all at once. It doesn't hit like a tidal wave and then retreat. It creeps in, seeps into the cracks, poisoning everything. And when you've already been cracked wide open, you don't notice how deep it's buried until you're drowning."

Present-Day Scene: One Month Later

I don't remember taking the pills.

Not really.

I remember the burn of whiskey on my tongue, the static in my chest, the emptiness in my bones.

I remember looking at the little orange bottle, shaking out one, two, three, four...

And then—

Nothing.

A void.

The next thing I knew, I was waking up back in the hospital, blinking against the fluorescent lights, the steady beep of a heart monitor in the background.

Déjà vu.

This time, I was the danger.

The Hospital Room

"Well, Nea," a voice drawled from the chair beside my bed.

I turned my head slowly, feeling a dull ache behind my eyes, the weight of the world pressing down on my chest.

River.

His jaw was clenched, his knuckles white against his jeans, but his voice was calm, eerily so.

"What the fuck were you thinking?"

I swallowed, throat dry.

"I don't know."

It wasn't a lie.

I didn't.

I hadn't planned to die. I hadn't thought that far ahead.

I just wanted to feel nothing for a little while.

"Mom's outside," River continued, his voice sharper now. "They called her at two in the goddamn morning. She thought she was gonna have to bury her daughter today."

Guilt hit me like a slap.

I turned away, staring at the ceiling.

"I wasn't trying to die."

"Then what the fuck was it?"

I didn't have an answer.

Three Days with the Shrink. They kept me for forced observation, which was a nice way of saying, 'We don't trust you not to do it again.'

I spent three days in a sterile room, talking to a psychiatrist who wanted to dissect my pain like it was a puzzle to be solved.

"Do you want to die?" she asked me on the second day.

I thought about it.

I thought about it.

"No," I said finally. "I was drunk. I don't even remember doing it."

Which was true.

But also not.

Because I remembered the feeling.

The numbness.

The desperation.

The deep, aching loneliness that no amount of whiskey, loud music, or fake laughter could drown out.

She made me swear I wouldn't do it again before they let me go.

And I did.

Because I wanted to believe it, too.

The Weekend Parties

By the time I got home to the farm, River was waiting with a bottle of vodka and a cigarette, sitting on the hood of his truck like nothing had happened.

"Party next door," he said, nodding toward our best friend's house. "Kevin's there. So's half the rez."

I hesitated.

A part of me wanted to crawl under the covers and disappear.

But the other part?

The one screaming for distraction, for anything other than silence?

That part grabbed the bottle out of River's hand, took a long pull, and wiped my mouth with the back of my hand.

"Let's go."

And so the cycle began.

Every weekend, the house next door turned into a warzone of whiskey, weed, and loud music.

River, my cousins, Kevin, and half the rez drowned ourselves together.

I was the life of the party, shot in one hand, beer in the other, laughter spilling from my lips so easily it almost sounded real.

Almost.

But late at night, when the music died down and everyone stumbled home, I would lie awake staring at the ceiling, my pulse still pounding in my ears.

And I would wonder—

If I had taken just a few more pills, would I still be here?

"I wasn't living. I was surviving. And barely, at that. But that's the thing about rock bottom—you don't realize you've hit it until you've been there a while. And even then, climbing out feels impossible."

"But I wasn't safe. Not yet. Trauma isn't something that disappears when the bruises fade. It lingers, burrows into your bones, and whispers in the quiet. And Kai? He wasn't done haunting me—not by a long shot."

"Some moments brand themselves into your soul, carved in fire and regret. The night of the bar fight wasn't just a moment—it was a reckoning. It was the night I finally understood that Kai was beyond saving, and if I didn't get out, I'd burn with him."

I told myself I liked Kevin.

That he was good for me.

That he wasn't Kai, and that was enough.

But it wasn't.

Not really.

Because no matter how much I tried, I couldn't feel anything real.

The nights blurred together—drinking, parties, making out with Kevin to prove to everyone, to Kai, to myself that I was fine.

But I wasn't.

I was drowning.

One night, I came home, stumbling drunk, my vision hazy.

Mom was waiting.

She didn't yell.

I didn't scold.

She just looked at me.

And I broke.

"I can't see them anymore," I whispered.

Her brow furrowed. "See what?"

I swallowed hard. "The spirits, they don't talk to me anymore. I don't hear them, and I can't see them."

Silence.

Then—understanding.

I had lost my gift.

I had drowned it in whiskey and regret.

And the worst part?

I didn't even care.

"That night should have killed me. Maybe not physically, but something inside me shattered. And when I woke up in that hospital bed, I realized something—Kai hadn't just tried to take my life. The pain took my gift."

I was done with this pain, and I had at least felt my emotions and cycled through the stages of grief. I had enough of the pain, and the next day, I decided to pack the despair away and get back to life. Back to college, back to Kamloops, returning to the fight against the mine at Eagle Ridge, anything but that pain.

CHAPTER 23

The Calm Before the Storm

Moving back into real life, the fight for Eagle Ridge consumed most of my time, and college life had its rhythm. There was a sense of normalcy I hadn't expected to find when I returned. It wasn't perfect, far from it, but it was a routine I could rely on. I wasn't just an activist, a warrior in training—I was still a young woman trying to carve out some semblance of balance in a life that had been so full of chaos.

And, as much as I didn't want to admit it, part of that life included Kevin.

He was my library study buddy, gym partner, and occasionally my drinking companion. We were a pair that made sense—our camaraderie was so natural that I never had to force it. After classes, we'd head to the library, cracking open textbooks and pretending to study. However, more often than not, Kevin would get distracted and grin at me across the table, his eyes full of mischief.

"You're supposed to be reading," I mutter, trying to focus on my notes, my pen moving across the paper to regain some semblance of control over the storm of thoughts in my head.

Kevin would smirk and lean closer, his big forearms resting on the table. "I'm studying something way more interesting," he'd say, his voice light and playful but with that underlying warmth that made my heart do an involuntary flip.

I rolled my eyes, but my stomach still fluttered. The truth was, I wasn't sure what I expected from him. I didn't know what I wanted from him. But at that moment, in the quiet of the library, it didn't matter. The rest of the world felt distant, and things were simple in that bubble with Kevin.

Dancing in the Campus Pub

On weekends, when I wasn't back home at the rez fighting against the mine, we'd hit the campus pub. It wasn't a glamorous place by any means—the music was loud, the beer cheap, and the floor was always sticky from spilled drinks, but it was ours. And, for a few hours, it felt like everything else could wait.

Kevin was a presence. A magnetic force. All charm, muscles, and carefree fun. His laugh would fill up the room, and his energy was contagious. When he was around, I felt like I could breathe a little easier, like the world's weight was a little lighter. We'd dance, close, too close at times, his hands strong on my hips, my arms draped around his neck. The music rhythm wrapped around us like a comforting blanket, and for once, I could forget. Forget about the mine, my family, Kai, and all the tangled mess that came with him.

Kevin smelled like beer and sweat, but beneath that was the scent of his cologne, something warm and familiar. His lips would tease against my ear, whispering things that made me smile and laugh. It was lighthearted, but there was an undertone of something more. A deep connection that I didn't fully understand but couldn't ignore.

And then, outside, under the streetlights, he would pull me in for a kiss. Deep, slow, the kind that made my knees weak. It was tender, a stark contrast to the chaos inside me, but I didn't need anything else at that moment. I just wanted that kiss, wanted to forget the pain that tried to cling to me in quiet moments, even as I let myself melt into him.

The Gym & The Heat That Followed

We trained together, too. Early mornings in the campus gym, lifting weights, racing each other on the treadmill, pushing ourselves harder than we probably should have. Kevin loved to flex, to show off, and I pretended not to notice—but of course, I did. I'd watch him with a mixture of appreciation and something deeper, something I didn't want to label or understand.

It was a Saturday morning when the incident occurred. The gym was quieter than usual, the air thick with the scent of sweat and rubber. The sounds of weights clanging and treadmills humming filled the space, but Kevin and I were focused on the bench press. It began as a challenge—see who could outlast the other. I won, of course, but Kevin wasn't a good loser.

Still, there was a glint in his eye that didn't go unnoticed. Sweaty, still grinning, he pulled me into the locker room showers, the steam swirling around us like a cloud of heat. The sharp edges of reality began to fade, and the air between us grew thick with something else, something electric.

Kevin's lips found mine, his hands pulling me closer as the water sprayed around us, turning the air hot and heavy. Suddenly, studying was the last thing on either of our minds. There was no longer any pretense of being "just casual" or anything else. It was raw and untamed, and everything I'd been trying to bury was rising to the surface.

An Adorable, But Not Too Serious, Love

Kevin and I were good together—effortless, easy. It was the kind of relationship where everything seemed to fall into place. But deep down, we both knew it wasn't forever. I still carried my scars—the ones from Kai, the fight for Eagle Ridge, and all the battles I had fought and lost. Kevin, as sweet and steady as he was, wasn't the one to heal them. I was too broken, too tangled in my web of pain to let anyone truly see me.

Still, Kevin made me laugh. He made me forget, if only for a little while. I will always be grateful for that. He was the one who reminded me that joy was still possible, even in the mess of everything.

Kai, in the meantime, was long gone. He'd moved to Alberta to work in the oil patch, far away from Kamloops and the farm. At least, for now, seeing him was behind me. And that, in itself, was a kind of peace.

But that calm, as fleeting as it was, was deceptive. It was only a matter of time before everything simmering under the surface would come to a head. And when it did, I wasn't sure anyone, not even Kevin, could hold me together.

CHAPTER 24

The Campus Life & Kevin's Warm Embrace

Kevin wasn't just a gym rat or my study buddy—he was the university's star lacrosse player, the guy everyone wanted a piece of. He played with the reckless confidence of someone who knew he was damn good, and when he stepped onto the field, you couldn't help but watch him. It was impossible not to be impressed. He moved like the game was made for him, fast and fearless, like he was born with a lacrosse stick in his hand. After every game, there'd be a crowd—cheerleaders, students, alumni—waiting to celebrate with him. But through all the noise, he always found me first.

I'd watch from the sidelines, arms folded, pretending I wasn't impressed by how effortlessly he commanded the field, but I was. I always was.

The Jock & The Cheerleaders

The cheerleaders—perfect hair, perfect smiles—threw themselves at Kevin after every game. Their perfectly curled ponytails bounced as they fawned over his muscles, athletic status, and charm that was as easy as breathing. I could see why they were drawn to him. He was everything they wanted—a mix of popularity, confidence, and good looks.

But despite all the attention, he'd always find me at night's end. After the applause died down, after the crowd scattered, we'd slip away together, leaving the noise of the bar behind. He'd grab my hand, his fingers warm against my skin, and lead me into the quiet, the space we shared where no one could interrupt us.

Back in his tiny dorm room, which was barely big enough for him, let alone both of us, we'd fall into each other—breathless and tangled, laughing between kisses. It wasn't glamorous or romantic in the traditional sense. It was messy, real, and it was ours.

I'd look around his cramped room, noticing the posters of lacrosse games and old bands plastered to the walls, the cluttered desk filled with textbooks and empty coffee cups. It was a far cry from the life I had imagined for myself when I first arrived at college, but in these moments with him, I felt like I was exactly where I needed to be.

The Pub, The Hip & The Outfield

The campus pub became our scene, where we could just be. Kevin's arm was always around my waist as we stood shoulder to shoulder with friends, belting New Orleans is Sinking by The Tragically Hip lyrics. The music thumped through the bar, the vibrations underfoot matching the pounding of my heart. We'd stomp our boots on the sticky floor, singing along with Gord Downie like we were at a damn concert. It didn't matter that the pub was grimy or that the beer was lukewarm—it was ours, and at that moment, it was perfect.

Then, *The Outfield's Your Love* would come on, and everything else faded into the background.

"I just wanna use your love tonight... I don't wanna lose your love tonight..." The song's soft, familiar cadence was our anthem, and Kevin would grab my hand, spinning me around before pulling me close. The crowded space disappeared, and it was just us, caught in the rhythm of the music, the warmth of each other's touch.

When he kissed me, slow and deep, in front of everyone, I could feel the weight of every jealous glance. Some people wanted him, and I knew it, but when his lips met mine, I didn't care. We were there together, and that was enough.

Pizza, Beer & John Hughes Films

After the pub, we'd stumble back to his dorm and order pizza, cracking open a few beers. We'd sprawl out on his bed, the remnants of the night echoing around us as we watched *Sixteen Candles*. Kevin knew every damn line by heart, and we'd both yell at Jake Ryan for taking way too long to get his shit together with Molly Ringwald's character.

Kevin would stretch out beside me, his massive arms wrapped around me, his chin resting on my head. The smell of cold pizza lingered, but we ignored it, caught up in the warmth of the moment. We didn't need anything else. I didn't need anything else.

At least I had pizza, beer, and great cuddles. I could pretend nothing else mattered in that small, quiet space. For the first time in what felt like forever, I felt light.

It wasn't about escaping the past. It wasn't about running away from everything that had hurt me or everything I had lost. It was about finding a small piece of happiness where I could.

The Next Morning: A Simple Kind of Happiness

The morning came, and we woke up lying together, cuddled through the night, his fingers still caught up in my hair. Our hair was a mess. The world outside his dorm room didn't exist those first few moments. We lazily dressed, the day stretching ahead with no real plan except to be together.

We headed out for brunch, hand in hand, laughing as we walked. Kevin sipped his coffee, grinning at me over the rim of his cup, his eyes twinkling with that same playful energy that made him so easy to fall for.

"You know," he said, after a moment of silence, his voice warm and teasing, "I could get used to this."

I smiled, though I didn't quite know how to respond. Could I? Could I let myself believe that something as simple as a coffee with this sweet thing every morning could be enough to make me forget everything I had carried for so long?

But then again, maybe that was the point. Perhaps I didn't need to forget. Maybe I just needed to let myself live in this moment with him. For once, I wasn't drowning in the past. I wasn't thinking about Kai. I wasn't haunted by what had been.

I was here for the first time in what felt like a lifetime. In the present. With Kevin. With his warm embrace, teasing smile, and the simple joy of being close to someone who wanted me as much as I wanted him.

As Kevin left for practice, he pulled me in for one last playful kiss, and I sat there, content, watching him go.

I didn't know where we were headed or how long this calm would last, but in that moment, it was enough. For the first time in a long time, I could breathe.

CHAPTER 25

The Fight for Eagle Ridge

I was at college, but part of my heart was still home—pulled to the land, river, and people. Every lecture, every discussion, every campus event felt simple compared to what loomed ahead, as if I were living in a world that wasn't mine. My thoughts were always drifting back to the rez, where the fight for Eagle Ridge was slowly building into something bigger than anyone could have anticipated.

The proposed mine threatened everything. Eagle Ridge wasn't just any mountain—it was our sacred mountain, the backbone of our people. Setétkwe, the river beside it, wasn't just water—it was life. The idea of having tailing ponds dug near the river was a betrayal I couldn't stomach. Every other weekend, I'd drive back home, head to meetings, and try to rally our people against it. But the divide was deep, and the stakes were even higher.

The Divide: Betrayal and the Promise of Money

The community had been split right down the middle. Half of us were outraged. The mine was a violation of everything we held sacred, a direct assault on our land, our culture, and our future. The other half? They saw the money. They saw the promise of jobs, of a bright future with the illusion of prosperity. They couldn't see the long-term damage, the poison that would seep into the land, into the water, into our very bones, into the blood and bones of our children.

It was heartbreaking. Every time I walked into a meeting, I could see the tension in the air, the unspoken weight of years of hardship that had led some to believe that selling out our heritage for a quick fix was the only way forward.

And at the center of it all was Billy.

Billy: The Face of Betrayal

Billy had once been the smooth-talking older brother I remembered, who'd spend his time charming everyone, making them laugh. But now, he had transformed into a man who stood at the table with the mining company's executives, a big-shot lawyer, negotiating away our future. I couldn't believe it when I first heard about it. My brother was selling the very land that had given us life.

He was no longer the kid who had looked up to our Elders with wide eyes. No, now he was slick in his Chanel suit, rubbing elbows with the Treaty groups, acting as if he were bringing progress to the people. He stood proudly alongside chiefs, shaking hands with those who'd bought into the Treaty Process—the same process many of us saw as a way to relinquish sovereignty and sell our land.

I watched him at a community meeting, his voice smooth, dripping with promises of prosperity. He informed our people about the jobs the mine would create and how it would help lift us out of poverty.

And some were desperate for any hope of change who listened. They nodded, believing that this mine was their only way out.

But I could see through it. It wasn't just a deal with the devil. It was a betrayal of everything we had been taught and believed. Billy was selling our birthright, and there was nothing I could do to stop him.

The Warriors Arrive

Then, just when it seemed like the battle was already lost, the Native Youth Movement showed up. Dwayne, Wilson, and Tommy arrived at the farm one weekend, ready to stay and help us strategize. These weren't just activists—they were warriors trained in resistance, and they came with a fire that burned brighter than anything I'd seen in a long time.

Their uniforms weren't the usual student protest gear—no, these men wore quasi-military fatigues, combat boots caked in dirt, and patches on their jackets marked with the warrior flag. They were the real deal. And they weren't playing politics. They were ready to fight.

I introduced them to River and our cousins, Grampa Oliver, Mom, and Daddio, who eyed them respectfully and cautiously. That night, we sat around the fire, drinking coffee and strategizing for the battle ahead. The NYM boys weren't just here for the mine at Eagle Ridge—they had seen this same fight happen in other communities before, with different projects and other industries. This was a war that had been fought and lost too many times before, and now we had to fight it again.

"We've seen this before," Dwayne said, his voice low but sharp. "Same game, different mine. They offer money. People get desperate. Divide the community. Then they move in."

Wilson's voice followed, heavy with warning. "The trick is, once they break ground, they never leave. They promise 'clean extraction' and 'reclamation,' but look at Mount Peter. The tailing pond burst, poisoning everything for miles. You think they won't do the same here?"

River's jaw clenched. "The old people say the mountain is alive. There's something sacred up there. If they dig, it won't just be the land that suffers."

I turned my gaze to Billy, standing across the way, talking to a chief already deep in the Treaty Process. He was so confident, so sure of himself. He was now the enemy, standing with the mining company and the forces that sought to erase everything we had.

The Enemy Within

The enemy wasn't just the mining company. It wasn't just the politicians and the business people who wanted to exploit our land. It was our people who turned against us. Billy, my flesh and blood, stood on the opposite side of the battlefield, fighting against everything we had ever believed in.

The next day, at the community meeting, the fight truly began. It wasn't just a debate anymore. It was a war—one that would tear our community apart if we weren't careful.

Face-to-Face With Billy

After the meeting, Billy caught me outside, his expression almost pitying. I could see it in his eyes—the disappointment, the disdain. "You're dreaming, Nea," he said, his voice smooth and condescending, like he was doing me a favor. "You and your activist friends don't understand revenue and benefits. This is real money. Enough to change everything. You think our people want to live in poverty forever?"

I stepped closer to him, my hands trembling with anger. My voice was cold and sharp. "This land is not yours to sell."

For a moment, I saw a crack in the façade, a flash of guilt or maybe fear. But it was gone in an instant, replaced by his usual smirk.

Billy sighed, shaking his head. "You've been hanging around with the wannabe warriors too long."

I glared at him, my voice low but steady. "Better a wannabe warrior than a sellout."

His smirk vanished. His fists clenched. I thought he might lash out for a moment, but before he could say anything, River stepped forward, his voice quiet but dangerous. "It's time for you to go, Billy."

Billy looked at Dwayne and the others, then back at me. He shook his head, the smirk returning but now darker, colder. "You have no idea what you're up against."

With that, he turned and walked away, leaving my heart heavy with the weight of the betrayal. But we weren't done. The fight was beginning.

The Start of Something Bigger

That night, we gathered around the fire at the farm again, sipping coffee and discussing strategy. The NYM boys told us about other fights they'd been part of—pipelines, dams, sacred sites under threat. This wasn't just about Eagle Ridge. This wasn't just about us. It was happening everywhere, in communities all across the continent. They were trying to wipe us out, to erase us from the land, using money and agreements to divide.

Dwayne leaned forward, his eyes locked on mine. "You should come with us to Vancouver. We're setting up a training house, young warriors, educating people on their rights."

Wilson nodded. "We need voices like yours. People who aren't afraid to stand up."

I looked at River and our cousins, knowing I couldn't leave yet. Not until the fight for Eagle Ridge was over. But I felt the pull of something bigger, something beyond this battle. A seed had been planted, and I knew, deep down, that this was just the beginning.

A year later, I would be in East Vancouver. I would be standing at the UN Climate Change Conference a year later.

And that would change everything.

Including my heart.

CHAPTER 26

The Occupation of Eagle Ridge

The call came in the dead of night.

I woke with a start, my body half out of bed, instincts kicking in before my mind could fully process the urgency in River's voice. "Nea, it's happening. They got the permits. The trucks are rolling in."

His words sent a shockwave through my chest. I didn't need any more information. I'd known this was coming, had known deep in my gut that the mine would stop at nothing to dig its claws into our land. But now, it was real.

Kevin stirred beside me, groaning as he rubbed his eyes, still half asleep. "What's going on?"

I kissed his forehead, feeling the moment's weight press down on me. "I have to go. It's the mine."

I didn't say anything else because there was nothing more to say. Kevin didn't need an explanation. He knew the fight for Eagle Ridge was everything to me, and even though it scared him, he didn't try to stop me.

Within the hour, I was back on the rez. The air felt different—thick with tension, heavy with the threat of destruction. The sacred mountain was being torn apart before my eyes. The hum of heavy machinery and the sight of bulldozers digging into the earth sent a wave of nausea through me. Over a hundred people had gathered: family, cousins, Elders, and warriors, all ready to stand their ground. The land beneath our feet was being violated, and we would not let it happen without a fight.

Billy: The Betrayal in Plain Sight

I found Billy standing with the corporate suits, arms folded, wearing a black jacket that seemed too sharp for someone who had once been part of this land, this people. He was smooth, unshaken like he'd done this a thousand times. The same Billy who had once stood by my side, who had known the stories of our people, who had sat in the sweat lodge with us and helped Mom in the kitchen. The same Billy who had shared secrets with me as children, whispering about dreams of a better life. Now, he was the enemy.

Billy wasn't just a lawyer anymore. He was the face of everything that was being sold, everything that was being lost. He stood there smiling, proud of himself for being "successful." I wanted to scream, tried to tear him apart, but I held it in, my body rigid with anger.

I turned to Grampa, River, and Mom; Dad was still away working up North. Where was he when we needed him? "We have to stop this."

And so, the Eagle Ridge Occupation began.

The Camp: A War Begins

For 45 days, we held the line. Each day felt like a test of endurance and resolve. The Native Youth Movement warriors—Dwayne, Wilson, Tommy, and others—arrived first. These weren't just kids with signs and slogans; these were warriors. Their faces were hardened by battles fought in other communities, other lands, where sacred places had been desecrated for the sake of s. They had scars, not just physical ones, but scars that ran deeper, the kind that came from years of watching their people lose everything.

They trained us. They taught us how to build strong barricades to withstand the police force. How to protect our Elders, the keepers of our stories and wisdom. How can we stand in unity, shoulder to shoulder, when the RCMP comes? Their preparation wasn't just about physical survival and protecting our culture, identity, and future.

Every night, Mom cooked meals over the fire. She was calm, but I saw the tension in her hands as she stirred the pot. Dad finally back to help on the frontline, was always on edge. He spent hours sharpening axes, speaking in low voices with the Elders, and strategizing.

And Grampa, every morning, he prayed. He would place his weathered hands on the earth, whispering to the land, apologizing for the fight he knew we had to fight but wishing it could be different. I could see its weight in sorrow and determination.

But Billy? He was like a king on his throne.

"The Band Council supports this, Nea," Billy said one afternoon, standing by his shiny new truck, looking every bit the corporate lawyer he had become. "This is money for our people."

I couldn't believe it. I wanted to scream. I wanted to shove him down into the dirt and make him understand that he didn't represent us, that he didn't speak for the land, the ancestors, or the future of our children.

"You don't speak for all of our people, and there are other communities across Canada that don't support these mines," I said, my voice low and deadly.

His smirk faltered for a second, but then he recovered. His eyes didn't show guilt, didn't show remorse. They were cold. Detached. He had already made his choice.

The Raid: RCMP

On the 45th day, the RCMP tactical assault team arrived. They came at dawn, their black uniforms a stark contrast against the pale light of morning. The sound of their boots crunching on the gravel was like the march of an invading army. They weren't here to talk, to negotiate. They were here to crush us. They brought helicopters and surveillance planes. They declared it an exclusion zone for "public safety" and to prevent journalists from entering.

Armed with automatic rifles, riot gear, and batons, they stormed the camp, tearing through it with the precision of a military operation. Chaos erupted. People were screaming, rushing to protect the Elders, pushing barricades into place. But nothing could stop them.

And then they came for Grampa Oliver.

I will never forget the sickening sound—of a fist connecting with Grampa's face. The RCMP officer who struck him didn't care. He didn't care who he was hitting or what he was breaking.

That was when I snapped.

River and I rushed forward, adrenaline coursing through our veins. We took the officer down, fists flying, driven by something primal, something ancestral. I didn't even recognize the rage that consumed me, the fierce protectiveness. This wasn't just about the mine. It was about everything they had taken from us—the land, the people, the stories. This was a fight for our survival.

They beat us for it. The crack of the baton against my ribs was like a shockwave of pain, but I didn't care. I could hear River shouting beside me, the sickening thud of boots against his body.

When they finally dragged us away, our hands were bound with zip ties, our bodies bloodied, our spirits defiant. We were shoved into the paddy wagon, the cold metal pressing against my skin. I locked eyes with him as we passed Billy, standing with the corporate suits.

I spat blood at his feet. "You did this."

For the first time, Billy looked ashamed. He tried to rush over to Grampa Oliver, but the warriors would not let him near.

Jail, Kevin, and the Aftermath

I don't remember much about the drive to jail. I was in and out of consciousness, my ribs screaming with pain. I remember Kevin, though. I had been hit over the head with a baton and my vision was blurry, blood burned in my eyes.

We sat in the Kamloops jail for what seemed like days but was only overnight. Kevin was the first person I saw when I exited the jail. He was white as a sheet, his hands clenched into fists. His father—one of the higher-ups in the local, used his influence and pulled strings to get us released.

Kevin's arms were around me instantly, holding me steady as I nearly collapsed. He whispered, "I got you," and I let myself believe it momentarily. I let myself feel the comfort of his embrace.

But the mine? The mine was still happening. The bulldozers were still rolling. The destruction was still underway. The camp was gone. The police had won.

Billy? Billy walked away with a six-figure deal, a shiny new future built on the blood of our land.

River and I stood at the edge that night as the bulldozers began their work. It was dusty; their work and all the trees had been cleared. The earth was being torn apart beneath us, and I felt the loss deep in my bones. The sacred mountain was slipping away, and we couldn't stop it.

"Was it worth it?" I whispered, my voice barely audible over the noise of the machines.

River didn't answer. He just handed me a bundle of cedar, his eyes grim. Without a word, he led me to the sweat lodge.

I had two broken ribs, a concussion, a fractured spirit, and the sinking realization that this was just the beginning. The fight for Eagle Ridge wasn't over. And neither was the war for our land.

PART 2
The Wolves Becoming

CHAPTER 27

Mending Wounds, Building Resistance:

After the Occupation

I lay in bed, wincing as I tried to move. Broken ribs, a bruised body, and a fractured spirit. Every breath was a reminder of the RCMP raid, of the batons, of the police boots slamming into my side.

Kevin sat beside me, his strong hands carefully pressing an ice pack to my ribs. His eyes darkened whenever he looked at the damage they'd done to me.

"I should have been there," he muttered for the hundredth time.

"You had midterms," I rasped. "You don't belong in jail, Kevin."

But he wasn't listening. His jaw was tight, his muscles flexing as he gently rubbed my arms and my shoulders, easing the tension out of my battered and wrapped his arms around me carefully and protectively, careful, protective. "You scared the shit out of me, Nea."

For the first time since the raid, I let my guard down. I let him hold me. I let myself be small, just for a moment.

And then, as Kevin always did, he made me laugh. I winced; laughter was not a good idea with broken ribs.

"You know," he mused, brushing a strand of hair from my face, "we should take this fight academic."

Taking the Fight to the Classroom

Dr. Webbles, my anthropology professor, had been following the fight. He was outraged.

"They arrested you? Beat your Elders? Over a mine? In 1980, that might've flown under the radar. But this? This is a human rights violation."

I sat in his office, still sore and healing but more determined than ever.

"You want to fight this? We take it academic," Dr. Webbles said, pacing. "We publish. We get the media involved. We get the universities involved. You get people outside the rez to care."

So we did.

I wrote articles. Kevin, Dr. Webbles, and I gathered research on land stewardship, Indigenous resistance, and the environmental impact of copper mining. We got letters of support from professors, environmentalists, and even politicians. We shared copies with the movement in Vancouver.

By the end of the semester, our research was being cited in environmental law courses. The mine might have started, but we weren't done fighting.

The Native Youth Movement Rises

Meanwhile, the NYM was growing.

We weren't just a small group of warriors anymore. After the raid at Eagle Ridge, we were getting calls from other Indigenous communities across BC.

"Teach us," they said. "Help us fight."

We became the BC Chapter.

We trained.

Blockade strategies.

Legal rights in protest.

Survival skills for long-term occupations.

Dwayne, Wilson, Tommy—they were our core warriors.

But me? I was both a fighter and a scholar.

I was writing the movement's story while living it.

Kevin was there through it all.

Through late-night study sessions, tracing bruises on my ribs with soft fingers. Through press conferences, where he held my hand under the table.

Through the nights when I broke down, feeling like we were losing, feeling like nothing we did mattered, he was there.

But Kevin was about sports, university, and a career in coaching.

I was about the revolution.

And Vancouver was calling.

"Come with me," I whispered one night after another long day of fighting, writing, and planning.

He smiled sadly. "Nea, I can't."

Because he was safe here, he was a golden boy.

And I was already halfway out the door.

CHAPTER 28

A Last Hurrah & The Road Ahead After the Occupation

I was healing. Slowly but surely.

Kevin, River, and my activist friends were there every step of the way as I pushed through the pain to finish the semester.

Kevin helped me study, Doc Webbles checked in constantly, and River ensured I still found moments to laugh.

Then, the final moment is the Regional Lacrosse Championships.

The Last Championship

We all piled into cars, heading to watch Kevin and his team fight for the title.

The stadium was packed, the energy electric.

Kevin was in his element—fast, aggressive, unstoppable. A warrior on the field, dodging, weaving, striking with perfect precision.

When they won, the entire stadium erupted in celebration.

Kevin lifted his stick in victory, eyes searching for me in the crowd. When he found me, grinning, he pointed straight at me.

I cheered, my voice hoarse.

For one night, we weren't fighting. We were just young, wild, and alive.

A Final Hurrah

The pub was packed.

Sweet Child of Mine blasted through the speakers. The river was dancing with two girls, laughing, with a beer in hand.

Kevin had an arm around me, his mouth close to my ear.

"One last night?" he murmured.

I just smiled. "One last night."

Doc Webbles even showed up for a bit, raising a glass to me.

"Nea, you're not done yet," he said, pressing a folded piece of paper into my hand.

I unfolded it—a recommendation letter for an anthropology conference in Albuquerque.

I stared at him in shock. "Are you serious?"

"You belong in that room," he said simply. "You belong in a hundred rooms like it."

The road was stretching out in front of me.

And Kevin felt it, too.

He kissed me slowly that night like he knew I wasn't his to keep.

From Kevin's POV – The Night Before Nea Leaves for East Van

The rain drummed softly against the window, its rhythm steady, grounding. Nea's breath was slow, steady, warm against my chest as she lay curled into me. Her long hair spilled over my arm, strands tangling like threads of fate that I wasn't ready to unravel.

I watched her sleep, her body fitting against mine like she had been carved from the same clay. There was always something ethereal about Nea—like she lived between worlds, caught between the past and the present, the seen and unseen.

I had spent my life trying to understand things beyond the physical. The months I spent meditating in Nepal's high mountain temples had cracked something open within me. The monks had taught me about Anahata—the unstruck sound, the heart chakra, the energy of boundless love. Love without possession, love without chains.

But lying here, with Nea in my arms, I felt the pull of human love— the kind that ached, wanted, and longed.

I knew I would love her from the moment I met her, not just in this lifetime but across many. There was something ancient in how we fit together, something that whispered of other lives and promises made in forgotten tongues.

She shifted in her sleep, her brow furrowing as though she could feel me thinking too loud. I kissed her head, inhaling the familiar scent of cedar and wild earth.

I knew what was coming. She was leaving.

Nea belonged to the fight—the land, spirit world, and battles waged beyond my understanding. I was the anchor, the healer, the one who could keep her soft when the world demanded she be hard. But I couldn't stop her from going.

And I wouldn't.

Love without possession. Love with detachment. Love without chains. That was the lesson.

I tightened my arms around her, memorizing the feeling of her warmth against me, knowing that I would have to let her go come morning.

Their Lovemaking – Pure Light, Universal Love

There was no rush, no hunger that needed to be fed—only connection.

As Kevin kissed her, he whispered ancient blessings into her skin. Mantras he had learned in the high temples, prayers for love, protection, and peace.

Their bodies moved like waves meeting the shore, effortless, destined.

And then, as they reached the height of their love, light filled the space between them. Soft at first, then radiant.

They were glowing.

A golden hue pulsed from their joined bodies, filling the room with warmth, with something holy. The kind of love that transcended flesh that vibrated at the frequency of the divine.

Kevin felt it.

Nea felt it.

For a moment, she forgot every heartbreak that had come before, every battle still ahead. There was only this. This love. This presence. This moment.

The Rift Begins

The last few weeks were bittersweet.

We spent every moment we could together, but we both knew—

My road was leading elsewhere.

Kevin was a lacrosse coach at the university.

I was on the frontlines of activism amid war.

And after everything that happened at the rez, after barely escaping jail… I wasn't the same.

The NYM was shifting.

Some were turning to writing, using the pen to protest.

Some were training to kill.

River told me that Dwayne and Wilson had been partying harder and getting more reckless.

And East Van was waiting.

This was my road.

And I took it.

CHAPTER 29

Leaving the Land, Losing My Spirit

"I thought I was moving forward, but I was walking away. I left behind more than Kai. I left my language, medicine, and spirit behind, but my spirit was restless. My Mom said the spirit of the grizzly wouldn't calm."

The city was nothing like what I imagined.

Vancouver felt like a buzzing, unrelenting pulse that surged through every street and every person. Yet, somehow, it left me feeling smaller, more insignificant. The skyscrapers towered over me, their glass façades gleaming like a promise of something I could never touch. The noise was constant—traffic, voices, construction, the hum of thousands of people rushing to somewhere, anywhere. Everything moved fast here, but I couldn't catch up. It was 1996.

When I arrived in Vancouver, I was supposed to feel something—hope, excitement, a sense of new beginnings. Instead, I felt as though I was slipping away from the one thing that had ever truly grounded me: my connection to the land, my people, and the spirit of my ancestors. It was like the earth beneath my feet had been replaced by something that didn't hold me, something that didn't care if I existed.

I had told myself it was time to leave. It was time to escape the weight of the past, the haunting memories of Eagle Ridge, and everything I had fought for, fought against. But it wasn't just the fight that had torn at my heart—it was the loss of what I had once had. My culture. The language that had shaped me. The stories Grandpa Oliver used to tell me in quiet evenings by the fire. I thought moving to Vancouver would give me a clean slate—a chance to start fresh and rebuild.

But all I found was a gaping hole inside me, one I couldn't fill with the bright lights and fast-paced life around me.

I would go to the university daily, sit in lecture halls filled with students from everywhere and nowhere, and pretend I fit in. But the truth was, I didn't. I wasn't from here. I wasn't one of them. I felt like a stranger in my skin, caught between two worlds I didn't belong to.

At night, I would walk the streets, my thoughts swirling, the sounds of the city buzzing in my ears. I recall sitting by the waterfront one evening, watching the city's lights flicker across the water.

The lights reflected in the water, but it didn't feel like home. I missed the stars, the constellations I used to watch from Eagle Ridge, the quiet forest at night, and the sound of the river as it rushed past.

In the city, I couldn't hear the spirits anymore they had faded from the events of the past. The silence. The absence of the guidance I had once felt so strongly.

The Present: The Spiritual Disconnect

Now, I know what I couldn't understand then. My spirit was already unraveling before I even realized it. I had traded the quiet guidance of the land for the loud distractions of the city.

I stopped listening to the whispers of the wind, the stories in the rustling of the leaves, the rhythm of the earth beneath my feet. The spirits had gone quiet, but I was too wrapped up in my distractions to notice. I was busy with books and activism.

In Vancouver, I would stand in the crowd, surrounded by people, yet feel utterly alone. I was lost, not in the city, but in myself.

The more I pushed forward, the further I moved from who I was. I abandoned my language, the words I had spoken with my family, the prayers we had said together. I hadn't realized how much I needed them until they were gone. The language wasn't just words—it was the breath of my people, the rhythm of my ancestors' hearts. Without it, I felt like a piece of me had been stripped away.

I left behind my medicine, too—the teachings I had received from the Elders about how to care for myself, heal, and remain balanced in the face of chaos. I thought the city would offer me something better and faster, but it gave me a disconnected and hollow life.

And my spirit? I left it behind, too, without even knowing it. The sacred ceremonies, the sweat lodges, and the moments of prayer and reflection by the fire were the things that kept me whole and connected to my roots. But I was too busy to notice the gap and trying to build something that wasn't meant for me.

The City and the Silence

The first time I truly felt the weight of this loss was during a night when I was alone at the training house. A rare moment alone.

I was sitting on the floor, the glow of the city lights streaming through the window, but all I could hear was the buzzing in my ears. It was like the silence wrapped around me, pressing in from all sides.

I tried to pray. I tried to speak the words my grandmother had taught me, but they felt foreign on my tongue like they didn't belong to me anymore. The words felt too heavy to lift, and my connection to them felt thin, like a thread about to snap.

That night, I lay awake, staring at the ceiling, my heart pounding. I had convinced myself that moving here, leaving the land, was the right choice. But deep inside, I could feel the fracture. The pain of losing something so fundamental to who I was. It wasn't just about the land. It was about losing myself in the process. But I couldn't go back already. I knew I needed to evolve and that there were things I needed to see, learn, and do.

The Guilt and the Longing

There were times when I felt guilty for leaving for leaving after the fight at Eagle Ridge.

For abandoning my people. I told myself I needed to be here, learn, grow, and fight on a larger scale. But the truth was, I didn't know where to start. I didn't know how to bridge the gap between what I had lost and what I was trying to find.

Sometimes, I would close my eyes and imagine myself back at Eagle Ridge, standing at the edge of the mountain, feeling the wind on my face, hearing the sounds of the river, listening to the voices of my ancestors in the rustling leaves.

I would imagine my mom's hands in mine, her soft voice telling me the stories of our people, and the weight of her words anchoring me.

But that was a memory now. A memory I couldn't reach, no matter how hard I tried.

The Struggle to Reconnect

I don't know if I'll ever fully reconnect to that part of me. Maybe the city will never feel like home. Maybe the land is where I truly belong, where my spirit is rooted.

But even now, as I sit here in this unfamiliar city, I know I must return to it.

I have to find the words, the language, the medicine again. I must remember how to listen and hear the spirits once more. Maybe it won't be easy or happen immediately, but I can't keep walking away from myself. Not anymore.

The land may be far away, but it's still with me. It always will be.

CHAPTER 30

East Van Life

The city smelled different—wet pavement, cigarettes, cedar smoke curling from alleyways, and the salty air of the Pacific mixing with gasoline.

East Vancouver had a pulse.

It was nothing like home. There were still mountains to the North but no river whispering stories, but there was the vastness of the Pacific Ocean. And graffiti-stained alleys was humming with life, and the constant sound of sirens cut through the night.

I took a deep breath and stepped into my new life.

The Warrior House

The house was packed—full of warriors, activists, and revolutionaries.

Inside, every room told a story.

One room had maps pinned to the walls, marking pipeline routes, mining projects, and protest sites.

Another had a makeshift gym—punching bags duct-taped together, weights stacked in the corner.

The living room was a war room.

Dwayne, Wilson, and Tommy were smoking and debating strategy.

"We've got a blockade training this weekend," Dwayne told me, flicking a cigarette out the open window. "You'll learn quickly that Vancouver protests differ from the rez."

I smiled. "I think I can handle it."

Wilson grinned. "We'll see."

Training for the Frontlines

Day one was survival.

How to lock your arms in a blockade.

How to break a police hold.

How to move when the riot cops charge.

How to take a hit and keep standing.

Dwayne taught me how to go limp when arrested.

Wilson taught me how to spot undercover cops.

Tommy taught me how to run when shit went sideways.

By the end of the day, I was bruised, sore, exhausted.

And I felt alive.

The Divide: Peace vs. War

But something was shifting in the movement.

Some of us believed in peaceful resistance, media, and storytelling. The oral tradition of our ancestors.

Others?

They were training for war.

I saw it in Dwayne's eyes.

In the new people showing up—ex-military, ex-gang members.

Some nights, the house smelled like sage and cedar, and prayers were whispered before a rally.

Other nights, it smelled like gun oil and whiskey.

And I was standing right in the middle.

Albuquerque is Coming

One night, Tommy slid a flyer across the table.

UN Climate Change Conference—Albuquerque, New Mexico.

"We need someone to speak," he said. "You're it," I told them Dr. Weebles had gotten me on a panel on Indigenous resistance and land stewardship.

I swallowed. New Mexico.

Something about it pulled at me.

A whisper. A memory. A call from the land itself.

This was bigger than just the rez. This was bigger than just BC. This was the world. And I was walking straight into it.

CHAPTER 31

Rez Blues & Revolution: East Van NYM

The living room was packed.

Dwayne was perched on the couch, guitar on his knee, fingers plucking a slow, lazy tune.

"This one's for all the warriors, all the rez dogs turned activists," he said with a smirk, shifting into a blues riff, voice dipping low.

"They wanna steal the land,

Lay the pipeline down,

But we ain't movin', no,

We stand our ground."

Wilson drummed his fingers on the table, keeping rhythm. Tommy joined in, tapping an empty beer can against the wall.

I sat on the arm of the couch, laughing, but also thinking.

George Manuel's book, Our Manifesto, was spread open on the table.

The Fourth World and Brotherhood to Nationhood.

A guide, a prophecy, a call to arms.

We had underlined passages, dog-eared pages, and scrawled notes in the margins.

"This is what we stand for," Tommy said, pointing at a passage.

"We are Nations, not minorities," Wilson added.

But outside this room?

Outside this house?

The lines were blurring.

The Indian Bar

Friday night, we hit the Indian Bar.

It had brown faces, Warrior's t-shirts, long braids, and combat boots.

The DJ played everything from Willie Dunn to Metallica.

The boys were wild.

A group of white preps were sitting at the bar, whispering, glancing over like we were animals in a zoo. I was thinking they must have wandered into the wrong bar.

Tommy knocked back a shot of whiskey, squared his shoulders, and started walking.

I grabbed his arm. "Don't."

"Just gonna have a chat," he said with a grin.

I already knew how this night would end.

A fight. Cops. Someone in the drunk tank.

Again.

Holding It Together

By the time I pulled Tommy, Wilson, and two others out of the bar, it was almost 3 AM.

They were laughing, wiping blood off their knuckles, high on violence.

I was exhausted.

This was the other side of the movement.

The side that wouldn't change.

Gandhi vs. The Warriors

The next night, I stood in the living room, holding up a book on Gandhi.

"There's another way," I said.

Half the group nodded, murmuring their agreement.

The other half?

Wilson leaned against the wall, arms crossed. "You think a hunger strike's gonna stop a fucking mining company?"

Tommy scoffed. "Yeah, let's all hold hands and sing Kumbaya while they bulldoze our land."

Tension.

It was growing.

We were doing great work, but the cracks were showing.

I said with conviction, "We can find a way to do both; it doesn't have to be one or the other."

What Would Grandpa Oliver Say?

That night, I sat outside, rolling sage between my fingers.

I thought about Grandpa Oliver.

What would he say?

"Fire feeds fire, but water shapes the land slowly over time, and even the sharpest river rocks edges turn soft and rounded by water."

His words echoed in my head.

I was trying to be water.

But I was standing in a house full of fire.

Sweatlodge Before Albuquerque

Before I left for New Mexico, we had a ceremony in Vancouver.

The lodge was built outside the city, tucked away in the trees.

Grandpa Oliver was there. Mom, Dad, River.

I sat in the dark, the heat pressing against me, sweat rolling down my spine.

The water hissed as it hit the stones, sending steam curling into the air.

I prayed for guidance.

For strength.

For clarity.

Grandpa's voice rumbled through the lodge: "You don't have to carry it all, Nea."

I took a deep breath.

Because I had been.

And I wasn't sure how much longer I could.

CHAPTER 32

The Manifesto:

The Four Pillars & The Hopi Prophecy

We were gathered in a dimly lit room, the weight of history pressing in on us as we stared at the printed words on the paper. The walls seemed to breathe with the energy of the people before us—the warriors, the healers, the storytellers. Our ancestors, standing behind us, holding the line.

The manifesto was more than just words. It was a call to action, a declaration of intent. It was a promise to those who had fought before us and those who would fight long after we were gone. This was the beginning of something bigger, something far beyond what we could fully comprehend at that moment.

And I felt it deep in my bones—the gravity of what we were about to undertake.

1. The Land Is Not For Sale

"We do not own the land. The land owns us. We are caretakers, not conquerors. The Earth is alive, and we must listen to her. We are returning to the way of ceremony, the way our Elders taught us; as we pray to the Creator, we are grateful that all we have been given, the land, the waters, fish, and wildlife are our brothers and sisters, the trees and the plants speak to us. We have not forgotten how to listen."

As Dwayne spoke, I thought about Eagle Ridge. I thought about my mother's hands in mine, her teachings that had once guided me. How she had told me, over and over again, that the land was not something to be possessed but something to be cared for. Something to be honored.

The land had given us life. It had provided us with everything we needed—from the food we harvested to the medicines we gathered. The rivers were our veins, the mountains our backbone. And now, in the name of progress, it was being torn apart.

The Hopi Prophecy echoed in my mind: *"The land shall be poisoned. The rivers will run dry. The trees will fall, and the air will grow thick with sickness. The People will forget the old ways. But in the time of the Great Purification, the ones who remember will rise."*

At that moment, I realized the weight of the prophecy. It wasn't just a warning. It was a roadmap. We were the ones who remembered. We were the ones who had to rise.

2. Indigenous Sovereignty is Non-Negotiable

"We are not minorities. We are Nations. We have our laws, our governance, our way of life. We will not be silenced. We worked together, we sometimes battled other Nations to expand our territories but we heed our Elders. The Elders say whatever we do to our waters to our lands we do to the Nations downstream to us. We make decisions not on just our parts of the rivers, lakes and oceans we think about the impact on all. We must return to stewarding our lands, and governing for all those who are impacted not just one, we have vision and these colonial governments have lost sight of the long term of the 7 generations."

River stood beside me as we read the words, his jaw set in a way that told me he was already thinking five steps ahead. His commitment to our people was unwavering, even when the world around him seemed to pull us in different directions.

The Hopi Prophecy warned: *"The ones who seek power will make treaties with forked tongues. They will promise peace but bring division. The People must not fall for their illusions. They must stand together, speak with one voice, and remember who they are."*

I thought about Billy again. He had become the face of betrayal, sitting in meetings with corporate types, promising progress in exchange for our land. I had once believed that he might find a way to bridge the gap, but now I saw the truth more clearly: there could be no compromise. Our sovereignty was not for sale, no matter how slick the deals or shiny the promises.

The time for words was over. It was time for action.

3. Resource Extraction is Modern-Day Colonization

"They come with their machines, contracts, promises of wealth. But what is wealth without water? What is progress without life? Our salmon are dying in our rivers unable to travel upstream due to dams, due to the siltation of our rivers from forestry and clear-cutting, they cannot find areas to spawn. The salmon choke in our rivers and oceans unable to breathe as the water temperatures rise due to pollution and industry, cutting forests worldwide the loss of Old Growth forests our Ancient trees who have kept the air balanced for billions of years. When salmon the keystone species is gone, we will be next, the Elders have warned us for decades. We will all be lost if we don't change. "

I thought of the heavy machinery, the bulldozers carving into Eagle Ridge. I thought of the children running across the land, their laughter echoing through the air, unaware of the destruction that was being set in motion.

The Hopi Prophecy foresaw: *"When the Black Snake crosses the land, it will bring great destruction. The waters will turn to poison, the fish will die, and the People will fall sick. The Black Snake is greed, the pipeline, the drilling, the mining. It must be stopped, or the Earth will weep."*

We had seen the damage done by resource extraction in other places—tailing ponds bursting, rivers poisoned, land rendered uninhabitable. But we were told it was necessary. We were told it was progress.

But I knew better now. Progress was not measured in profits or extraction. Progress was measured in the health of the Earth. In the lives of our people.

4. The Future is Watching

"What we do today will echo for generations. We cannot afford to fail them. We see the 7 generations ahead of us. As the Native Youth of today, we are over 50% of the population, yet we have no voice in our communities; only our Elders and matriarchs listen to us. The decisions Chiefs and colonial governments make today will affect us and our children. We will not let those decisions be made without us. Where are our Hereditary leadership, Matriarchs, Elders, and Ceremony leaders? We look to you and walk with you in ceremony to find the way."

Dwayne's voice was steady, but I could hear the fire in it. This was personal for him, for all of us. We had seen our ancestors' struggle, and felt their spirits guide us, but this? This was the moment when it would all come to a head.

The Hopi Prophecy is called *"The time of the Rainbow Warriors has come. They will be of many colors and from many Nations, but they will know the same truth. The Earth must be protected. They will rise, and the People will follow."*

And there it was. The prophecy was unfolding in real time. The world was shifting, and we had a choice: to remain silent or to rise. We had the chance to stand on the right side of history. The future, the next generation, was watching us.

We could not fail them. We would not fail them.

We stood back, the weight of the manifesto settling on our shoulders. His hand was still on the table, and Dwayne looked around at each of us, his eyes burning with conviction.

"Then let's make them listen," he said, his voice low but powerful.

The path was clear.

The battle had begun.

Dwayne had always been the strong force in our group. He was a natural leader with a way of words; when he spoke, people listened, but his actions always spoke louder than his words. He was a leader and a warrior. He had a history that none of us fully understood, a past that shaped the warrior he had become. Growing up in a family that had fought against the system at every turn, Dwayne had learned early on that change didn't come without sacrifice. He had lost family members to the fight and had seen firsthand what the world was capable of, and it had only made him more determined.

But it wasn't just about fighting for the land—it was about fighting for something greater. For the future. For the children who would never know what it means to be connected to the Earth unless we take action now.

I looked at River, who stood beside me, his face etched with the weight of the fight and his unshakable love for our people. He wasn't just fighting for Eagle Ridge, for the land. He was fighting for us— our culture, language, and way of life. He had always been the protector, the one who held the group together, who knew when to speak and when to listen. But I saw a new fire in him now. This fight was personal. He was now working with our Nation's leading work on fisheries; when he wasn't working, he came to East Van to be part of the movement and was my rock.

And I realized, as the words from the manifesto sank in, that it was personal for me, too. This wasn't just a fight for the land—it was a fight for the essence of who we were, for everything we had lost and still had to protect.

We were the Rainbow Warriors. We were ready to rise.

CHAPTER 33

The Lodge & The Manifesto:

Before the Occupation

The fire crackled outside the lodge.

The sacred space had been prepared—Grandpa Oliver overseeing every step, River tending the fire, the NYM boys watching, waiting.

Wilson, Tommy, Dwayne, and the others were restless—warriors in their own right, coming from Nations across Canada: Ojibway, Cree, Coast Salish the sweatlodge wasn't traditional for all of them.

Inside, the air was thick with heat, the scent of cedar and sage weaving into the rising steam.

I knelt beside Mom, River, and Grandpa Oliver. Daddio was off again, working up North in camp.

The others filed in, their voices hushed, their bodies tense.

It was time.

The Four Rounds of Prayer

First Round: The Ancestors

Grandpa Oliver spoke first, calling to the Ancestors.

"We ask for their guidance, their wisdom, their strength."

The heat pressed in.

Sweat dripped from my brow, soaking into the earth beneath me.

I closed my eyes, feeling the spirits stir.

I saw them vaguely, slightly shifting and unclear in the darkness—shadowed figures standing beyond the veil, watching, listening.

The ones who walked before us.

Second Round: The Sacred Feminine and Mother Earth

I found my voice in the round.

"She has given us everything. And now, we must protect her and all women everywhere, the women who give life, the women who have been lost and disappeared on these city streets."

The heat burned through me, but I sat firm.

This was my purpose.

I looked around the darkened lodge at my brothers and family.

We all carried the same fire.

Third Round: The Men and the Warriors

Wilson spoke next, his voice sharp, edged.

"We fight because we must. We stand because we have no other choice. We pray for the men who have been lost to us who suffer on these streets from addiction, and we fight for our lands, warriors to the end."

The NYM boys nodded, murmuring their agreement.

This was their path.

Some would fight with words.

Some would fight with action.

But the battle was the same.

I pressed my palms against the earth, grounding myself.

Fourth Round: For Ourselves and The Future Generations

Grampa Oliver started to speak quiet but clear.

"We don't fight for ourselves. We fight for the ones not yet born. But we pray for our souls that we connect with the Creator, our ancestors, and the land, and they give us strength to do our inner healing so that we may take the right action."

The stones hissed as more water was poured, the steam rising, enveloping us.

I thought of the children, the ones yet to come.

Would they inherit a world of forests, rivers, and sacred lands?

Or would they inherit dust and concrete?

Grampa Oliver sang the Healing Song. I cried for myself, everyone here, and everyone lost. I asked Creator for forgiveness for any I had hurt and to help me find forgiveness for those who had hurt me.

The Peace Pipe & The Pact

When we stepped outside, the night was cool against my skin.

The stars stretched endless above us, the fire flickering in the clearing.

Grandpa Oliver sat cross-legged, lighting the sacred pipe and singing the pipe-loading song.

The smell of kinnikinick filled the air as he took the first pull, holding the smoke and sending it up to the sky.

Then he passed it.

We took the pipe one by one, inhaling the smoke and exhaling our intentions.

> "We will all work in different ways."

> "We will honor each path."

> "We will stand together."

Some of us would write.

Some of us would speak.

Some of us would fight.

But we would all carry the fire forward.

Drafting the Manifesto

That night, we gathered around the kitchen table.

George Manuel's books lay open beside us.

The notes from our movement.

The teachings from the lodge.

The blueprint of our fight.

We had one night to craft a message for the UN Climate Conference.

One night to make them see.

The Manifesto: The Four Pillars

1. The Land Is Not For Sale

> "We do not own the land. The land owns us. We are caretakers, not conquerors. The earth is alive, and we must listen to her."

2. Indigenous Sovereignty is Non-Negotiable

> "We are not minorities. We are Nations. We have our laws, our governance, our way of life. We will not be silenced."

3. Resource Extraction is Modern-Day Colonization

"They come with their machines, contracts, promises of wealth. But what is wealth without water? What is progress without life?"

4. The Future is Watching

"What we do today will echo for generations. We cannot afford to fail them."

We sat back, staring at the words.

They were more than just a statement.

They were a battle cry.

Dwayne grinned, slamming his fist against the table.

"Let's see them ignore this."

We had our message.

Now, it was time to take it to the world. But first, the occupation at the Treaty office.

CHAPTER 34

The Treaty Table with Empty Chairs

The massive hotel banquet hall smelled of fresh coffee, industry, and polished shoes. Overhead, fluorescents buzzed like restless mosquitoes, their white light slicing through the dim air and glancing off the glossy plastic nameplates arranged in a long line of panelists and speakers.

Nea paused at the threshold. Her breath caught in her throat.

The tables.

They were round, but they weren't ours.

Each seat bore a name. Not one of them was hers.

Not hers. Not her mother's. Not Auntie Jean's, who still taught language softly in the old trailer by the rec field like so many others in communities across Turtle Island. Not the medicine keeper who'd packed cedar-smoked salmon for the feast. Not the young ones who organized the roadblocks last month. Not the Elders who had refused to sign those modern treaties.

The people who lived on the land were not at the table.

They had been given chairs to sit *behind,* if at all. Most wouldn't waste their time.

Observers.

Listeners.

Silent witnesses to the negotiation of their inheritance.

Nea stepped across the threshold and moved along the perimeter, her boots whispering across waxed linoleum. Motions practiced. A few heads turned. A few bowed. She passed men in dark suits who had memorized legal briefs but not the names of the rivers. Pens clicked. Lips curved into polite smiles that never reached their eyes.

The space felt tight. Choked with the breath of bureaucracy.

Along the far wall, an Elder stood. Their shoulders squared despite the lean of his cane, arms crossed like a gathering storm. His face was creased by wind and years of ceremony. When their eyes met, he nodded once—firm, quiet.

Nea nodded back. She pressed her tongue to the roof of her mouth to still the tremor in her chest.

This wasn't just a meeting.

It was a funeral.

The table was a coffin.

And the Treaty Process—a script read aloud without a soul.

1996.

The year they called it progress. The year they signed away pieces of the sky. Nisga'a had inked their deal in British Columbia, and Canada had toasted itself with press bulletins and champagne flutes. Delgamuukw lingered like a question mark in the courthouse hallways, poorly understood by the judges tasked with implementing it. UNDRIP was just a draft on distant desks in Geneva, laughed out of Ottawa's committee rooms.

But here, beneath lights too bright and chairs too white, Nea felt the truth:

This wasn't recognition.

It was erasure dressed in protocol.

She found a folding chair along the back wall. No nameplate. No microphone. She opened it. Sat down. Spine straight. Hands folded in her lap.

And listened.

The meeting began.

An assistant stamped an agenda and handed out crisp copies, each marked with the silver crest of Indian Affairs. Nea glanced at the back page. A small blank margin waited there—clean, untouched. A space she would fill.

The speakers rotated.

They used phrases like weapons: *certainty*. *Extinguishment*. *Certainty* again. Repeating the words like spells that might make them true.

One chief spoke too gently as if the land could no longer hear. His voice carried the careful cadence of compromise:

"We recognize the need for certainty. We acknowledge past errors. We invite collaboration on a framework for the future."

Nea's hands itched.

She imagined standing. Calling out names:

Auntie Jean, who taught language in secret.

Maudie, who healed with salmon broth and cedar smoke.

The girls who chained themselves across highways.

The grandmothers held ceremonies deep in the trees long after the priests had forbidden them. They beat the children in Indian Residential School.

She wanted to shatter the room. Split the speakers' table in half. But she stayed seated.

Watched.

Listened.

The Elder across the hall never wavered. She remembered his stories—of regalia buried in moss, river crossings made in silence, and sacred bundles carried through the snow. His bloodline was woven into the land like cedar roots.

And now they were being asked to sign it away.

The afternoon dragged on. Legal counsel recited clause after clause. Their voices were flat as ledger entries. The word *extinguishment* came again—monotone, dry, final.

Nea imagined the table as a casket—the ink on those papers like fresh blood.

Then came the minister: gray suit, polished words.

"This framework," he said, tapping the mic, "will ensure clarity. It will serve not only our generation but also generations that are yet unborn. This is historic and transformational for the future."

Generations yet unborn.

The phrase landed in Nea's chest like a stone.

The meeting ended. The pens clicked shut. Chairs scraped. Briefcases zipped. Delegates left with practiced nods and shallow applause.

Nea remained.

One woman. At one empty table. Holding space for everyone they had refused to see and listen to.

She reached into her coat and pulled out her pen. Uncapped it.

On the back of the agenda, in deliberate script, she wrote:

We were never at your table.
But we never needed to be.
The land remembers us.
And so do the Ancestors.

She folded the paper. Placed it in the exact center of the table.

Then stood.

And walked out—past the nameplates, suits, and heavy door that had once kept her out.

The latch clicked behind her.

Outside, the evening air wrapped around her like a drumbeat. The breeze stirred through spruce, carrying the scent of cedar and soil. She closed her eyes and breathed it in. Heard the voices in the wind: the rivers, the roots, the prayers buried under treaty lines.

She walked home to East Van, a place she knew and understood beneath the stars, her steps echoing like a ceremony.

The treaty table was behind her now.

But the land?

The land walked with her still, and the city spread before her.

CHAPTER 35

UNDRIP Isn't a Dream

The hotel loomed across cracked asphalt like a steel mountain quarried from someone else's dream. Fluorescent windows glared at Nea as she stepped from her old pickup, the ribbon skirt at her waist whispering against leather boots. She touched the earth beneath her soles, feeling its pulse—a distant drumbeat that thrummed beneath the conference center's concrete pad. The wind carried faint echoes of cedar smoke and eagle calls as if her ancestors were poking holes through the hotel's sterile walls to watch her arrive. She squared her shoulders. She had come for this summit, yet she carried a medicine woman's heart and a warrior's spear in her bones.

Inside, the lobby's polished marble forbade any sound, but the sandals scraped on the tile. White-suited delegates murmured around digital kiosks displaying treaty logos like corporate badges. Neon signs flickered overhead, announcing "Nation-to-Nation Unity." Yet Nea felt the building's breath slow as she passed—a held exhale, waiting to see what she might do. Beyond the revolving doors lay the ballroom: an arena of colonial theater where promises were paraded and buried.

She paused at the threshold. Round tables draped in starched linen stood like silent judges. Water pitchers glistened, sweating upon agendas printed in glossy ink. The hum of conversation dribbled around her, polite and perfumed with inertia. At the front, three flags hung limp: Canada's red maple leaf, British Columbia's union jack rising from a crown of sunbeams, and a generic Treaty Nation logo rendered in corporate clip art. None stirred. The land felt absent, held at bay by cheap carpeting and fluorescent lights.

Nea knelt. She pressed her palm to the floor, tracing an invisible line where ancient trails once met in council. The spirit of Raven brushed her ear, whispering: "Remember who walks here." She bowed her head and offered a silent prayer to the bones of hereditary chiefs buried beneath that very ground, to the children who'd played among those trees before the bulldozers came. Then she rose and settled into a chair at the back—no nameplate before her, just her ribbon skirt shining like a blood-red stream. The fire in her belly flared up in the cool room.

Across from her, a young minister tapped notes into a tablet, oblivious to the small drumbeat echoing in Nea's mind. A cluster of white consultants huddled over a land portfolio that divided that ground into squares, each stamped with a price tag. A fatigue-worn Chief fingered his lapel pin, the gold glinting like a cage. A single journalist sat poised with a recorder, smiling politely as if they all belonged to the same story. Yet Nea knew the myth of this gathering: it was a ritual of erasure, expertly choreographed to render thousands of years of sovereignty into legal footnotes.

The facilitator stood at the podium—a pale-faced man in a navy suit—with a microphone cradled like a holy relic. He cleared his throat. The hum of the air conditioners ceased for a heartbeat. "Welcome, everyone," he intoned, voice polished like distant thunder. "We gather today in the spirit of reconciliation to advance our Nation-to-Nation relationships. After our opening remarks, the floor will be open to community observers."

Nea felt the room tilt. Chairs squeaked as she rose. A ripple ran through the delegates, a faint disturbance in their choreographed grid. The old lights flickered, and for a moment, Nea caught a flash of dancing silhouettes at the windows—shapeshifting forms that looked like wolves and ravens, ghosts of her people's metamorphoses, watching. She clutched the microphone like a medicine staff, its weight warm in her hand.

"I'd like to speak," she said, voice low but steady. Dwayne and the boys in their fatigues beside her. The echo of her words bounced off the walls, stirring the still air. Some heads turned, and others remained fixed on their tablets. The facilitator blinked, then nodded. The microphone slid across the podium like an offering.

She raised the staff to her lips. "This isn't consultation; this isn't free, prior, and informed consent," she began. "It is choreography. You call this a Nation-to-Nation summit, but there are no nations here— only ministries and mandates. You speak of modern treaties as if they were healing balms. You invoke the Nisga'a as though their journey were a universal cure. Still, you ignore that their deal was forged in blood and broken promises. What you present today is a blueprint for extinguishment, a contract that turns the inherent title into a footnote, our rights into something you can file away."

The man in the blue tie stopped scribbling. A consultant's lips parted; the journalist straightened, pressing record. A Chief across the aisle shifted, crossing his arms, his face hard as driftwood. Nea saw fear ripple through the room like wind pushing across still water.

"I have walked the ridges where our ancestors' bones lie buried beneath the forest floor. I have stood at survey flags that pierce our sacred springs. I have heard your lawyers speak of 'fee simple' as though the land were a page in a ledger—and as if the spirits who dwell there were deaf."

A hush fell. Even the air conditioners seemed to hold their breath. Nea drew a deep breath, feeling the old spirits crowd around her: Raven with his cunning smile, Bear with fierce protectiveness, and Raven's sister Eagle gliding high but ever watchful.

"My great-grandfather did not carry the land title. He carried law in his bones and memory in his hands. Ballots did not elect my auntie— the spirit world chose her to guard our ceremonies and summon the water birds when the salmon were scarce. None of them asked for certainty. They asked to be remembered and shared through story and ceremony, not the meaningless of paper."

Her ribbon skirt gleamed. The lamplight caught the beadwork of her deerskin vest, made by her Mother: traditional quillwork across the front, done in the traditional style. Each stitch held a story older than any government document. She wore the pants off a brown, felt hat popular among all the activists. Now, those stories pulsed in the fluorescent glow of this hall.

"Don't speak to me about extinguishment and call it progress," she said. "You offer us a paper treaty, bound by ink and fine print, and expect us to swallow our children's inheritance in a single breath. You say we must adapt or be left behind. But what you call progress, I call erasure after a history where our ceremonies were banned until 1951, while my Grandfather, my Mother, and my aunts and uncles were beaten for speaking the language. At the same time, your government-run Indian Residential schools ran rampant with abuse. Your lawyers fill this room at $500 an hour, tallying up invoices billed against these treaties. Those puny millions will go to those lawyers and never reach our communities. You think we don't see this long con, but I can tell you right now, we see it: the Elders and the Native Youth Movement see every one of you."

She paused and felt her hands tremble slightly—not from fear, but from the restraint of centuries and adrenaline pumping in her ears. Her heart hammered like a water drum. In her vision, she saw the pipeline tubes coiling through her homeland like serpents, the clear-cut scars on the mountains, the uniformed officers chasing Elders from healing ceremonies. The RCMP rounded up children to take to the Indian Residential School. She saw the land weeping.

"I have walked where the cedar and pines used to stand. I have heard our prayer songs become silent under the roar of bulldozers. I have knelt at the cold stones of our lost villages and heard the bones of our people cry out for justice. This land is not for sale."

The edges of the room darkened. The flags behind her billowed as if stirred by an unseen wind. The minister's face went pale; the audience shifted in their seats. Somewhere behind her, a window cracked, a spiderweb of fracture blossoming in the glass.

"You can sign your agreements," she continued, voice echoing like a canyon call. "You can stack signatures and stamps across these pages. But the land remembers every treaty you've broken. The water remembers every chemical spill you've hidden. The trees remember the firebombs you dropped to clear them. And we remember, too. We remember the names of our ancestors. We remember their songlines traced across these peaks and valleys. We remember that the land was never ceded."

A single clap broke the silence—short, hesitant, then stifled. Nea lowered her gaze. The journalist kept recording; the scribbler in the blue tie looked lost for words. One older woman, seated in the far corner, nodded once, slowly, her eyes moist with recognition.

Nea exhaled, feeling her warrior spirit settle around her like a cloak. She set the microphone back on its stand as a crown returned to its pedestal. Then she turned and walked away. Dwayne and the boys surrounded her. Each step resonated through the silent hall, like a heartbeat calling the land back to itself.

In the corridor, the air was colder, truer. Nea touched the stone wall and felt the earth's sigh rise through her fingertips. Outside, the sky was undone by a sudden wind. Her skirt billowed, tugged by unseen hands—those of Raven, her grandmother, and every spirit breathed beneath cedar canopies.

She raised her face to the swirling clouds. A flock of ravens darted overhead, their wings sharp silhouettes against bruised dusk. They cawed a greeting and a promise: that the land would not forget, that her words would echo in forest hollows and riverbeds in every soul who dared to listen.

Nea walked on, her heart steady with knowing. She had spoken truth to the spaces that tried to hide it. Behind her, the ballroom receded into fluorescent shadow, a vessel emptied of pretense. Ahead lay the vast, living world—her true stage. And on that land, the medicine woman warrior would continue her song, unbound by paper, unconquered by clause. Because some fires cannot be extinguished, and some lands can never be sold.

CHAPTER 36

The Occupation

The concrete front of the BC Treaty Commission looked like every other government building in Van—gray, forgettable, pretending not to hold power. But inside, the walls had heard it all: extinguishment clauses whispered in airless boardrooms, consultation scripts rehearsed like lullabies, land packages wrapped in corporate apologies and sharp black ink.

Nea sat cross-legged on the foyer's cold tile floor on the eighth morning, her back pressed to the glass doors they'd blocked with lawn chairs and banners. The flag of the Native Youth Movement fluttered overhead, duct-taped to a vent—red and black, a fist raised in lineage. The air carried the lingering tang of burnt sage, winding through the sterile building like a prayer no one knew how to answer.

Beside her: flattened pizza boxes scrawled with marker slogans—*STAND UP, WHO'S YOUNG?*—leaning against a cedar-wrapped prayer bundle. Dwayne paced near the window wall, his breath fogging the glass. Through it, you could see the early sun cracking through the Vancity haze, painting steel-gray rooftops gold.

His jaw was tight. His eyes were sharp. He hadn't slept in days. But his voice still burned.

"We didn't come here for optics," he said that morning. "We came because they don't speak for us. Because we're not tokens. We're not future economic stakeholders. We're the ones who remember."

Nea watched him. The way his shoulders carried weight he should never have had to hold—the weight of Cody, Jax, and Leon, all flanking the foyer like tired warriors. Cody fiddled with a beadwork medallion. Jax spun his lighter in restless loops. Leon sat cross-legged in silence, hood up, eyes fixed on the inner door like it might breathe.

They had been raised by aunties who taught them to survive. They had stitched together their nations out of trauma, fire, and memory. And they followed Dwayne like he was the last drumbeat in a forest gone still.

Nea believed in what they were doing. Every cell in her body vibrated with it. But this morning, something in her tightened.

She remembered Day Four—the lawyer in the army coat. No tie. Just a satchel full of binders and hushed warnings. He'd pulled Dwayne aside near the medicine bundle, voice low. Crown prosecutors. Public safety units. Occupation vs. trespass. Youth criminal records. High-stakes press fallout.

And Nea—who had grown up between spirit lodges and subway trains, between Elders and alley graffiti—began to feel the thin line beneath them quake.

Not for herself. She could carry it.

However, for those who have court dates next month. Who had baby sisters waiting? Who already had more on their files than they deserved.

"They'll try to make examples of us," she whispered one night to Dwayne as the lights dimmed and the boys slept on braided mats, their jackets for pillows.

Dwayne looked at her, his face unreadable. "Our Elders were examples, too," he said. "They took the hits. They carried the blame. They stood. And we—we're standing because they did."

That morning, as light seeped through the east-facing windows, he climbed the reception desk and faced the foyer like it was a longhouse. Cameras flashed. Press filtered in. A few Elders arrived silently, nodding to Nea as they passed.

Dwayne cleared his throat and began to speak.

"We are not here to barter rights you never gave us.
We are not negotiating the title. We are defending memory.
Your treaties are not tools. They are traps—extinguishment by consent. The Trick or Treaty Process.
You redraw maps with every meeting, but we carry the old ones. In our songs. In our scars.
You hold pens. We hold law.
You don't recognize us, but we are the inheritors.
We are not guests here. We are the ones who stayed."

Nea stood behind him. Quiet. Steady. Her ribbon skirt glinted under the lights like a warrior's flag. Her breastplate of bone and glass beads whispered every time she breathed.

Outside, police drones hummed over the skyline. Inside, Dwayne's words echoed like a ceremony being remembered.

Ten days.

In those ten days, the media spun them into heroes or threats, depending on the hour. The Commission released a statement emphasizing the importance of valuing Indigenous voices. And the RCMP hovered over but never touched.

By Day Ten, most of the city had heard about it. Some mocked. Some offered food. Some came to kneel at the glass and leave tobacco.

Nea walked the room's four corners on that final night with her smudge bowl, cedar and sage smoke curling through the vents. She pressed her hand to each wall. Thanked the ancestors. Thanked the floor for holding them.

She left a braid of sweetgrass where Dwayne had stood. Folded a note between the light switch and the door frame. In a delicate script, it read:

We were never lost. We were only waiting.

At dawn, they packed quietly. The lawn chairs folded. The banners rolled. The pizza boxes were stacked in neat piles of ash and ink. Cody carried the drum. Jax held the flag as if it were a heartbeat.

Leon stayed last, eyes scanning the skyline like he was memorizing it.

Together, they stepped outside.

The sky was soft with morning fog. The tower stood still behind them. Just glass and steel, pretending nothing had happened.

But Nea felt it. The shift. The hum in the land. The echo of voices too long silenced now stirred awake.

And somewhere in the marrow of the city, the Ancestors sang.

CHAPTER 37

The Shot Fired

The sky over the Treaty Commission tower had turned a bruised purple by mid-afternoon, streaked with the last gasp of sun and the first breath of rain. Nea stood on the edge of the raised dais—an oaken platform scuffed by a hundred protests, its grain etched like scars—with her ribbon skirt whipping around her calves, beads clacking like distant Morse code. The tower behind her was glass and steel and phosphor veins, humming with the city's data streams, but today it felt like a fortress under siege. Journalists in wind jackets and suits huddled before her, their lenses uncaring bayonets hungry for blood and drama.

Behind Nea, the flags of Canada and British Columbia drooped in the breeze, flanked by a pock-marked brass sign reading "Partnership Through Process." Someone had sprayed over it in bright ochre: LAND BACK. The paint dripped like fresh wounds.

Dwayne hovered at her shoulder, arms folded, his tall frame a steel-reinforced promise of defiance. His eyes, black coals of fury, scanned the perimeter—uniformed detachments in dark vests, riot shields catching stray glints of light, and a barricade ring separating humanity from the chrome tower. Behind them, youth with drums, Elders in cedar-weave hats, aunties pushing strollers draped in red cloth, babies nestled against them like seeds waiting to sprout. They were here for more than a sound bite. They were here to stake a claim in the bones of this land.

Nea inhaled the metallic scent of city air—exhaust, ozone, and the faint undernote of fresh-cut cedar from the basket of tobacco she'd placed at her feet. The wind tugged at her braids, and loosened the ends so a few hairs grazed her collarbone. She closed her eyes for a heartbeat and summoned the ancestors humming through her blood. Then she stepped forward, clearing her throat with a soft crack—like an old radio flickering on.

"I'm not here to give you the quote you want," she said, voice steady but raw, each word a pulse in the silence. "I'm here to speak the truth."

Flashes spilled from camera lenses. Reporters leaned forward, pens poised, recorders blinking. The world held its breath.

"You want to know why we occupied the Treaty Office?" she asked, gaze sweeping the crowd. "Because every negotiation you watch from behind plate glass is another attempt to parcel up land that was never ceded. Because every press release about progress is an elegy for our children's future. You talk Nation-to-Nation, but your statutes never utter our language. Your policy frameworks squelch our ceremonies. You build tables for us to sit at—already set to swallow us whole."

A murmur rippled through the press corps.

"You ask us to be reasonable. To be civil. Explain to me—is it reasonable that the land was stolen? Was it civil when our grandmothers were sterilized in hospital basements no one speaks of? When the carving of your hydro dams drowned our salmon runs? When our songs were outlawed, our children ripped from our arms?"

She paused, letting the wind fill the void. Up there, the sky bruised darker still, as if the heavens themselves were listening, mourning.

"We're not here to sign another treaty. We're here to remember. To witness. And we will not let you forget."

The applause wasn't thunderous—but it came from deep places: aunties clapping with worn hands, drums rolling like distant thunder, the youth stamping their boots in unison. It was the sound of land waking.

Then—somewhere beyond the perimeter—a shout cracked.

"Back up! Get back!"

Nea's head snapped toward the barricades. Across the slick plaza, flash-bang drones chased shadows. Protesters surged forward, fists and hearts clenched. The RCMP line advanced, shields rising like metal wings. One officer lifted a device—half camera, half strobe. Another knelt.

A crack split the air.

Time fractured.

Billy had been on the fringe of the crowd, leaning against a barricade hidden in half-light. His navy blazer looked polite—out of place among hoodies and moccasins—but he carried weight: heritage, guilt, hope under that suit. All morning, he'd hovered behind the youth he once distanced himself from. He said nothing. Spoke no slogans. Just watched. Maybe he is waiting for his moment.

Now, he stumbled.

Nea's breath caught in her throat. The world slowed. Rain began to fall—slanted needles that sizzled on metal. The riot shields jerked as officers raised their arms.

Billy clutched his chest, fingers splayed like a wounded bird struggling to fly. Blood bloomed through the fabric of his blazer—deep red, slick against concrete gray. A dark pool spread beneath him.

Nea lunged forward, boots scuffing on stone. "Medic!" she screamed. Dwayne barreled past, voice a bellow calling for Leon, our medic, our lifeline. The crowd recoiled, a wave of horror and rage. Drums stopped. Cameras whirred on. Someone gasped. A woman dropped her cedar drum; it hit the ground with a hollow crack.

The RCMP line hesitated, shields lowering. Tides pulling back, trying to wash away their first wave.

Nea sank to her knees beside Billy. Rain dripped from his hair. His eyes fluttered open, unfocused. He gripped her hand surprisingly—an ember of warmth in the chill.

"I didn't mean it—" he rasped, voice ragged.

"I know," she whispered, leaning close so only he could hear. She raised her other hand and pressed tobacco from her pouch into it, a prayer in leaves. Leon arrived then, kneeling with his bag, hands steady despite the pounding in his chest. Dwayne loomed over them, shielding the paramedic from the uniformed ranks inching forward.

The world flooded in: sirens wailing somewhere down the street, the hiss of rain, the press corps shouting questions nobody wanted answers to. A drone hovered directly overhead, its red light blinking. It filmed the blood as if it were poetry.

By the time the medics loaded Billy onto a stretcher, his chest rose and fell like a dying tide. He didn't speak again. Not as they carried him away, not when they strapped him into the ambulance.

Nea sat alone on the cold stone, the dais now deserted, the tower's lights mocking her with their distance. She pressed her palm against the spot where Billy had fallen. The stone was wet and slick. She let her tears blur the rain.

Behind her, the crowd evaporated. Barricades collapsed into twisted steel. The RCMP retreated, disappearing into the city's veins. The press pack disbanded—some chasing ambulances, others chasing quotes from shaken officials.

In the aftermath, the Commission went silent. The Minister clammed up. Press offices have turned into locked rooms, with the lights off and phones unanswered. But on the streets, the story refused to die. Youth-tagged murals with Billy's name. Aunties sang songs of healing in church basements. Elders drummed beneath overpasses. Words slipped into social feeds: "They shot one of us." "Bodies in the way of history." "Resistance bleeds."

And Nea?

On the eleventh night, she came back. The plaza was empty except for shattered glass and those gritty bits of spray paint. She knelt by the blood-dark stain and lit a candle—its flame a stubborn flare against the wind. She laid tobacco in a neat pile, cedar-green and sweet, then sang softly in her tongue. The words were as old as the rocks, rising and falling like a heartbeat.

Above, ravens croaked from the tower's ledges, their glossy heads cocked. They watched her—witnesses in black.

Nea closed her eyes, letting the chant carry her. Somewhere in the marrow of the city, beneath concrete and neon and data streams, the land remembered the crack of that shot—how it tore through skin and promise alike. The earth trembled in sympathy.

She sang for Billy's breath, for every stolen treaty, for ancestors whose names were carved only in memory. And when the candle guttered, she let it burn out, a spark swallowed by the night.

Tomorrow, the campaign would continue. The occupation might ramp up. The world would demand statements—verbal teardrops from polished officials. But Nea knew what words could do. She'd spoken hers into the wind, etched them into stone and blood. This was the line drawn in public: not one more foot of land given away, not one more body struck down without answer.

Because to resist was to remember. To remember was to live. And as long as those ravens perched on steel and stone, and as long as the land held that echo of a shot fired, the story would never die.

CHAPTER 38

When River Returned

It was days into the occupation, but it felt like each moon had bled into each other. Inside the tower, the air crackled like powwow drums in a thunderstorm. Too many prayers were stacked on each other—whispered in hallway alcoves, scrawled on crumpled scraps of paper, muttered under breath over screens glowing with digital witness—too many hearts unspooling, unraveling at the same raw seam. Static sat heavily on our skin as if the world had turned inside out and we were all hooked up to the same live wire.

Nea hadn't slept since Billy went down. Hell, she'd barely eaten. Her hands—warrior-rough from pounding drum skins and gripping cold concrete banisters—were crusted with calluses the color of clay. Two nights ago, her voice had cut through the lobby like a war cry; now it rasped, ragged as a dull blade. That edge was gone, worn away by too much truth.

We'd been in that lobby—on sacred ground—to over twelve days. The drummers who'd set us rolling had quieted; their rhythms thinned to cautious taps. The grandmothers who came with kettles of sage and rose hips, smiling, looked at us like we were tired warriors who had lingered too long on the battlefield. News cameras had shifted their lenses to the next viral spark—but we couldn't leave. Not now. Not ever. The smell of burnt sage stayed under the vents like a ghost we couldn't shake. Treaty maps lay on the stone floor, edges reddened and friable, smeared with ash and fresh ink—our hopes scribbled, scrubbed out, rewritten.

Nea sat by the west-facing windows—where the moonlight pooled in silver tiers—cradling a tin cup of cedar tea gone tepid. Her spine was curved, each vertebra a battered tree branch bending beneath snow. She stared at the tea, but her eyes traced constellations in the chipped paint of the sill. Somewhere behind her, Cody and Jax argued in low tones over who'd call for more pizza. Someone hacked a cough into a shawl. Everything felt too loud.

Then the door cracked open.

There are no rolling drums. No horns. Just the slow, sure footfall of boots on stone. And River walked in.

Nea lifted her head, and the air shifted. You could feel it—like the first gust before a storm. His jacket—slick with rain from outside—hung heavy on his shoulders. His braids, dark as raven plumage, clung wet against his neck. One hand held a medicine bundle wrapped in deerskin; the other gripped a canvas bag that thumped softly. His eyes, the color of gathering storms, scanned the room. I swear you could see memory crackle behind them.

Nea stumbled up so fast her knees shook. Before she could jab a word, River crossed the floor in three long strides and folded her into his arms. For a second, all the noise in her head died. She didn't know how close she'd been to shattering until his heartbeat pressed her back together. Then the water broke. Tears spilled out like runaway salmon—no warning, just liquid truth.

"I thought you weren't coming back," she whispered, voice dissolving.

He held her a moment longer, then eased back. "I had to," he said, voice quiet but iron-strong. "You've been carrying too much weight, Nea."

He knelt and unfurled the deerskin bundle. Inside lay a small brass bowl, dulled by time; a braid of sweetgrass, pale as twilight; and a jar of salve that smelled of bear root and sacred smoke. River's fingers trembled as he set the items in her lap.

"Grampa Oliver would've skinned me alive if he saw you burning out," he said, eyes meeting hers. "Not like this. We have a lot already."

Nea slid to the floor beside him, palms open, feeling every hollow in her bones.

He gazed at the treaty maps, the fine white ash flecking the lines, then back to her. "You remember what they did to him? That day on the mountain road?"

She nodded, slow as winter was melting. "They didn't want him praying." Her voice cracked. "They said he was a threat with songs instead of guns."

River's jaw tightened. "They beat him anyway. Even though he carried nothing but medicine in his pack and a song in his heart. You were fifteen and threw yourself in front of those batons."

"They broke my ribs," she said, lifting her chin. "I felt it crack."

"They almost broke my arm," River admitted, lips pressed tight.

They sat in silence, memories drumming in the dark. The tower felt alive—branches and roots winding through the stone floor, humming with everything we'd lost and everything still breathing.

"And we were the lucky ones," River said finally. "Some barely made it off Eagle Ridge."

Nea swallowed. "I still hear him singing, even when my head hits the pillow." Her voice was a ghost-note. "He sang for the Ancestors."

River lit the sweetgrass with a small match that flared a golden hue. He waved the smoke—slow and deliberate—over her hands, then her chest. Sweetgrass curls around the fingertips, creeping between knuckles. They inhaled and closed their eyes, letting the medicine drift into their lungs.

"Grampa knew his songs would travel," River murmured. "Even if they tried to beat him silent in this world, his voice would carry in the wind, the roots, and the stars. He trusted the Ancestors to finish the work."

Nea's shoulders loosened, tears still streaking down. "But I keep picking up the drum."

River's gray eyes softened. "You've done enough fighting, sis." He touched her shoulder. "It's time to root. Let Dwayne call the chants. Let the kids pound the drums. You don't gotta prove you're fire—you already burned the sky wide open."

Fire. She blinked, startled. The word hit her like a cedar needle piercing her skin. "Then what am I if I'm not the spark?"

He tipped his head, a smile flickering. "You're the seed." He pointed at the maps. "The fight grows from you—but seeds need soil. They need rest, water, dark. That's the lesson they never taught us."

They sat, watching the lights from their phones flicker across the treaty lines like distant constellations.

"I'm flying to Albuquerque next week," Nea said, voice stronger. "They want me to speak at that big gathering."

River didn't blink. "Then speak. But speak as a mountain, not wildfire. Let them hear how deep your roots go."

She nodded—hands trembling—this time not from fear but from thawing. Warmth seeped into her chest like a sunrise over a glacier. She felt taller and grounded. Once hollow and echoing, the cavern of her heart now held something solid.

He stood and gathered the bundle. River draped the sweetgrass braid over her wrist, set the brass bowl by her side, and dabbed salve on her cracked skin. The scent of bear root and smoke rose, sweet and sharp.

"You reminded me what I am," she whispered.

He winked, half-grin mischievous. "It's what Grampa Oliver always said: 'Blood remembers. Bones remember. You gotta give them a moment to speak.'"

Nea closed her eyes. She felt the hum of the tower shift. The stone floor softened under her legs like the earth was leaning in. From somewhere deep beneath, a low vibration—like distant thunder—stirred the treaty maps. Their lines glowed faintly red as if the ancestors themselves were tracing routes through the stone.

She cracked an eye open. Cody and Jax had paused arguing. The grandmothers watching from the far corner looked calmer, their faces shining with lamplight. A hush fell, punctuated only by the rain.

Nea stood tall and unbroken. She brushed her hair back and met River's steady gaze. He tipped his head—proud, relieved.

"Let's finish this night right," he said, voice hushed.

They gathered in a loose circle. River lifted the brass bowl and dripped in cedar tea. He murmured a blessing in the old tongue—words like sparks leaping off the rock. Then, he stirred the tea with a staff carved from an elder cedar branch. Steam curled in the lamplit air.

Nea knelt before the maps. With slow reverence, she sprinkled the salve—just a pinch—along each treaty line. The salve sank into the parchment, feeding the cracks. Each map rippled as though breathing, like the ash and ink were waking.

By the time dawn tiptoed through the windows, the lobby felt different. The static was gone, replaced by a pulse—like the earth's own heartbeat. The drummers tapped again, slow and sure. Grandmothers hummed old songs under their breath. The cameras outside spun their wheels, but our spirits were weightless inside.

Nea lifted her chin and met River's gaze one last time. He nodded. No fanfare. No drumbeat. Just two siblings standing on ancient ground, roots intertwined beneath the stone.

She closed her eyes, breathing in cedar, sweetgrass, and promise and speaking as a mountain. Knowing that no matter how far she flew—Albuquerque, Ottawa, wherever—they'd always find their way back. Because blood remembers, bones remember. And as long as the earth holds breath, so will they.

CHAPTER 39

Smoke & Paper

The smoke didn't rise, not at first.

A thin, unseen fog of grief and surveillance hung low over the city. Nea could feel it more than see it—the weight of it in her lungs, the quiet tremor beneath the sidewalks, like the land itself was holding its breath. When the news cycle called it a tragedy, the story had already been told and twisted a hundred times. RCMP spokespeople stood behind podiums with empty eyes, calling the protest "unlawful" and the incident "regrettable." The Commission issued a brief statement expressing its regret at the disruption of dialogue.

Dialogue.

That's what they called it.

Nea didn't speak for three days.

Not out of fear. Not out of shock. But because there were no words left that hadn't been stolen, softened, or shoved through the teeth of bureaucrats until they lost their bones.

She sat in the ceremony instead, in a dark room lit by fire and cedar and the breath of old songs. The Elders came in ones and twos. Some spoke. Some didn't. One laid a feather across her shoulders and said nothing else. That was enough.

Outside, the city convulsed. Youth hit the streets. Candlelight vigils flared under overpasses. Billy's name appeared in red spray paint across treaty offices and government doors.

Some Chiefs went silent.

Others stepped in front of microphones, their words too careful, as if their scripts had been handed to them.

Dwayne didn't sit still. He paced from rally to healing circle to press call, voice tight with fury, hands always half-clenched. The boys—Cody, Jax, Leon—stuck close. They moved like shadows between gathering spots, carrying bundles, lighting sacred fires, and watching every squad car with predator's eyes.

Nea stayed back. The wound was still too open.

She knew how this played out. She'd seen it before. The Crown would float language like smoke: de-escalation, dialogue, review. There would be investigations with redacted findings. The land defenders would be labeled "agitators" in official memos. And somewhere, behind a desk in Victoria or Ottawa, someone would sigh and sign another deal.

Billy had tried to come back and had stood near the truth. And the cost of that moment now bled through concrete.

On the sixteenth day, she lit a fire in her way. She took her brush pens and painted a mural on the alley wall beside the Friendship Centre. Not for media. Not for art. For the ones still walking, still watching.

It was a wolf, half-emerging from a burning longhouse. Behind it is a trail of songlines and children's footprints.

Underneath it, just five words: **"We are not your paper."**

People began to gather there. To sit in silence. To leave medicine and photos. No one tagged over it.

By the end of the week, a new phrase had begun to circulate.

Smoke & Paper.

It was part joke, part elegy. Protesters began writing quotes from Nea's speech and taping them to building doors—literal acts of paper resistance. They burned copies of old consultation frameworks in drums outside the Vancouver courthouse. Someone mailed a pile of shredded treaty documents to the Commission.

When the Minister finally spoke, her voice was hollow.

"We are committed to a thorough review of the incident. We continue to believe in the treaty process as the path to lasting peace. We see the need to engage more young people and the national Aboriginal organizations are developing youth councils as we speak in answer to this call."

Peace and youth engagement.

Nea walked alone to the tower that night.

She brought nothing but a bundle of tobacco, and her ribbon skirt wrapped tight under her coat. The bloodstain was gone—power-washed away like an inconvenience—but the crack in the stone where Billy had fallen remained. She knelt and pressed her palm to it.

The concrete was cool. But beneath it, the land was alive.

She could feel it.

Not anger. Not revenge.

A thrum of memory. A kind of grief that had long since hardened into something sacred.

She stood and faced the mirrored windows. In them, her reflection rippled like smoke. She raised her hand, fingers splayed.

"I am still here," she whispered.

The words didn't echo.

They embedded.

At that moment, Nea understood the cost. Not just speaking. But of *witnessing*.

She would carry it because she had to.

Because there was no going back to the ceremony without carrying the fire forward.

Because some truths don't live in speeches.

They live in silence.

In murals.

In blood.

In smoke.

And in paper that will never burn.

CHAPTER 40

Chairwoman of the Landless

Nea leaned into the corner of the plywood room, curled on the edge of her thin mattress like a fledgling hiding under her mother's wing. Her ribbon skirt—hand-stitched strips of ember-red silk and ochre cotton—pooled around her ankles in silent praise, soft confetti of ancestors' colors spilling over the warped floorboards. The low lamp at her feet cast its gentle buzz across the squat, illuminating the thin wisp of smoke curling from the last ember of her spirit. That fire—the one she'd carried in her throat through every vigil, every council hall, every fiery speech to governments who still heard the word "Aboriginal" and rolled their eyes—now flickered so low it was barely visible even to her memory.

She called the answering machine at the training house. One message from Kara Lin, the reporter from The Northern Star who wanted everything yesterday. Three messages from Bobby—her comrade deep at the pipeline blockade, probably waiting to know if Nea would show up. She looked at pictures. In the grainy picture, the faces of young people curved around each other in a circle of solidarity, edge to edge, like migrating birds against a gray city backdrop. Spray-painted in bleeding white letters: WE ARE NOT YOUR PAPER. Beneath that, an arrow toward the crumbling territorial marker: No treaties in BC, all this stolen soil.

She stared at that message as if the photo could rise and burn the plaster off the walls. Her ribs ached. Her shoulders felt wound tight, like a fishing line that might snap. And her heart, holy ghost of a heartbeat, felt heavy with too many names—Billy Two Feathers, Rachel Crane, the forty-eight water protectors beaten at the impound lot last week.

Her finger hovered, trembling, calling from the landline.

"Dr. Weebles?" she whispered into the crackle of the line.

"Nea," came the reply, warm like tobacco in winter, steady like the north star. "I was wondering when I'd hear from you."

"I can't sleep," Nea said, voice cracking on the words like frozen glass. "Every time I close my eyes, I see smoke and broken bodies. But my skin buzzes like somebody's turned the dial when I try to stay awake. I'm… I'm so damn tired. Not just my bones. My soul feels like a bird trapped under some heavy glass."

Silence. Not the empty silence of phones left off the hook, but the kind of silence that holds you — like a cradle — making space for words you haven't found yet.

"Your body knows the cost of speaking the truth," Dr. Weebles said. "It doesn't forget. Even words that heal will burn you from the inside out. Especially those."

Nea closed her eyes, letting her head fall against the chipped paint of the wall. She tasted cedar smoke on her tongue, the salt of tears she didn't know she'd cried. "Billy got shot he got lost in the fray between some other militant groups we didn't even know just trying to escalate and the police, one of them shot a gun in the air," she breathed. "The police shot back and hit him in the shoulder, but they were aiming for the chest."

"I saw the news," Dr. Weebles said softly. "I'm sorry, my girl."

"They're calling us heroes one minute," Nea's voice lowered to a rasp, "and criminals the next. The papers—white papers—talk about policy change. Still, they don't talk about blood on the asphalt."

"I know," came the quiet response. "I know."

Nea wiped her sleeve across her face. She could taste grit and sorrow. "I'm supposed to be in Albuquerque in a week," she said. "The climate summit. They expect a speech from me. But right now, every syllable feels like an insult. What do I even say to a room full of diplomats who hand out treaties sealed in red tape?"

Then Dr. Weebles' voice softened as though a breeze had slipped through the line, stirring the hair at Nea's temples. "Let your bones speak," she said. "Your body has wisdom. So does the land beneath you. Remember: leadership isn't just your words from a podium; it's your heartbeat in the soil. It's the slow drum of feet walking back home."

Nea didn't answer. She just listened to Dr. Weebles' breathing on the other end, each inhale a warm blanket laid across her chest. No instructions. It's just that ancient reminder that healing and justice both unfurl in crooked lines, not straight ones.

She was about to say goodbye when a call came in on the other line. A number she didn't recognize. An overseas exchange, the country code for Indonesia. Bali.

Kevin's line. That soft voice that sounded like daybreak filtering through banana leaves. The one who hadn't shown up at the ceremony last month—said he had surfboards waiting and a plane to catch. Now: an island retreat, breath-work circles around night fires, shamans, and wind-chants. Of course, he'd be halfway across the globe while she slogged through tear gas in treaty land.

Nea let it ring until the sixth buzz. Then she picked up.

"Yo," she said. It came out half-gruff, half-pained. "What's going on, Kev?"

"Nea," he breathed, greeting an old prayer. "Hey. I just saw the news back here in Ubud. Are you all right?"

She snorted. "Define all right."

He hesitated. "Alive?"

"I'm alive," she said, shoulders lifting in a single let-down. "You?"

"Still in one piece," he promised. "I'm with a group doing candlelight meditations, night-fire ceremonies, breath-work that's supposed to open your heart chakra or some shit. I see your face burning like lantern light in the darkness every time I close my eyes. I wanted to call and see if you needed someone."

Part of her ached to crumble into Kev's arms, let somebody else carry her grief for once. But part of her bristled—Kevin had hovered at the edges of her world, surfing those tropical waves while she stayed to fight in the trenches.

"I appreciate the call," she said, careful. "But I leave for Albuquerque in two days. Summit opens next Thursday."

"Oh," he said. Then: "Can I call you back?" A note of hope, like a teenager asking to borrow a mixtape.

"You can try," she said. "Maybe after Albuquerque. I'll see if I survive the delegates."

He laughed very softly. "I'll hold you to that." Then, "I love you, lady."

"Don't start Kevie, we'll talk later," she said. And hung up.

She exhaled. Her breath came out slow for the first time in days, like a river releasing itself from ice. There was space again in her lungs, room for an ember to catch.

Nea rose, head still spinning with phone voices, urgent faces on newsprint, and the roar of assembly halls. She moved toward her battered travel bag: the one patched up with ceremony leather straps, the one that held her grandmother's shawl—woven with the patterns of twin serpents, the old story of water and air entwined. She folded her ribbon skirt with ritual care, like smoothing out ancestral songlines. She tucked in her cedar pouch—sweet under her palm—and slipped in her small leather journal of policy briefs, her father's ledger of treaty obligations, and a single feather from an eagle that circled the pipelines under construction.

And then she paused, sliding her hand across the rough wood floor. She pressed her palm flat as if she could imprint her energy into the floor. The ripple of past gatherings haunted the walls: neighbors passing bannock at sunrise, older adults singing the water song, and the hush before a breakout session on forestry rights. She wanted to leave a bit of herself behind, a blessing on the beams.

They—the media, the suits, the conference halls—had started calling them "the BC Native Youth Movement Chapter." Dwayne had become their de facto spokesperson, booming chants that trembled like thunder. Every vigil he led, every banner unfurled, he carried the spotlight. And Nea… Nea had been the spark, the rebel poet who risked arrest to read the names of fractured waterways. But now she was stepping back. Not because she was weak but because she'd learned the hard way that the flame of a spirit can only burn long if it's allowed to rest. You can't pour from an empty chalice.

"I'm done asking for a seat," she murmured to the ceiling. "I'm the damn table."

The next morning at YVR International, she walked in her mocassins through security, the icy tile floor pressing into her arches, reminding her of glacier-chilled riverbeds back home. The boys on an earlier flight. The guard's eyes flicked from her bare feet to the ribbon skirt folding at her ankles and back again, that little flash of confusion when you see someone who doesn't fit the rulebook. She let them stare. She let the cold steal the last of her hesitation. She let their curiosity be a testament to belonging she didn't have to ask for.

Once airborne, the engine's thrum was like a heartbeat she could lean into. She pressed her forehead to the window well—barely glancing at the drifting clouds. Instead, she closed her eyes and reached out, in mind, across the land. Beneath her, the rivers still wove their way between floodplains and sediment. The mountains still sang—those rumbles of tectonic lullabies from eons past. Somewhere in that vast mosaic, Billy was in a hospital bed, counting his breaths. Kevin lay on a bamboo mat somewhere beneath a sky full of dying stars.

Nea breathed deeply. She whispered the water song her grandmother taught her: a syllable of blessing, a vow of remembrance. She could hear all the murmured promises of treaty land in her ear. She wasn't landless. She was land-bound—bound to every creek and cattail, to every crack in the sidewalk stained with spilled oil. Bound to rise again, like sap in a frozen root.

She wasn't boarding that summit as just another delegate droning on about carbon caps. She was going as a witness, a standing mirror to their talk of policy that too often traded our watersheds for corporate profits. She was a Chairwoman of the Landless—bearing forward grief and hope in equal measure and bearing every open wound of stolen earth in her chest. And the land—ancient, breathing, unbroken—had already given her its vote.

"Hey, Albuquerque," she whispered, loosening her fingers from the cloth window. "I'm coming."

CHAPTER 41

Albuquerque & The Storm Waiting to Happen:

NYM and the Conference

The dry heat of Albuquerque hit us like a wall as we stepped out of the airport. It smelled different here—sunbaked earth, sagebrush, and something ancient lingering in the air. Something I couldn't name. It was beautiful when I looked up, and the sky was the most transparent, bluest colour as far as the eye could see, with not a cloud in sight. To the east of the city rose the Sandia Mountains, beautiful in their pinkish, earth-toned hue. The town was spread out, with no glassy high-rises like Vancouver. Most of the buildings were made of adobe, and many were a warm, earthy pink in color. Cars drove by, and Hispanic and Latin music in Spanish was everywhere. To my amazement, most of the people here were brown like us. They were from Mexico and parts of Latin America, with a history of Hispanic influence, and many different Indigenous tribes, including the Navajo and Pueblo, as well as Indigenous people from across Turtle Island. I could feel the electricity in the air, the power of this place, its connection to deep history, and a supernatural intensity in the energy of the earth and sky. It was hypnotic.

Dwayne slung his duffel over his shoulder, they had waited for her to arrive, his ever-present military-style fatigues hanging loose on his tall, wiry frame. "Feels like home," he muttered, squinting against the bright desert sun.

Tommy stretched, cracking his neck. "Yeah, if your home is inside a sweat lodge on full blast."

I smirked. "You're the one who wanted to come, city boy."

Tommy shoved me playfully, and we approached the waiting shuttle to take us to the conference. The UN Indigenous Climate Conference.

We weren't just here as attendees. We were speakers.

We had a manifesto. A prophecy. A war cry.

The conference center was a mix of suits and regalia—Elders in ribbon shirts, women in jingle dresses, warriors in camouflage, and academics in tweed.

We were among our people but also outsiders—young, loud, uncompromising.

The Native Youth Movement had sent us because we were willing to say what many wouldn't.

Dwayne, Tommy, and I set up at a table covered in resistance materials. Copies of our manifesto, pamphlets on land back, and a stack of books by George Manuel—the warrior-scholar first named the Fourth World.

A woman in a sharp blazer stopped at our booth. "You young people are doing good work."

I nodded. "We're doing what needs to be done."

She glanced over our materials, her eyes lingering on the Black Snake prophecy. "Be careful," she said softly. Then she disappeared into the crowd.

Dwayne exhaled. "That was vague and ominous."

I shrugged. "Story of our lives."

Then I saw him.

Maw'Tsain.

He was smaller than the men I usually noticed. But there was something about him.

A presence. A fire behind his eyes.

He was standing near a group of Kiowa delegates from Oklahoma, laughing. Still, his eyes flickered toward me like he could sense me watching.

Maw'Tsain.

That wasn't his real name, but that was what everyone called him.

A wrestler. A warrior. He is a leader in his own right.

Dwayne elbowed me. "Don't even think about it."

I rolled my eyes. "What? I wasn't thinking anything."

Tommy snorted. "Yeah, sure. You've got that look."

I did. I knew I did. Because I already knew how this would go.

It would be fast. Intense. Devastating.

And I would love him completely.

And it would end in fire.

But I stepped toward him anyway.

CHAPTER 42

The Fire In My Throat

They stood side by side on the raised dais, the heat of Albuquerque sunlight leaking through the floor-to-ceiling glass walls behind them, pooling at their feet like molten gold. Through the transparent panels, one could see the jagged Sandia Mountains beyond—pink at dawn, fiery at noon, and cool lavender in the dying light—bearing witness to this moment. Inside the vast hall, the air was warm with anticipation, scented faintly with the aroma of sage smoke from the smudge bowl at the entrance, carried in by the ceremony bearers earlier that morning. The United Nations Indigenous Climate Summit had drawn delegates and knowledge keepers from across Turtle Island and beyond: Haudenosaunee from riverside longhouses; Mapuche from the wind-whipped southern pampas; Dene from taiga and tundra; Inuit from ice floes and polynyas; Quechua from the soaring Andes; and many more whose ancestral voices wove together into a tapestry of living languages and living lands. But in that hushed moment on the stage, it was just Nea and Dwayne and the promise of Grampa Oliver's spirit standing tall between them.

Nea felt the beam of sunlight press against her back like a reminder of centuries of sun-baked trials and triumphant resistance. She closed her eyes for a heartbeat, recalling the soft crackle of the lodge fire where she spent long nights recounting the old stories, the way the flames danced like ancestors calling across the smoke. Her fingertips curled around the metal neck of the microphone, gripping it with both hands as though it were the handle of Grampa Oliver's healing drum. Under his careful guidance, she had learned that one must root oneself in the earth before speaking truths too long buried. Her heartbeat echoed in her ears as clearly as a war drum.

"The words we carry," she said, voice low and steady, "come not from policy rooms or ivory-tower think tanks but from the land itself—woven into every ridge and valley, the soil in our hands, the sap in the trees. From blood and bone. From stories burned and treaties broken."

She felt Dwayne shift beside her. He stood tall, shoulders squared, wearing a red scarf tied by his wrist. That scarf had once wrapped Grampa Oliver's hand during ceremonies at Eagle Ridge—a vibrant slash of crimson against the high desert sky. The old man's talisman against despair was a signal of hope when the world seemed determined to silence him. Now, the fabric fluttered gently in the air conditioning's breath, a living memory around Dwayne's wrist.

"Our Elders fought," Nea intoned, his voice deep as riverbed rock, "so we could stand here and be heard. Grampa Oliver stood on that ridge with only his drum in his hand praying. They beat him, jeered at him, and tried to break his spirit. They nearly killed him. But he would not yield. They could not take his voice. So we speak today in his name."

Nea's voice wavered for a single breath, a tremor like the fluttering wings of a mourning dove. Then she found her footing again—roots twisting deep into the red clay of memory, tapping into wells of resilience. She lifted her chin, leveled her gaze at the great assembly before her, and began to read, her cadence deliberate:

The Four Pillars of the Youth Manifesto:

1. The Land Is Not For Sale.

It is not a commodity. It is not negotiable.

We revere the mountains that cradle the clouds and the rivers that carry salmon through generations. Each foothill is a story, each valley a library. Putting a price tag on land means reducing our ancestors' whispers to sterile ledger lines. We must defend these places as we would defend our hearts—because they are unique.

2. Indigenous Sovereignty Is Non-Negotiable.

We do not need permission to exist.

Our people thrived long before colonial borders were drawn across our territories and long before maps marked lines to serve distant empires. We remember our languages, our medicines, our kinship laws. Outside voices have tried to legislate our very being. We will not ask for leave to breathe or for license to pray. Our right to self-determination is inherent in our creation.

3. Resource Extraction Is a Modern-Day Form of Colonization.

They don't take just the ore—they take the future.

Strip mines gouge scars in the earth that take centuries to heal. Pipelines snake through untouched forests, fracturing watersheds and poisoning life beneath the soil. This is not progress; it is the same old hunger for gold and oil that once funded gunboats and wars. We refuse to be collateral damage in a scheme that prioritizes profit over people and the planet.

4. The Future Is Watching.

And we refuse to be the generation that stayed silent.

Our children's eyes are upon us—eyes bright with curiosity, eyes heavy with inherited dreams. Will they inherit a world where Indigenous voices speak truth to power? Or will they sleep under skies thick with smog and longing? We choose legacy. We choose courage. We choose to be the people who stood, spoke, and changed the course of history.

As Nea named each pillar, echoes rolled through the hall: hushed murmurs in Quechua, nods among the Haudenosaunee delegation, hands drifting to sacred necklaces strung with wampum and coral. The words seemed to vibrate in the air, awakening hope in those who had begun to believe hope was fragile.

When she finished, silence descended for an instant so profound it felt like the world had stopped breathing. Then the audience erupted—not in polite applause, but in a deep-throated rumble that reverberated through the glass walls, the hall's columns, and carried outward across the broad desert beyond. It was the sound of thunder born from truth, rolling from mouth to mouth, heart to heart.

Dwayne stepped forward, letting the red scarf dance free as though it were the banner of a new era. "This isn't just a declaration," he said, voice rising with unwavering conviction. "It's a warning. We will not go quietly. We will not disappear like smoke in the wind. The lands our ancestors entrusted to us are not forsaken. The waters coursing beneath these mountains are not up for grabs. We will stand guard with every bone in our bodies."

Nea felt warmth bloom in her chest as a tear slipped down her cheek—clear as melted glacier ice. It was not a tear of sorrow. It was a tear of legacy, a silent acknowledgment of every grandparent whose toil had made this moment possible, of every child whose future depended on it. It burned with the fire she had carried silently in her throat all these years, now unleashed in full voice.

They stepped back from the microphone as the thunder of approval subsided into a sustained hum of solidarity. In the front row, an elder grandmother raised her lined hand in blessing, her shawl of indigo and copper glinting like evening stars. Her eyes, clear as pond water, brimmed with quiet pride. Across the room, someone struck a single drum, and the reverberation joined with the hum, weaving into a new rhythm of resilience.

On the very edge of the podium, a butterfly alighted—wings iridescent with hues of turquoise and amber. It lingered for a heartbeat, then flapped its delicate wings as though to say, "Listen." In many of their traditions, a butterfly symbolised transformation and renewal, acting as a messenger. Here it was—tiny yet mighty—echoing the promise that growth often begins in the most delicate forms.

Nea turned her face upward and closed her eyes, feeling the heat of the desert sun through the glass and the cool murmur of the crowd flow through the floorboards at her feet. She could almost hear Grampa Oliver's voice, firm and patient, cutting through the din: "That's enough now. Let the land speak." And so they did. The glass walls seemed to vanish, and for a moment, the hall was nothing more than wind whispering through sagebrush, the steady pulse of the drum calling the people home.

Overhead, the ceiling lights shimmered like distant galaxies. The United Nations flags—each a testament to politics and diplomacy—hung silently in the rafters. But the true might in the room, Nea knew, came from the voices gathered here: voices of ancestors, voices of grandchildren yet to be born, voices of the land itself. And those voices, once ignited, could never be silenced.

As the hall lights dimmed and the presenters gathered their notes, delegates rose to their feet, no longer solitary figures representing distant nations but a unified chorus answering a call too urgent to ignore. Outside, beyond the glass, the afternoon sun began its slow descent, painting the mountains in strokes of crimson and gold. In that radiant glow, every promise made on the stage felt woven into the very bones of the earth.

The Youth Manifesto carried on the breath of ceremony and the firelight of countless discussions. It had found its moment under the high desert sky. And as Nea and Dwayne walked off the stage side by side, their shadows long and unwavering, they carried with them more than words. They weighed unbroken promises, the echoes of ancient drums, and the luminous spark of a future determined to be heard.

CHAPTER 43

Arrival in Albuquerque

The Next Chapter Begins

After the conference, I did it. I accepted an offer to attend college in Albuquerque. It was a big step but I was ready. My car, stuffed with what I could fit, rolled into town late, wheels grinding against the cracked pavement of a city that seemed as restless as the stars above. The air felt different here—dry, sharp, electric, as if the desert had absorbed centuries' energy. It was ancient, that land, and it spoke in the language of dust storms and sunburnt earth.

It wasn't the wet earth and cedar of home, where the trees whispered and the rivers sang. This place had its rhythm and voice, and as I stepped off the bus, I couldn't help but listen to the desert wind that cut through the air.

I didn't belong here—not really. I could feel my skin prickling and my bones aching. Albuquerque was where the past didn't linger like it did at home.

The pull of my family, the land, the heartbeat of my people was still a part of me, but it felt distant now, like an old dream I couldn't quite reach.

I stood still, the weight of my heart like a small anchor pulling me down. I was so tired, hours spent driving but also from the physical exertion. It was the kind of exhaustion that came from running away from something you didn't want to face. It was the kind of exhaustion that comes from carrying the weight of memories, losses, and regrets.

And then, I heard her.

"Nea!"

The sound of my name cut through the night, sharp and familiar, and something inside me stirred for the first time in what felt like forever. I turned just in time to see Q, her silhouette framed by the harsh glow of the streetlights.

Her cowboy boots clicked against the pavement with that confident, rhythmic step that made her impossible to miss. She was a storm in human form—her long, dark hair flowing behind her like the wild trails of a midnight wind, arms wide open, a mischievous grin plastered on her face.

She didn't even slow down as she ran toward me, and before I could do anything, she had me in a bear hug, squeezing the air out of me.

"Girl, you're home now," she said, her voice light and teasing, but there was a warmth in it—something that made me feel like I might belong here, for a moment at least.

I wanted to laugh and say something clever back, but the words caught in my throat. Home? I wasn't sure about that. I wasn't even sure what "home" meant anymore.

All I knew was that the heat of the desert sun was already starting to seep into my skin. For the first time in a long time, I felt the tug of something familiar, something I hadn't realized I was missing.

I wasn't sure if Q meant it in the way she said it, but the possibility of it—that I might *belong* somewhere, even if it was just for now— felt like a fleeting promise. It wasn't the same as the earth beneath my feet back home, the land I'd fought for and bled for. But this... this was different. It was strange, like stepping into a new world that felt alien and welcoming.

Q stepped back, giving me space but not letting go, her eyes scanning my face with that knowing look she always had. She saw everything, and I hated that about her sometimes. She could see right through me, into all the places I buried deep—places I thought I had shut off long ago.

"You okay?" she asked, her voice softening.

I didn't answer right away. How could I? I wasn't sure if I was okay. I wasn't sure if I ever would be again. There were pieces of me scattered across the land I'd left behind, scattered in the broken places where I'd fought for something that slipped through my fingers like water.

Q's arms were still around me, and I let myself lean into her for a moment in the quiet that followed. She had always been there, even when I was too stubborn to admit that I needed her during my first month in Albuquerque, attending the conference and then deciding to stay for school and return. The world made you believe you could handle everything independently, but she had never bought into that lie. She knew the value of family and belonging in ways I couldn't quite grasp.

"You know," she said after a moment, pulling away just enough to look me in the eye, "I knew you'd come. I could feel it."

I blinked at her, confused. "What do you mean?"

She shrugged, that familiar, carefree motion that made her seem so much younger than she was. But there was a depth to her that most people never saw. "I've been waiting for you, Nea. You're part of this. Part of what's coming. You didn't know it yet."

Part of what was coming?

I looked around at the streetlights, the empty roads, and the shadows stretching long across the pavement. The air was thick with possibilities, but I couldn't tell if they were good or bad. The weight of everything I had left behind, all the pieces of myself that were scattered across the land, tugged at me.

Q must have read the uncertainty in my eyes because she smiled, a slight, understanding curve of her lips. "It's alright. You'll figure it out. You always do."

The thing about Q was that she had this way of making you feel like the world was bigger than just your problems, bigger than your losses. She believed in things. In causes. It is the power of people to change the world, one step at a time.

And for the first time in a long while, I wanted to believe in something too.

"Come on," she said, grabbing my duffel bag from my shoulder and slinging it over hers. "I'll show you the place."

I hesitated momentarily, staring at the empty stretch of road ahead, the desert night humming with a strange life. I didn't know what I was walking into, didn't know what my future held here in Albuquerque. But with Q beside me, her confidence bleeding into my veins, it didn't seem quite as daunting.

"Okay," I said softly, more to myself than to her. "Let's go."

And in that moment, it felt like the first step of a new chapter—one that I wasn't sure I was ready for but one that I knew I couldn't avoid. For better or worse, I was here now. And maybe I was starting to believe I could find a new place to belong.

With Q leading the way, I stepped into the unknown.

CHAPTER 44

Maw' Tsain & The Wild Year in Albuquerque

I t started with a challenge.

I was at a bar with my date, one of the guys I had met through the conference—casual, easy, learning about the local nations. Then he turned to him and grinned.

"I'm going to steal your girl."

It was cocky as hell, but somehow, it didn't sound like a joke.

His friend laughed, but I met the Maw'Tsain's gaze. A bolt of electricity shot through my arm when we shook hands.

I should have run right then.

I didn't.

Playing it Cool

I kept my distance. I was in Albuquerque for the conference, then attending school, focusing on advocacy, learning, and trying to keep my passion alive without getting consumed by someone else's.

But he was everywhere.

The pub, playing pool, drinking beer, dancing to blues.

The jazz and blues bars, the country bars, the places where the music seeped into your bones and made you move before you could think.

We all ran in the same circles—activists, engineers, land protectors, troublemakers. Maw'Tsain was all of the above.

When I wasn't in class, I was with him. When I wasn't at protests or writing reports, I was hiking up in the Jemez mountains with him, cliff-jumping into icy waters, riding horses at his best friend's ranch, throwing bales, feeding cattle, watching the sunset on the desert horizon.

For a couple months, I remained calm.

Then I fell. Hard.

Loving a Fire That Would Burn Me - Maw'Tsain

He was from Oklahoma. A wrestler. A warrior. An environmental engineer who could talk science and ceremony in the same breath.

At night, I practically lived at his place, drinking beer, laughing, curled up on his cousin's couch, watching the ceiling fan spin.

I worked at the Midnight Rodeo bar when I wasn't in school. A wild, rowdy cowboy joint where the music was too loud, and the beers were cheap. When our shifts ended, we partied until dawn.

I thought I was the one.

Until I wasn't.

One day, I was at his place when the phone rang.

A message played. Angel.

"Hey, Maw'Tsain. We met at the gym. I can't wait to get together."

My stomach dropped.

I had thought we were exclusive.

I had thought I was enough.

But I wasn't.

I felt him distancing. The calls are getting shorter. The time between seeing each other stretched longer.

I stayed longer than I should have because the good times were so good.

Because we had a year of fire, adventure, laughter, and freedom.

And when it was time to go, I didn't look back.

I hadn't heard from Maw'Tsain in three weeks. The space between us had grown wider, stretched by his silence, my overthinking, and that damn phone message from Angel.

So I went to his house. I thought at least a real goodbye was better than this.

I stood on his porch, heart hammering, hands clenched into fists. Knocked.

No answer.

I knocked again.

Finally, I heard his voice—muted, distant, irritated.

"What?"

I swallowed, forcing my voice steady. "I need to talk to you."

Silence.

Then, a laugh. A woman's voice—smooth, older, smug.

"I'm here with him."

My stomach dropped.

I stumbled back off the porch, tears burning down my face. I didn't know who she was. I had an idea, but I learned everything I needed to know.

CHAPTER 45

Maw'Tsain's Perspective

Almost, But Never Enough

Maw'Tsain leaned back against the bar, the cool wood of the counter pressing against his spine as he lazily spun it, the empty whiskey glass in his hand. The dim glow of the neon lights outside bled through the windows, casting long shadows across the room. Albuquerque had a way of feeling both electric and stifling at the same time. It was a place that hummed with life, but there was an undercurrent of something oppressive, something suffocating in the air. Even as a kid, he had always felt the heat of the desert mingling with the bitterness of broken dreams.

And yet, tonight, it was quieter than usual. His usual haunts seemed to hold less of the spark they once did, as though the city had drained him, piece by piece, over the years. But then his eyes found her.

Nea.

She was at the far end of the bar, leaning in with one of the Native Youth Movement guys. She was animated, her voice rising and falling in the familiar cadence of someone speaking about something they truly believed in—passionate, intense, and full of fire. Maw'Tsain couldn't help but watch her, his gaze lingering, the familiar pull inside him. There was something about the way she burned. She wasn't like anyone he had ever known. She didn't just exist; she lived, every word, every gesture, every decision a testament to the cause that moved her.

And, damn, he liked that about her.

Hell, if he was being honest, he liked her more than he should.

But love?

Love was a whole different thing.

The Chase Was Fun

The first time they had met, she had been someone else's girl. That hadn't mattered at the time. It had only made things more interesting. He had turned to his buddy, smirked, and without missing a beat, had said the words out loud, the cocky bravado that he'd honed over the years slipping out effortlessly.

"I'm gonna steal your girl."

It had been a joke at first, an offhand comment made with the usual charm that got him by in most situations. The easy, confident way he carried himself, as though the world was his to take. But when their hands first touched in that handshake, a jolt of electricity shot up his arm, sharp and unexpected. He hadn't been prepared for it, hadn't been prepared for *her*.

That was when he'd known it wouldn't be just another conquest.

She was different. And that difference intrigued him, gnawed at him in ways he couldn't quite explain.

He leaned into it—long nights at the pub, endless games of pool, the drives that meandered up into the Jemez mountains, each moment steeped in a sense of something undefined. There was always the way she looked at him when she thought he wasn't paying attention, the way she'd let the silence stretch just a little longer, allowing him to fill the void with words.

Maw'Tsain knew she wanted him. It wasn't a matter of doubt; he could see it in how she moved around him and how her body responded when they were near.

And why wouldn't she?

He was a catch. Smart, successful, fun as hell.

But, he saw something beyond reach when he looked at her and examined how she carried herself. Something that made her more than just a conquest. Something that told him she would never be like the women he was used to.

The Problem with Nea

The problem with Nea wasn't that she wasn't beautiful because she was. She had that raw, untamed strength that came from years of surviving and learning to fight for everything she had.

No, the problem with Nea was that she was *too much*.

She wasn't soft. She didn't need him to protect her. She didn't need him at all.

She was too strong. Too independent. Too whole.

She was too *fucking* strong.

He couldn't help but think back to how she looked—so lithe and lean, her body taut with muscle, the hard lines of her arms, the definition in her abs. She wasn't built like the women he had been with. Angel had curves, a softness to her that had been so easy to slip into. Angel had been predictable, steady. She had wanted to give him the world—promised him a place in it, handed him her life on a silver platter, willing to bend and break for him.

Angel had been everything Maw'Tsain thought he wanted.

But Nea? Nea didn't need him to bend. She wasn't here to cater to him or build a life around his needs. She was already whole. She had her fire, her purpose. And he? He couldn't handle it.

Not like he thought he could.

The Night It Ended

Maw'Tsain wasn't sure when it had gone wrong. One minute, they were together, wrapped in the haze of heat and desire, their bodies entwined. Nea had been so sure of herself, her hands gripping his back, pulling him closer, her voice in his ear, promising nothing but everything all at once. It was the kind of passion that burned white-hot and left you gasping for air.

But then... she was gone.

There had been no fight. No screaming, no accusations. It wasn't dramatic. It wasn't a grand, cathartic release of everything they hadn't said. She had just slipped away, leaving him with an emptiness he hadn't been prepared for.

And yet, the weird thing? He almost respected it.

She had felt the shift. She had sensed the distance in him, the part of him already halfway out the door before he even realized it himself. She hadn't needed to fight for him because she had never been the one to lose herself to anyone else. She had her own life, her fire to feed.

He could've fought for it. Hell, he could've fought for *her*. But in the end, Maw'Tsain knew the truth: Nea wasn't meant to be his. She wasn't the kind of woman who fit into his world, not in the way he needed. And deep down, he had always known it. And love, he didn't believe in love. He had felt it only once, and she was taken too soon from this world, so he wanted no part of it. He was 26 with a whole life ahead of him.

So, when she left, it wasn't with the sting of rejection. It was just… quiet. A silent understanding. It was almost like they had both known it would never be enough.

The truth was, Maw'Tsain had always been a man caught between two worlds—the life he had built for himself in Albuquerque and the ties that bound him to his people, his heritage. He had always been a physical and emotional wanderer, never fully connected to any place or tethered to anyone.

And yet, Nea had somehow pulled him closer to a place he had avoided for years. She had challenged him in a way no one else had.

She had made him question everything—his life, choices, and desires.

But in the end, he couldn't change. Not in the way she needed him to. Not in the way she deserved.

And now, sitting in that bar, watching her from across the room, he realized that no matter how much he had wanted to be someone else for her, no matter how much he had tried to pretend he could be something more than he was, it had never been enough.

Not for Nea.

CHAPTER 46

Midnight Rodeo & Wild Nights

The first time I walked into Midnight Rodeo, I thought I had stepped into another world—one where the rules didn't quite apply, where the usual weight of responsibility, of struggle, was momentarily suspended.

The thick haze of cigarette smoke hung in the air, mixing with the sharp scent of whiskey and sweat. Neon lights cast a fluorescent glow over everything, giving the place an almost surreal, dreamlike quality.

It was loud—the clink of glasses, the laughter, the hum of country music twanging through the speakers. The rugged and rough Cowboys moved in smooth rhythms, their boots scuffing against the worn wooden floor as they danced the two steps like they were born to it.

But it wasn't just the men who fit in. Q, with her effortless confidence and wild energy, was in her element. She owned this place in a way that made it seem like it had always been hers.

Her long, dark hair swayed as she moved, her laughter rising above the noise like a spark in the dark. She didn't just belong here; she commanded the space. She'd walked into this bar like it was the only place she'd ever wanted to be, and somehow, it made sense that she was a part of it all—her spirit as free as the wild desert winds I was starting to get used to.

"Stick with me, Nea," Q grinned, handing me a tray of drinks that seemed ridiculously heavy in my hands. "It's just like a protest, except the cops are drunk, and you make tips."

Her words sent a laugh bubbling up from somewhere deep inside me. I wasn't sure if it was the absurdity of it or the fact that Q always knew how to make anything seem less daunting.

For the first time in a long time, I wasn't thinking about the struggles I'd left behind or the battles I'd fought and lost. I wasn't planning or strategizing. There were no speeches to make, no lands to defend, no families to save.

I was just here. Just existing. And that felt strange. Good, but strange.

We worked the tables, serving drinks with practiced ease. At first, I was awkward and unsure of the dance that came with balancing trays and navigating the crowded space. But Q was a natural, moving effortlessly between customers, chatting with them like old friends, making them laugh and feel seen.

It was easy to fall into her rhythm. Before long, I found myself laughing with her, dodging the occasional flirtation with a smile, and collecting crumpled bills in my cache, stacking them like I was learning a new art.

But it wasn't just about the work. It was the little moments between that went unnoticed by everyone else but felt like lifelines to me. Q's warm hand was on my shoulder as she passed by.

Her wry smile when a guy at the bar made an inappropriate comment, the way she'd shoot him down without missing a beat, her words sharp as a whip. We were a team, even if we didn't have to say it out loud.

And when our shift ended, we didn't rush home. Instead, we pulled off our aprons and tossed them aside, no longer the workers but the wild souls we were always meant to be. The music had shifted by then—more upbeat, a faster tempo—and Q grabbed my hand without asking, pulling me into the crowd. Jumping in with a group of cowboys.

"You ready?" she asked, her voice daring, her eyes alight with mischief.

I could feel it before I even stepped into the dance circle—something was intoxicating about this place. The freedom. The abandon. Here, no one cared who you were or what you had been. All that mattered was the now. And tonight, I wasn't burdened by the past. I wasn't a fighter or a protestor, a daughter of the land with a heavy heart. Tonight, I was... living.

We twirled, laughed, and spun in tandem with a group of cowboys in town from Texas letting the music carry all of us. The bright neon lights blurred around us, the heat from the bodies surrounding us mixing with the desert air that pressed in from the open doors. We were living—no fights, no struggles, no weight to carry—just the pure joy of the moment.

For the first time in years, I felt like I could breathe.

There was a wildness to the way Q moved, an untamed spirit that I had always admired from afar but never fully understood. She didn't need to explain herself. She didn't have to fight for attention or validation. She existed, and that was enough. It made me wonder, as I caught my breath and we laughed together, if—I could learn to do the same.

The night stretched on endlessly as we danced until the sun began to rise, the sky turning from deep indigo to soft pinks and oranges. My legs ached, but the good kind of ache came from feeling alive, from feeling the pulse of the world beneath your feet.

As the music slowed and the last few dancers filtered out of the club, Q leaned in, her breath warm against my ear.

"You did good tonight, Nea," she said, her voice soft but firm. "You needed this."

I didn't answer right away, but at that moment, I realized she was right. I hadn't known how badly I needed just to let go, to stop fighting for a second. To live. For a while, I could forget about everything—the mine, the fights, the endless battles I had waged. I could forget about the weight of my heritage and the expectations of my people and just be.

Just be me.

And for the first time in a long time, it felt like enough.

CHAPTER 47

Holidays with the Greyeyes

Finding Belonging

The warmth of the Greyeyes family home wrapped around me as I sat at their long, wooden dining table. The scent of roasted corn and sage mingled in the air, the kind of earthy aroma that felt like it was woven into the fabric of the land itself. It reminded me of home, the mountains, the river, the earth I had left behind, but with a subtle difference. This warmth wasn't just physical but carried the weight of belonging.

I glanced around the room at the faces of the family gathered there. Q talked animatedly with her cousins, and her laugh was infectious and free, like music.

I could feel the rhythm of their lives—the easy familiarity from years of shared stories, traditions, and love. It was beautiful, almost like watching a dance I was learning the steps to, one where I wasn't yet certain where I belonged but was willing to learn.

At the head of the table sat Stan Greyeyes, Q's father. A towering figure in both stature and presence, Stan was the kind of man who spoke with authority but not through force—he spoke with conviction, with a history carved deep into the lines of his face. His hands moved as he said, expressive and purposeful, as though the stories he shared were just as much about painting with words as with his art. Everywhere I looked in the room, his work was there—bold, vivid strokes of Indigenous resistance, beauty and survival, stories untold, and wounds healed.

And then there was me—sitting at the table, on the outside, trying to fill a space that felt both new and painfully familiar. There was comfort in the laughter, the ease with which they teased one another, and the shared looks that spoke more than words ever could.

But underneath it was a rawness, a gnawing emptiness that followed me from place to place. I hadn't realized how deeply I craved this belonging until it surrounded me.

Stan turned his gaze to me, and for a moment, it was as if the world fell away. His eyes were full of wisdom, perhaps, or a depth of understanding I didn't quite have the words for. He watched me in a way that made it feel like he could see into the very heart of me, past the layers of fight and fire I'd built up over the years.

"Your voice is like that, Nea," he said softly, his words wrapped in quiet reverence. "You paint with words. I heard you at the climate conference a while back."

I froze for a moment, unsure how to respond. His words felt like a revelation—a truth I hadn't been ready to hear. It wasn't just the compliment that struck me. It was how he said it, as though he had known me and had seen a part of me that I hadn't even acknowledged.

I shifted uncomfortably in my chair, the weight of his words pressing into me. I had spent so many years fighting, trying to carve out a space for myself in the world, so many years using anger as my fuel. I had forgotten there could be another way—a quieter way, a more deliberate way of creating change, of making my mark.

I had learned how to wield my voice like a weapon, sharp and pointed, but now Stan was suggesting something else—something gentler, more powerful in its own right. I didn't know how to be that person yet, but it felt possible in this room, surrounded by these people.

The warmth of their home, the stories, the laughter, the connection—it was something I hadn't felt in years. I had been so used to running, fighting, and pushing against the current of my existence. But now, with the Greyeyes family, I felt like I could breathe. I wasn't just a fighter.

I wasn't just an activist, a warrior, or a burden to the world. I was something else, something softer yet no less powerful. I was part of something again—part of a family, part of a community, part of a narrative bigger than just me.

As dinner carried on, I found myself listening more than talking. The stories flowed easily, mixing past struggles, triumphs, and simple moments of joy. Q's siblings bantered back and forth, their voices rising in playful argument before bursting into laughter. Sam and his partner, Maria, shared glances that spoke of decades of history, their unspoken language more meaningful than any words could ever be.

And there, amid it all, I realized something: I had been running so long, fighting so hard, that I had forgotten what it felt like to... belong. I want to let go of the fight, even for a moment, and be part of something bigger than myself.

I didn't have to prove anything in this house at that moment. I didn't have to justify my existence or explain my purpose. I was enough.

Stan's voice interrupted my thoughts, bringing me back to the present.

"Your voice matters, Nea," he said, more firmly this time. "It's not just about what you fight for—it's about what you stand for. You have stories to tell. And you're ready to tell them."

I could feel the weight of his words sinking into me, resonating deep in my chest. It was as though the world had shifted just a little, and I could finally see a future where I wasn't just a product of my struggles but a creator of my narrative.

The fire inside me was still there, but it didn't have to consume me anymore. I could use it to build, inspire, and speak—with force and meaning.

I allowed myself to hope for the first time in what felt like forever. I dream of a life where I don't have to fight every day and can just... be.

As the evening wore on, the conversation ebbing and flowing around me, I felt a sense of belonging and peace settling in my chest, like the final brushstroke on a painting. It wasn't a perfect picture, but it was mine. And maybe, just maybe, I was finally ready to embrace it.

CHAPTER 48

Todd & The Peyote Church

A New Kind of Ceremony

The first time Todd brought me to the Peyote Church, I hesitated.

It was one of those moments where my instincts screamed to turn away, to avoid something unfamiliar that felt foreign to the fight I'd always known. I had met him at the conference; he was from a Pueblo nearby and had grown up in Arizona before moving to Albuquerque for work.

But Todd had a way about him—steady, calm, the kind of person who didn't rush but moved through the world like he already knew the steps. He had seen my restlessness, the way I flinched from peace as though it were a threat, and maybe that's why he'd invited me.

"It's not like anything you've done before," he warned me, his voice soft but steady. "It's not about fighting. It's about listening."

I didn't know how to listen anymore. My whole life had been a battle, an endless series of protests, clashes, and internal wars, and every moment of my existence had been about pushing, demanding, and forcing change.

I had never learned how just to *be*. So, when Todd spoke about listening, it felt like I was being asked to surrender something I wasn't sure I was ready to give.

But here I was, standing at the edge of something new.

We walked toward the tent, the darkening sky pressing down on us, and I could already feel the weight of the earth beneath my feet. The land here—so different from home, yet strangely familiar—seemed to hum with its energy, something older than time.

The air was sharp, clean, and smelled of the desert, but also something else. A deep, ancient aroma that was more than just the soil or the plants—it was the scent of something spiritual, something sacred.

Inside the medicine tent, the fire crackled, sending a soft orange glow up against the walls. There was a steady rhythm of drums—deep, persistent, calling something from within. It wasn't just music. It was a pulse, like the heartbeat of the land, and somehow, I could feel it inside me.

The sage twisted in the air, wrapping around me like an old friend, reminding me of something I had forgotten.

I sat on the floor, unsure of what would unfold. I didn't know the rules, the rituals, the steps. I had never been one for organized medicine ceremonies. Everything in me screamed against the structure, the traditional way of doing things. I was always the outsider, the rebel, the one who questioned everything.

Todd sat next to me, his presence solid and reassuring. He didn't try to explain or ask me to be anything but who I was at that moment. He handed me the medicine—a small, humble piece of peyote, the sacred cactus—and I accepted it, though I wasn't sure what would come next.

As I chewed the bitter cactus, the world around me seemed to fade into a strange, swirling calm. I could feel the drumbeats reverberating in my chest, faster now, louder, almost overwhelming. The medicine took hold, slow at first, like a gentle tide lapping against my mind. Then, as the veil began to lift, I saw.

The land, my ancestors, the future waiting to unfold.

It wasn't a vision in the traditional sense but a deep, profound *knowing*. The land I had fought for, the mountains, the rivers, the earth itself wasn't just a place. It was alive, breathing, watching. And it was patient.

I saw the spirits of my ancestors, faces that were familiar yet unknown, their voices woven together with the sound of the wind and the whisper of the trees. They weren't angry. They weren't demanding. They were... there. Waiting.

My breath caught in my throat as I realized something I had never understood: It wasn't about fighting. It wasn't about war, about standing on the frontlines or shouting into the void. It was about remembering. Remembering the old ways, the wisdom passed down long before my time.

It was about listening to the land, spirits, and ancestors who had lived and died on this soil long before I was born. They had never stopped speaking. I had just stopped listening.

The drumbeat carried me deeper everyone sitting upright it had been hours. The fire flickered in the corner of my vision, casting long, stretching shadows on the canvas walls of the tipi. The heat from the fire mingled with the cold desert air outside, creating a strange tension —a balance. I could feel it in my bones—this space between worlds, where the past and present collided and merged, where the future waited patiently for its turn to unfold.

I saw the faces of the people who would come after us—my children, their children, generations of warriors not with guns, but with hearts open wide, not with fists, but with a deep respect for the earth beneath their feet.

I saw a world where the land was no longer viewed as something to conquer but as something to honor and protect. The Earth was not a commodity to be used and discarded. It was a partner, a living being who gave and received in equal measure.

And for the first time, I understood that the fight I had been so caught up in—the anger, the resistance, the demand for justice—wasn't the only path. There was another way. A way came from listening, honoring the world's rhythms, and reconnecting to something older than myself. I felt a peace I hadn't known in years, a deep release, like the weight I had carried for so long, was slowly lifting.

The ceremony continued until morning, and I drifted in and out of that space between the waking and vision worlds. I heard the voices of my ancestors again, this time clearer, more distinct. They didn't speak with urgency.

They spoke with patience, with the quiet wisdom of ages. They told me that I was part of a larger cycle, that my struggles, my pain, were but a fraction of the story that had been written long before my time. I was a thread in a larger tapestry whose hands had weaved I could never truly touch but whose influence was still felt.

When the ceremony ended, I felt something shift inside me. It was as if the fight had left me, not in defeat, but in a surrender, a release. I had always fought for the land, justice, and my people—but now I realized I wasn't just fighting for them. I was fighting with them, with the land, with the spirits, with the very fabric of the earth.

Todd sat quietly beside me as I absorbed the experience, his presence a steady anchor. He didn't ask how I felt or push me to speak. He just let me be, letting the silence stretch between us.

After a long pause, he finally spoke. "You okay?"

I nodded, still feeling the weight of the experience in my bones. "I think I've been fighting the wrong fight."

Todd smiled, a slow, understanding smile. "Sometimes the hardest thing is to listen. But when you do, everything else makes sense."

I didn't have all the answers yet. But I felt like I was on the right path for the first time. Not the path of resistance, not the path of conflict—but the path of remembrance, of reconnecting to something deeper than myself. The journey wasn't over. It was just beginning.

CHAPTER 49

Indian Kids Leadership Camp

Becoming a Mentor

They're gonna eat you alive, city girl," Todd teased as we pulled up to Indian Kids Leadership Camp.

I shot him a playful glare, half-amused, half-nervous. The idea of this camp had both intrigued and intimidated me. Indian Kids Leadership Camp wasn't just a place for kids to run wild and escape their daily lives; it was a place where young minds were shaped, where resistance wasn't just something spoken of in hushed tones but actively practiced.

The camp was an institution that combined tradition with activism, a meeting of generations where the stories of the past were handed down to the future. Donations from individuals like Robert Redford and Val Kilmer funded it. Still, more importantly, it was a space where young Indigenous people could learn about leadership, heritage, and community in a world that often seemed intent on stripping them of those very things.

Todd had been here before, so he knew the drill. Me? I was a little uncertain of what to expect. As I tried to convince myself I belonged in this space, a small voice kept whispering, Who are you to teach these kids? I had spent my whole life fighting to survive, fight for justice, and reclaim what was lost. But now, it was time to shift gears. I wasn't here to fight for them. I was here to teach.

We exited the truck, the summer sun hot on our skin, the dry earth kicking up beneath our boots. The camp was tucked into the folds of the land, surrounded by mountains that seemed to have witnessed the passage of centuries.

The kids were everywhere—laughing, running, pulling each other into playful headlocks from grade 8 to grade 12; they were all ages. Some were barefoot, others with baseball caps perched on their heads, eyes wide with excitement, full of youthful energy that could light up the world's darkest corners.

I expected to feel out of place. I'd spent many years standing on the sidelines, fighting for causes I believed in, but I'd never been a mentor. And now, here I was, expected to impart knowledge, to guide a generation that, despite their youth, was already more connected to the land than I had been in a while.

Todd gave me a quick wink, clearly amused by my nervousness. "Don't sweat it. Just be yourself. They're not here for some shiny, polished version of you. They want real."

That was easy for him to say. He had always been the one who fit into any space, whether it was the streets of Albuquerque or a camp filled with teenagers.

For me, though, the pressure of leadership felt heavy; the weight of every misstep magnified in my mind. What if I couldn't teach them what they needed? What if I failed them?

But as soon as we entered the main circle of the camp, something shifted inside me. The kids saw us, and their faces lit up. There was no judgment in their eyes, no expectation of perfection—just curiosity. The camp was a space where mistakes were another part of the learning process. We were there to show them that they could attend university too and achieve success for the betterment of our communities.

The first thing I noticed about the kids was their intensity. They were bright, hungry for knowledge and something more than what the world had already tried to offer them. There were no fake smiles, no pretending to fit into a mold they didn't belong to. These kids were rooted in who they were, even if they hadn't fully realized the depth of that connection yet.

I was introduced to my group, a mix of teenagers from many different tribes in the southwest, all with the fire of resistance in their eyes. Some were quiet, others boisterous, but each had a story and battles. Some had already tasted the sting of racism; others had yet to realize how deep the world's injustices ran. However, they all shared one thing: the seed of leadership was already within; it just needed nurturing.

As I stood before them, trying to calm the jitter in my stomach, I realized that my authenticity was the one thing I had in abundance—perhaps more than any of the polished, well-meaning adults they'd encountered. I wasn't here to discuss something I read in a book or learned in a lecture. I was here to tell them stories, to teach them the ways of our people, the resistance we had endured, and the legacy they were inheriting.

My first lesson was simple: storytelling.

I began with a story that Grandpa Oliver had told me, one that had been down through generations. It was the story of the trickster, the coyote, who could outwit the gods and carve paths where there were none. The trickster wasn't always the hero, but he was a survivor, a symbol of resilience. I told the story slowly, feeling the weight of every word, watching the kids as they listened, their eyes wide with attention.

It felt different, to tell these stories to a new generation. It wasn't just about entertainment. It was about teaching them who they were, about weaving their identity into a narrative of power. In the past, I'd only told these stories to myself to comfort myself, to remind myself that we had endured, fought, and were still here.

But now, as I spoke, I realized the weight of what I was passing on. These stories weren't just mine to carry anymore—they were theirs.

The next day, we moved on to language. We spoke in our traditional tongues, the words flowing from my mouth like forgotten rivers. And some of us shared drum songs we learned from our families.

But it wasn't just the stories and the drum that connected us—it was resistance. The next lesson I imparted was about resistance in all its forms. Not just the big battles, the public protests and movements, but the quiet, everyday acts of defiance. The refusal to be invisible. The fight to keep our culture alive, even when the world around us tried to erase it.

I shared my story—the occupation of Eagle Ridge, my experience in the sweat lodge, the battle for the land. But I also shared the stories of others—Elders who had fought in different ways, the women who had stood up, and the children who had picked up the torch when the older generations had been silenced. And why I was pursuing education.

The kids were mesmerized. They understood. They saw themselves in the struggle, in the resistance. They knew they had their battles to face, but they also knew they weren't alone. They were inheritors of something greater, something unbroken.

By the end of the week, something incredible happened. These kids—who had come to the camp as individuals, unsure of their place in the world—had begun to form a community. They stood taller and spoke more confidently, and their eyes gleamed with purpose I hadn't seen before. They were the future, and I realized my role here wasn't just mentoring them. It was to guide and help them find their voices and stand in their power.

And for the first time in a long time, I felt the weight of responsibility settle in me like an old, comfortable coat. I wasn't just a fighter anymore. I wasn't just a survivor. I was a mentor.

Maybe that had always been my purpose—to guide, teach, and pass on what had been given to me. I had spent many years looking for warriors to stand beside me. Still, now I understood something important: the warriors were already here. The next generation was already in place.

All they needed was someone to help them see it.

And maybe I was meant to be that someone.

CHAPTER 50

Jonathan, Harvard Law & The Hopi Prophecy

Jonathan sat across from me, and an old mahogany desk between us was a symbol of the world he lived in. He was a professor in the law program at UNM and had been an eloquent, enigmatic speaker at the conference. His fingers were steepled, his eyes sharp—so sharp they seemed to slice through the air, cutting straight to the heart of the matter. The kind of gaze you might expect from someone who'd climbed the highest academic ladders, who had spent years in the pristine halls of Harvard Law, weaving together the intricate threads of justice and privilege. He had become a different version of himself since we'd last met—not the conference speaker but a young professor, a leader amongst his peers, a version who now wore the weight of a future too big for the rest of us to comprehend.

He was a puzzle to me—someone I had always struggled to understand fully. Jonathan was born into privilege, his parents were successful lawyers and environmental activists from Hopi pueblo they protected their most valuable asset—water. But even as a child, he had felt the gnawing emptiness of that life. This disconnection came with growing up with everything in a small, struggling community. We had shared a few late-night conversations in the past, moments where he'd confided in me about his struggle with identity. He was an outsider in his skin, and though he had carved out a place for himself in the world of law, part of him was always searching for something deeper rooted in the soil of his ancestors. Although his life was law, he told me vague stories of the medicine ceremonies of his pueblo but very little. Their ceremony was deeply held in secret, sacred knowledge, so I never fully knew the depths of his spirituality, only what he could share.

"Do you know about the tablet the Hopi have held for 10,000 years?" he asked, his voice low, almost reverent.

I shook my head, my stomach sinking as the words landed heavily between us. The Hopi. They were an ancient people whose wisdom I had always respected. Still, the idea that they had a sacred tablet kept for millennia felt like something out of a myth I had never been told.

Jonathan leaned forward, his gaze fixed on me with an intensity that tightened my chest. "It's an artifact. A tablet passed down through generations. The Hopi believe it holds the knowledge of the world's cycles—the rise and fall of civilizations, the turning of the ages." He paused, his voice lowering even further as if the words themselves were too powerful to speak aloud. "It tells of what's coming. The breaking of the world. The Unsettling."

The word *Unsettling* hung in the air between us, thick and oppressive. My heart beat a little faster, a shiver creeping up my spine. I had heard whispers of prophecies, stories told around campfires, about times of great upheaval, when the world would be forced to change when the earth would reclaim what had been taken from it. But hearing it from Jonathan, with that intense certainty in his voice, made it feel real in a way I wasn't ready for.

The silence stretched between us, long and heavy, as I tried to process what he was saying. Jonathan had always been a man of logic who would dissect an argument until nothing was left but cold, hard facts. He had been a speaker at the Climate Change conference. A young, up-and-comer. But now, there was something deeper in him than his legal mind could explain away.

"And what does it say about people like us?" I finally asked, my voice quieter than I intended. The question felt like a weight, a desperate hope for something to hold onto during the storm that seemed to be brewing around us.

Jonathan's lips curled into a faint smile, the kind of smile that always made me wonder what he was thinking. It wasn't one of arrogance or pride but something far older, something more knowing.

"That we're the ones who will survive it," he said, leaning back in his chair. His words were slow and deliberate, as though they were both a declaration and a warning.

I sat back, letting the weight of his statement settle into my bones. Survive. The word felt like a burden, heavy with implications. The

Hopi prophecy, the tablet, the breaking of the world swirled together in my mind, knotting itself into something I couldn't yet untangle. We were all being swept along by something bigger than ourselves than any of the movements we had ever fought for. The Hopi had seen it coming—the collapse of systems, the unraveling of civilizations, the reckoning of humanity. And somehow, Jonathan and I—people like us—were supposed to stand firm when everything else crumbled.

But why?

What made us different? Was it the battles we had fought? The blood we had spilled? Or was it something else—something inherent, something woven into our very beings, something that connected us to the land, to the ancestors, to the ancient wisdom of the Hopi and the other Indigenous peoples who had seen the cycles of time unfold?

I swallowed hard, feeling the enormity of the moment. With all his legal training and polished intellect, Jonathan had always been able to dissect the world into neat, manageable pieces. But now, even he seemed unsure. This was different. This was beyond the law, beyond reason. This was about something bigger than us. It was about survival—not just as individuals, but as a people, as a collective consciousness that was awakening.

"How do you know?" I asked, my voice barely above a whisper.

Jonathan's eyes softened for the briefest moments, the hardness in his gaze fading just enough for me to see the vulnerability underneath. "I don't," he admitted, his voice quieter now. "But I feel it. I feel its weight every day. It's like… like the world is on the edge of something. And we're all just waiting for the first spark."

I looked at him, at the man who he was, who a deep, unshakeable need for purpose had consumed. He had found that purpose in law, in the system, but now, it seemed that the world was pulling him—pulling all of us—toward something far more profound.

The tablet, the prophecy, the Unsettling. These weren't just ideas. They were warnings, signs, guides. The Hopi had known that a reckoning was coming for thousands of years. And now, it seemed, it was our turn to heed the call.

I met Jonathan's gaze, feeling the weight of everything pressing in on me. For the first time in a long time, I wasn't sure where the road ahead led. But I knew one thing—whatever came next, we wouldn't face it alone. We were part of something much larger than ourselves.

And somehow, we were meant to survive it.

CHAPTER 51

Prayers in Death Valley

The desert stretched for miles, its silence heavy, its vastness pressing in from all sides. The horizon was a blur of heat and dust, the colors shifting beneath the sun's intense light. There was no shelter here, no refuge from the open emptiness, just the dry wind that whipped across the land like a whisper from the past. I had wanted to travel here to Monument Valley to connect with the sacred place.

I knelt in the dirt, the earth's heat seeping through the fabric of my jeans, grounding me in a way I hadn't felt in years.

The dry dust stuck to my skin, a reminder of how far I had come from the green, lush forests of home—the places where the trees whispered secrets and the rivers sang songs of ancestors long gone. Only the stillness, the raw, unrelenting desert stretched forever.

I pressed my palms to the earth, the roughness of it against my skin, the jagged rocks and sand, and the ever-present weight of the silence. This land was ancient.

It had witnessed civilizations' birth and death, empires' rise and fall, and the slow, steady march of time. The land was older than any of us, older than the battles we fought and the words we used to try to make sense of it all.

I prayed.

But it wasn't a war prayer. Not for justice or vengeance. In the heat of battle, I had prayed for those things once, with fists raised and my heart full of fire.

I had been consumed by the need to fight, claim something, and push back against the world that had stolen so much from us. But now, kneeling in this vast and desolate place, I realize that my prayers need to change.

I wasn't sure what it was that had brought me to this moment, to this desert, but I knew it had to be something bigger than me. Something older. Something that couldn't be fought with guns or laws or contracts.

I prayed to understand.

I didn't need answers. I didn't need to make any adjustments. I needed to understand the land, myself, and the path that had led me here. The answers would come in their own time. But I needed to quiet the noise inside me first.

The wind picked up, a gust that sent the dust swirling into the air. I closed my eyes and breathed it in, trying to connect with the deep, ancient rhythm of the land.

The prayers of my ancestors were buried here, in the dirt, in the rocks, in the bones of those who had walked this earth long before me. They were waiting to speak. All I had to do was listen.

When I opened my eyes again, the world had shifted. It was just after sundown now. Everything looked still and silent. How long had I been here praying?

There, on the horizon, was a black shape. It stood against the orange sky like a silhouette—still, unmoving, but there, unmistakable. At first, I thought it was a mirage, the heat playing tricks on me. But no, it was real—a presence. Something is watching me.

My breath caught in my chest. The shape was large, its form angular, as though it were something that didn't quite belong in the world of flesh and blood. My heart began racing, and my mind fought to understand it.

The air turned cold, an eerie chill slicing through the desert's heat. It was a sudden drop in temperature as if the land itself had breathed in something dark that didn't belong.

I wasn't alone.

The realization hit me like a wave, heavy and crushing. The desert had always been a place of solitude, where I could get lost in my thoughts, away from everything and everyone. But now, I knew it wasn't just the land I had to contend with. There was something here—something ancient, something primal.

I stood slowly, my legs shaking slightly as I faced the black shape in the distance. I didn't know what it was. I didn't know if it was real or a vision, but I felt its gaze heavy, like a weight pressing against my chest. It looked like a large bat with wings, but I couldn't see its face.

It wasn't fear that gripped me, not exactly. It was something else—something that made my heart beat faster and told me I was on the edge of something far bigger than myself.

I had prayed for understanding. And now, it seemed that the land was answering.

But what did this presence mean? Why was it here, waiting, watching? Was it a sign? A warning?

I had no answers. But I knew this: my journey wasn't just about me anymore. It never had been. I was part of something larger, something older, and whatever was watching me from the horizon was part of it, too.

I took a deep breath, grounding myself in the moment. There was no running from it, no escaping it. This was my path. And I had to walk it, even if the answers I sought were still hidden beneath the earth, the silence, and the weight of what had come before.

The shape remained on the horizon, unmoving, and I felt the desert itself hold its breath. And for the first time, I knew I was no longer just a person walking through the world. I was part of something. Something vast. Something ancient. And the land was waiting for me to understand.

CHAPTER 52

The Skinwalker

It started as a whisper, faint at first, like the breeze through dry leaves. But it wasn't the wind. I could feel the shift in the air, the prickle on the back of my neck. My heart began to race, and my breath caught in my throat. It was too quiet. The world seemed to hold its breath, waiting.

Then came the laugh.

It was not a sound that belonged to any human being but something deeper and older. It reverberated in the pit of my stomach, something that pulled at my soul, twisting it into knots. The laugh echoed through the stillness, too sharp and too cold. My instinct screamed at me to run, but I stood frozen. My feet felt rooted to the earth, but my mind was already a hundred steps ahead, running through every story I'd ever heard.

The Elders had warned me.

They always warned us about the Skinwalker.

The stories were always vague, half-told, with sharp edges that never fit together. A creature born of darkness, of twisted magic—

something that could change its shape, slip between worlds, and come in the form of anything it desired. A man. A wolf. A bird. It could mimic voices and steal faces. It dwelled in the shadows, where the land felt amiss, and the balance had been disrupted.

Do not speak its name. Do not look too long. Do not let it follow you.

But even as the warning echoed in my mind, I couldn't shake the feeling that it was already here and had been with me all along, lurking in the space between every breath I took. Testing me and watching me.

I turned, slow and deliberate, my pulse pounding in my ears.

Nothing.

The desert stretched out before me, barren and endless. The day's heat had begun to fade, but the night still felt heavy, like something unseen pressed down on me, waiting to strike. My eyes scanned the horizon, but there was nothing—no shape, no figure. Just the darkness stretching out like an ocean of black.

Still, I couldn't shake the feeling that I wasn't alone.

The Skinwalker was old. Older than the world I knew. Older than the stories we passed down. And there was something about it that knew exactly where to find the cracks, where to slip into your thoughts and twist them, turning them into something unrecognizable. Something dangerous. Something that could make you doubt yourself, your memories, your sanity.

I had learned long ago that the land had its rhythms. Its heartbeat. But now, it felt like the earth beneath me was pulsing with something unnatural. A friend told me not to be here in the desert after sundown.

I could feel the weight of its presence, pressing in from every direction, wrapping itself around me like a cloak. It was close. Too close.

I took a deep breath, gathering what little courage I had left. The Elders said that fear was the Skinwalker's greatest weapon. If you showed fear, it would only grow stronger. But how could I not be afraid? How could anyone not be scared of something that could take your shape, that could look like anyone, that could become anything?

In the darkness, I heard it again—the soft padding of feet on the earth, the unmistakable sound of something moving just out of sight. The air seemed to grow colder, the space around me narrowing, pressing in. I could feel the temperature drop as though the land itself was recoiling from what had come to haunt it.

I turned again. And there, just for a moment, I saw it again.

A flicker of movement. Something is shifting in the shadows. The flash of eyes gleamed like glass, catching the light in a way that didn't seem right. It was quick—too quick—but I caught sight of it. I saw a barely human figure bent at an unnatural angle, a shape that wasn't quite right.

And then it was gone.

But it wasn't. It never really was.

I swallowed hard, trying to steady myself. This wasn't just some creature. This was a thing from the old stories, a force of nature itself—a being that existed beyond the limits of the world I knew, beyond the stories I'd grown up with. It manifested fear, the embodiment of everything broken, twisted, and forgotten.

As Grandpa Oliver taught me, I called in my ancestors and guides.

It tested you. It made you question your mind. Your memories. Your understanding of what was real and what wasn't.

I had no idea how to fight it. I have no idea how to face something like that.

But the thing was, I *knew*—deep down—I would have to.

The desert had always been a place of power. Of mystery. But it had also been a place of answers, a place where the past could be called upon, where the ancestors' wisdom still lived in the stones and the wind. And if the Skinwalker was here, then it meant something. Something bigger than me.

I had no choice but to confront it. To face it head-on.

I closed my eyes for a moment, grounding myself in the earth's rhythm. The land had always spoken to me before. It has always guided me.

And now, I had to trust it again.

The wind picked up once more, sending a shiver down my spine. The desert was alive, thrumming with energy. The Skinwalker was a test—a trial. But it was also an opportunity—an opportunity to prove something.

I was no longer the girl who had run from fear. I wasn't the girl who had buried herself in protest, resistance, and battle. I was something else now. Something more.

And when I opened my eyes again, the desert was waiting.

The Skinwalker was still there, somewhere, but I wasn't afraid anymore.

Not of it. Not of anything.

Because, in the end, the land always had the answers. And the truth would come. Whether I was ready for it or not. I could feel my ancestors surrounding me and the wolf in my veins rising – my protectors were still with me, no matter where I was.

CHAPTER 53

The Choice – Scholar or Warrior?

The email arrived early the next morning, just as the sun began to rise. The heat of the New Mexico desert was already starting to creep into the day, but I felt cold. A shiver that had nothing to do with the weather.

SUBJECT: Congratulations, Nea - UBC Environmental Studies Program.

I stared at the words on the screen, my heart drumming in my chest. My hand hovered over the mouse, my finger hesitant, as if I could somehow stall the decision just by not clicking. The moment I opened that email, everything would change. And yet, somehow, it already had.

I took a deep breath and clicked.

Dr. Webbles had written my recommendation. "She is not just a student. She is the future."

I'd always been told that the fight, the struggle, the passion for the land—that was what defined me. But Dr. Webbles had seen something else. A future, perhaps one that didn't require me to bleed for it. One that wasn't waged in protest or anger but in knowledge, study, and *understanding*. But that wasn't me.

I stared at the words on the screen, my mind swimming in memories of barricades and bulldozers, of the endless battles I had fought for the land. I remembered the faces of the people I had stood with—the warriors, the Elders, the youth. Every face reflected my burning desire to protect something that could never truly be owned. The land. My people. My spirit.

And then, River was the sudden sharp reminder of how much had been left behind. Daddio, Mom, and Grandpa Oliver and all the East Van Crew. People who had become my family and my anchors. Was it time to leave the desert and go back to Vancouver?

I had always been at war. From the moment I understood my purpose in this world, it had been clear: I was meant to be a warrior. Not just a fighter for land but for identity, culture, and justice. I had carried that responsibility in my bones, in my blood. My role was clear, and my purpose was defined.

But now... the future stretched before me like an endless desert, as barren and uncertain as the night sky.

Stay in the fight.

The words echoed in my mind. I had spent my life *fighting*—for my people, the earth, and justice. I knew the names of the battles, the scars of the wars I had fought. It had been my identity, my purpose. But what would I be without the fight? Without the resistance? Could I survive outside the walls of the protest, the barricades?

Could I let go of the urgency, the fire that had kept me moving for so long?

Or...

Change the war entirely.

Could there be another way? Could I learn to fight from within the system rather than against it? The idea of changing the system from the inside—of using knowledge as a weapon rather than my fists—was a concept that felt almost foreign to me. But the more I thought about it, the more I realized that maybe it wasn't just about changing the fight. Maybe it was about shifting the ground itself, finding new ways to bring about the change that had eluded me for so long.

The reality of the email settled over me like a weight. This wasn't just a decision about a career or education; it was a life-changing choice. This decision was about who I was and what I wanted to become. Could I leave the fight behind longer and finish my studies? Could I trust that I could still make a difference, even if it wasn't in the way I had always imagined?

The weight of that decision dragged me down for weeks after I clicked 'accept.' I could barely focus on my final exams, as if I were walking through the motions of a life that no longer felt mine. I was there, physically present in the classrooms. Still, my mind was already gone, drifting to the idea of what could be, what I could become. I didn't know if I was running toward something or away from everything I had fought for.

I didn't tell anyone. Not Q. Not Todd. Not Jonathen. I couldn't explain it to them—couldn't find the words to justify why I was leaving when there was still so much at stake and so many battles to fight. The pull to stay was powerful, but so was the need to step away, find my path, and contribute. The complexity of that decision nearly broke me.

On the morning I left, I packed my bags with the same hesitation I felt when clicking 'accept.' Everything I owned fit into a couple of suitcases, a small representation of the life I was leaving behind. The desert stretched beyond the horizon, as empty as my chest felt.

Q and Maw'Tsain had always been a home for me for a time, but I could feel the desert swallowing another piece of my heart, as it had with every love I'd tried to hold onto. I was leaving behind not just a place but a part of myself—the fire, the fight, the certainty that had defined me for so long.

I boarded the plane, feeling the weight of my decision in my bones. As the plane ascended and the heat of New Mexico faded behind me, I couldn't help but wonder if I was leaving for good—or if I was heading toward another battle.

I had made my choice, yet I wasn't sure if I had chosen the right side of the desert or closer to my homeland. In the end, I figured home was always the answer.

But in the end, *maybe* that was the point. In life, there was never a single path to walk. The choice wasn't about which road to take but about accepting that you could forge your way, even if it meant leaving people behind and stepping into a world that might not recognize your fight.

I wasn't chasing ghosts anymore. This time, I was choosing to live.

But what that meant, I didn't know yet.

Like the rest of my journey, the desert would have to wait.

PART 3
The Grizzly Sleeps

CHAPTER 54

Rising From Ashes

Home was a brief pause, a moment to let go of my old life in Albuquerque, heal, and sit in a ceremony with Mom, Grampa Oliver, and River.

But I wasn't meant to stay.

I was back in Vancouver within weeks, pouring myself into work, school, and the fire of ambition that refused to let me fall apart.

I threw myself into the Urban Native Youth Society, determined to build something, help, and make a change. My life became a mix of policy meetings, youth programs, and advocacy work—early mornings and long nights.

I finished my degree at the University of British Columbia at 26, the first in my family to do so. Then, I dove headfirst into a Policy Think Tank on Indigenous Issues, a project that consumed me for five years.

The days blurred into each other—papers, research, conferences, panels, flights. I immediately enrolled in my Master's program in Leadership and Training at Royal Roads.

There was no time to stop.

Success had its price: sixty-hour work weeks, coffee-fueled ambition, and an endless loop of strategy and execution. I was climbing, fighting, leading.

And on the weekends?

I danced until dawn in the gay clubs of East Van, gin and neon lights, my heart half wild, half detached.

For a while, I had Danielle.

She was sharp, confident, unapologetic. A woman who kissed me like she meant it, who pulled me into a world where labels didn't matter.

We were on and off for a year.

Dancing in dark, pulsing clubs, bodies moving to bass and rhythm, but never quite finding something solid.

Danielle was a moment, a lesson in love that felt different but ended the same.

I didn't have time for deep love—I barely had time for sleep.

The work came first.

And then, at 30, walking down the street with my best gay friend, I met the father of my children.

That moment shifted everything.

The Night Fate Intervened

The neon hum of Davie Street flickered above us, casting long reflections on the damp pavement. The night was young, the city alive with the reckless energy of possibility. Music throbbed behind us, the ghost of bass-heavy beats still pulsing in my chest as AJ and I stumbled out of Celebrities, drunk on laughter, on movement, on the fever-dream haze of a night not yet ready to end.

And then, I saw him.

Leaning against the takeout window at Tsu Huang Village, ordering food with his best friend. It was a moment so unremarkable, yet somehow, it changed everything.

I slowed my pace, something in the air shifting.

The two wore long black wool coats over jeans and polos—as they had just stepped out of a fraternity recruitment poster, looking effortlessly polished and unbothered by the late hour.

I smirked. "Where's the frat party?"

They turned. And in that instant, something ignited.

Laughter. Banter. A twenty-minute sidewalk debate about everything and nothing at all—the kind of conversation that makes time irrelevant and binds strangers into something more. None of us wanted to leave.

We crossed the street to Blendz. AJ and his friend drifted off into the night, but we stayed.

For hours.

Aleksander: The Man Who Would Change Everything

He stood at 6'3, golden-haired, green-eyed—a study in contrasts. His gaze was sharp and watchful; he saw more than he let on and understood the weight of the spaces between words.

Russian and half French. Lean, fit, but never ostentatiously so. He was witty and sharp, with a cutting intelligence that could be charming or caustic, depending on his mood.

There was a push and pull between us, an unspoken gravity. He was reserved, cautious, a man who measured his words while I was all fire and motion, my energy pulling him into the light.

He worked as a manager at a high-end men's tailor—always dressed in sharp, crisp collars and well-fitted suits, as if the world would bend to his presence. Graduated from UBC with a commerce degree at twenty-two.

And he was twenty-five—**five years younger than me.**

But age had never been a language I spoke. Not when the connection was this effortless.

From that night forward, he was everywhere.

He slipped into my world like he had always belonged there. Weekends stretched into weekdays, clothes left behind, routines forming in the quiet spaces of familiarity. We danced around it, pretending we weren't falling, but the truth sat between us, undeniable.

And then, five months later, we stopped pretending.

We moved in together.

He carried himself with an effortless charisma that made him both untouchable and entirely within reach. A paradox. Unfazed yet intense, unshaken yet deeply knowing.

He was the kind of man who could command a room without raising his voice, whose silence held more weight than most people's words.

I didn't expect to fall so fast.

But Aleksander wasn't a slow burn—he was wildfire. Consuming. Absolute. A force of nature, a gravitational pull I couldn't resist.

It started with one date.

A rooftop patio, the warm hum of city lights, the quiet intimacy of deep conversation stretching into the early morning hours.

Then another.

And another.

Until suddenly, he was my world.

We moved quickly—love like lightning, striking before we had time to prepare.

And then, one day, everything changed again.

The Leap to Ottawa

After the first year, our love settled into something solid.

The kind of love that wrapped around you like a wool coat in the dead of winter—warm, secure, promising. A feeling that had a weight that felt safe.

Then, the call came.

Ottawa.

A Senior Policy Analyst position. A dream job. The kind of career move that could shape everything, a path paved by opportunity.

I should have been thrilled. I should have jumped without hesitation.

But there was him.

Aleksander.

And suddenly, the life we had built on Commercial Drive—the ease, the familiarity, the weight of something unfinished—felt more permanent than I had ever expected.

"Come with me," I said.

I expected hesitation. Resistance. A sign that I should stay.

But to my surprise, he didn't want to let me go.

He agreed.

And just like that, the road stretched before us again.

Another leap into the unknown.

Leaving Vancouver Behind

I sold the apartment on Commercial Drive, leaving behind the scent of cedar and rain-slicked streets, the hum of late-night conversations drifting from café patios, the life we had once known. We packed up everything we owned—every book, every photograph, every half-written dream stuffed into boxes—and with it, the last remnants of who we had been.

For the first time, we weren't just a couple fumbling through love and late-night promises. We were partners, bound by something deeper, something weightier than passion. The road stretched eastward, each mile unspooling a future we had chosen together.

Ottawa was nothing like Vancouver: no mountains, no ocean breeze, no scent of salt. Instead, the city stretched in quiet dignity, its bones built from Parliament and power. It was a city of order and austerity, where the pulse of politics thrummed beneath the surface, shaping lives in both visible and invisible ways. Suits and lanyards filled the cafés; the news cycle dictated the rhythm of the day. Conservative, measured, a place where history pressed against modernity, where the ghosts of prime ministers still lingered in the stone corridors of Parliament Hill.

But Ottawa was beautiful in its way. The Gothic spires of government buildings stood solemn against the sky, watching over the city like sentinels of the past. The Rideau Canal wound through its heart, freezing solid in the winter, transforming into the world's longest skating rink—a silver ribbon cutting through the city's cold, unforgiving winters. Summers were hot, the air thick and still, as if the entire city held its breath before the next seasonal shift.

I bought a small house with a crooked fence and a garden that would take years to tame. Our first real home. A place where walls could hold laughter, where rooms could breathe us in and remember us. Aleksander finished his CGA, stepping into a world of pressed suits and government corridors, a life carved from numbers and stability.

For a while, it was enough.

We were happy.

Content.

Or so we told ourselves.

CHAPTER 55

The Unexpected News

Life in Ottawa had settled into something steady, predictable—a rhythm built on early mornings and quiet nights, on the soft click of dress shoes against government office floors, on the comforting weight of routine. It was a city of structure, order, and politics shaping the air we breathed.

And then, in a single moment, everything shifted.

I stared at the pregnancy test, my breath coming in shallow, uneven waves. Two pink lines. A verdict. A before and after.

Pregnant.

The word sat heavy in my chest, unreal and absolute simultaneously. My fingers tightened around the plastic stick as if holding it harder might change the result—a baby.

My body already knew. The exhaustion, the strange pull of nausea in the mornings, the sudden, inexplicable craving for oranges—all signs I had ignored until now.

I wasn't expecting it.

Neither was Aleksander.

When I told him, he went still, his face draining of color as if the words had stripped something from him.

"You're sure?"

"Yes."

For a moment, the air between us thickened, dense with something unnamed. Not fear, exactly. Not excitement, either. Something in between—uncertainty, hesitation, the slow unraveling of what we thought our future would be.

Aleksander exhaled sharply, running a hand through his hair, his jaw tightening as he paced. He was twenty-seven. We had only just arrived at this version of ourselves—this life, this career, this city that was supposed to be ours.

I watched him move back and forth across the living room, the tension rolling off him in waves. He was always composed and calculated; his world was built on logic and careful planning. But this? This was chaos.

And then, without warning, something in him cracked.

He freaked out.

Not in the dramatic, shouting kind of way. Aleksander was too controlled for that. But his mind spiraled fast, his thoughts tumbling out in clipped, frantic syllables.

"We aren't ready for this. We barely have savings. A baby?" His voice was sharp and strained, as if he were trying to force the weight of this into something manageable. "This changes everything, Nea."

It did.

He sank onto the couch, elbows on his knees, hands pressed together like he was trying to pray his way through it. His eyes—dark, stormy—stared at nothing in particular.

And I just stood there, watching the man I loved unravel.

I had expected shock. I had expected hesitation. But I hadn't expected this.

I had never seen him afraid before.

A strange, hollow quiet settled between us, stretching long and thin like a thread about to snap.

And suddenly, I wasn't sure what scared me more—the life growing inside me or the possibility that I might be stepping into this alone.

CHAPTER 56

The Storm Before the Calm

"I don't know if I'm ready. I don't know how to be a father."

"We're still young."

"This changes everything."

The words hung in the air long after he had spoken them like echoes trapped in the walls of our little house. Then he was gone. Not in the permanent sense, not in the way that left doors slamming or bags packed, but in the quiet way a man disappears into himself when the world tilts too fast beneath his feet.

For the next twenty-four hours, I barely heard from him.

I told myself he needed space. This was Aleksander—the man who analyzed before he acted, who made decisions like he built his career: carefully, methodically, with an eye on the long-term.

But logic did little to quiet the storm inside me.

I sat alone in our small house, in the silence of a life that was no longer just mine, pressing a hand to my stomach as if that could make sense. A heartbeat I couldn't yet feel, a presence that was both familiar and completely foreign.

And in the stillness, the questions whispered: would I be doing this alone?

Then, the next evening, just as the sky softened into dusk, he walked back through the door.

Different.

Calmer. Clearer.

He stood in the doorway momentarily as if measuring the weight of the words he was about to say. Then, finally:

"Okay." A slow exhale. A decision was settled. "We're doing this."

And just like that, something in the air shifted.

We sat down at the small kitchen table, the same place where we had once planned weekend trips and grocery lists, and instead, we charted the course of our future.

Where we would live.

How we would raise our child.

What life would look like now that everything had changed?

And just like that, he was in. Fully.

Aleksander wasn't perfect. He had never been. However, he remained steady and never abandoned his responsibilities.

For the first time, I felt it—the fragile, tentative weight of building something real.

Not just love.

Not just passion.

But a foundation.

And maybe that would be enough.

CHAPTER 57

A Wedding, A Home, and a Growing Family

We planned a small wedding that felt like home—intimate, warm, held within the walls of our little house in Ottawa. No grand venues, no extravagance, just love, laughter, and the handful of people who truly mattered. The scent of fresh-cut flowers filled the air, mingling with the laughter of family, the low hum of conversation, and the clinking of glasses.

Daddio had been sick, and I had feared—deeply, silently—that he wouldn't make it. But he did. He was there, smiling, his deep, knowing laugh rolling through the room like thunder on a summer night. That alone made the day perfect.

For a brief, fleeting moment, life felt whole.

Then, as if the universe had been waiting for its next great shift, Spring Equinox arrived, and with it, Talia.

Our daughter.

The moment I held her, the world rearranged itself. Every certainty I had once carried dissolved into something softer, unspoken, but profoundly real. The weight of her in my arms, her breath warm against my skin, the quiet, steady pulse of a new life—everything before her felt like a prologue.

A Dream Home, A Surprise Twist

Not long after, we left our little starter house behind and stepped into something bigger that felt like the promise of all we had built together.

Our new home in Westboro was a dream—a beautifully renovated rancher, its high ceilings stretching toward the sky, light pouring through the wide windows like it belonged there. The backyard unfolded into a space meant for summer days and childhood memories, a kidney-shaped pool shimmering beneath the sun.

It was a house that felt like a beginning.

The perfect place to raise a family.

And then—ten months later, life shifted again.

I remember the moment as clearly as the first. Sitting in the bathroom, staring down at another positive test, adjusting to life with Talia, figuring out who I was as a mother, and thinking, How did this happen so fast?

Aleksander just laughed, shaking his head that easy, effortless way as if the universe had simply handed us another chapter before we finished writing the last.

"Guess we're doing this again," he said.

And just like that, May was on her way.

CHAPTER 58

A House Filled with Joy

Summer stretched long and golden, seeping into your bones and making time feel endless. The air in Ottawa hung thick with heat, pressing down like a heavy, familiar hand, but it didn't matter. Not when the backyard was a world of its own—a sun-drenched sanctuary where childhood bloomed wild and free.

The pool shimmered under the blistering sky, and Talia and May ruled over it like tiny queens of their water kingdom. They ran naked through the yard, their sun-kissed skin glistening, their laughter ringing like wind chimes in the hot afternoon air. Sprinklers spun in dizzying circles, spraying arcs of cool relief over the dry grass, and they shrieked as they dashed through, limbs flailing, fearless and unbothered.

The grill was always hot, the scent of charred meat and spiced marinades drifting through the yard like an invitation. BBQs became a ritual, an unspoken tradition where friends became family, and the boundaries between work and home blurred in the best way. Aleksander's colleagues, who had started as casual acquaintances, soon became fixtures in our lives, their voices mixing with ours, their children tangled up in the chaos of Marco Polo games and impromptu water fights. Someone always brought a cooler filled with beer and ciders. As the sun dipped, the conversations stretched long into the evening. Stories were told, hands gestured wildly, the occasional burst of laughter too loud, too sudden—the joy that spills over when life is good, and you know it.

And then there were the nights when the city called.

The Heart and Crown was our favorite escape, where the music was always loud, the pints of Strongbow crisp and cold against the heat of the dance floor. Whenever family was in town, we made a night of it. Guinness and whiskey flowed, stories were retold louder than necessary, and the music pulled us into movement. We danced in that easy way that came with familiarity, knowing that even though life had settled into parenthood, responsibilities, and routines, we were still us.

And then winter arrived, draping the city in white, turning everything still and quiet.

Christmas brought Mom, Daddio, and River, their presence filling the house in a way that made it feel whole. Daddio would shake his head at the bitter cold, muttering about "the kind of weather that could kill a man." At the same time, ever the adventurer, River found magic in the deep snowdrifts and the sharp scent of pine. The house smelled of roasted turkey, sage, and cinnamon and warmth that only the family could bring.

When the holiday rush softened into slow winter days, we took to the canal, skating together in the cold, the world around us wrapped in the hush of fresh snow. Talia wobbled, gripping my hands, her cheeks flushed pink beneath her knitted hat. May—small but fearless—took off in wild, uneven strides, her laughter echoing against the frozen surface. Steady and patient, Aleksander skated alongside them, his hands outstretched and his voice gentle with encouragement.

In those moments, I knew.

This was the life we had built.

It is not perfect, but it is not without its struggles; it is full.

Full of laughter, of movement, of love so deeply woven into the walls of our home that even in silence, you could feel it.

And as I watched my daughters glide across the ice, the glow of streetlights flickering against the frozen canal, Aleksander's laughter rising in the cold night air, I thought—this is happiness. This is home.

CHAPTER 59

Loss, Grief, and the Breaking Point

Life had settled into a beautiful chaos that felt manageable, even exhilarating, in its rhythm. May was nine months old, her small world expanding with each new step, each curious reach toward something beyond her grasp.

She was a child of summer, her skin kissed golden by the sun, her laughter rising over the splash of pool water, and the low hum of conversation.

During those months—when life was full, brimming with movement and purpose—I boldly decided to begin my PhD.

It would be a seven-year journey, one that would demand everything of me: my time, my energy, my intellect, my patience. But I was ready. Or at least, I believed I was.

Life was busy, but it was good.

Our home pulsed with momentum. Summers unfolded in sunlit afternoons, the scent of grilled burgers and sunscreen thick in the air as May toddled across the backyard, her tiny feet navigating the warm concrete with unsteady determination.

She was growing too fast, and I was trying to capture every moment while keeping pace with the relentless forward motion of our lives.

I was deep in school. Aleksander was working hard. We were building something—something sturdy, structured, and responsible.

On paper, it looked perfect.

But perfection is an illusion, and illusions are fragile things.

I booked a trip home for the summer with the kids before. I needed to be on the land, press my palms into the earth, and breathe in the scent of pine and river before burying myself in academia.

Something was grounding about returning to where I had come from, something that reminded me of who I was beyond deadlines and research papers, beyond motherhood and marriage.

I hadn't realized I was walking straight into heartbreak.

A cruel silence comes before tragedy, a stillness that lets you believe, just for a moment, that everything is as it should be.

It lulls you, holds you in a false sense of security, and lets you move through your days unburdened by knowing what is coming.

I remember stepping off the plane, the heat of the tarmac rising in waves, the sky impossibly wide. I had no idea that the world I had known was about to crack open beneath me.

Because loss doesn't come gently; it arrives like a storm, sudden and unforgiving, tearing through the fabric of the life you thought you had.

And when it does, nothing is ever the same again.

CHAPTER 60

The Summer That Changed Everything

Some moments split your life into two parts—before and after, past and present, and the person you were and will become. I didn't know it then, but the summer of my father dying was the breaking point. The moment everything fractured, I would spend the next fifteen years piecing myself back together.

When I stepped onto the rez, Talia balanced on my hip. May was in the stroller, and the air was thick with something I couldn't name: a weight, a knowing, a shift in how the world moved around me. The land felt different beneath my feet, as if it, too, was bracing for what was to come.

"Daddio's in palliative care" said Mom.

The words landed with the force of a body blow that knocks the wind from your lungs and leaves you reeling. I had known he was sick—we all had—but knowing is not the same as accepting. A small, stubborn part of the heart always refuses to believe that time is running out. That the person who raised you, shaped you and carried you through childhood will one day slip away.

For most of that summer, I barely left his side.

I sat beside his bed, watching the man who had once been larger than life shrink into something fragile, something breakable. I bathed him when he was too weak to move, the roles reversing in a way that felt both natural and deeply unfair. I held his hand, traced the callouses of a well-lived life, and memorized how his fingers curled slightly even in sleep.

I played his favorite songs. The old ones, the ones that carried history, the ones that made his foot twitch in rhythm even when he could no longer speak.

And every morning, I woke up knowing I was watching my father die.

Talia and May: His Greatest Joy

But there was one light in those dark days, one thing that cut through the grief settling over our family like an early frost.

Talia and May.

Talia, only two, and May, only nine months old, still full of newness, their world expanding in wide-eyed wonder. And for Daddio, they were everything.

Meeting his first grandchildren was one of the highlights of his life. Even as his body weakened, even as the illness took more from him with each passing day, he beamed with pride whenever they were near.

He would watch me bathe May in the living room, where his hospital bed now stood, his tired eyes filled with something I hadn't seen in a long time—pure, unfiltered joy. He had always been a quiet man who carried his love in actions rather than words, but with them, it was different.

He spoke to Talia and May, his voice soft but steady, telling them stories of the land, the family, and the world they would grow up in. He laughed when May splashed in the warm water, her tiny hands slapping the surface in delight. With wide eyes, Talia sat on the couch near him, smiling. And when I wrapped May in a towel and lifted her from the basin, he would reach for her, his fingers brushing her soft skin, his touch lingering as if trying to memorize her and staring long and sweetly at Talia beside him.

They gave him something to hold onto in those final weeks.

The girls gave us all something to hold onto.

Even in the quiet of his decline, there was love.

The days stretched long and slow, marked by the quiet rituals of waiting. There was an unspoken understanding between us—no need for grand speeches, last-minute confessions, or regrets. The love had always been there, woven into the fabric of our lives in a way that did not need words.

Sometimes, he would open his eyes, that same sharp glint still there beneath the haze of illness, and he would squeeze my hand as if to remind me that he was still here. That he was still him.

And I would smile, even as my heart splintered, and say, "I know, Daddio."

When the leaves began to turn when the air carried the first hint of autumn's bite, the world outside his hospice room kept moving forward, even as mine stood still. We had to move him there when the pain became unbearable, and he was no longer able to move.

I had to go back to Ottawa. The PhD. The life I had built there. The responsibilities are waiting for me.

I bent down, kissed his forehead, warm and familiar skin beneath my lips, and whispered, "I'll be back soon."

A promise. A lie I didn't know I was telling.

Then I walked away.

I never saw him alive again.

The Call That Shattered Everything

On Remembrance Day, the call came.

It was Remembrance Day when the world tilted.

Nea still living in Ottawa at the time, the wind biting and sharp, her coat wrapped tight over the red poppy pinned to her heart. She had made tea with Elders, shared stories with Senators. It was supposed to be a day of remembering.

Instead, it became the day her father slipped into forever.

The call came just before she boarded the red-eye. Her mother's voice shook through the line. "It's time."

Nea promised she would be there. She would come home. She would hold his hand.

In Calgary, during the layover, her phone rang again.

"Nea, your Dad is almost making his final journey. I'm putting the phone to his ear."

Her voice broke as she whispered into the static: "Daddio, I love you so much. Everything I am, everything I've done is because of you. All the time fishing, hunting, out in the farm, haying, camping out on the land... You're my heart. I will see you on the other side. I'll always be with you."

She landed in Kamloops in the early hours. River picked her up, holding baby Talia in silence. No words passed between them. The grief had already settled in.

At the hospital, she reached him moments too late. His face was still, his chest unmoving.

She collapsed onto the bed, sobbing. Screaming in love, in rage, in grief.

Her mother held baby May and Talia, both of them crying in the room that held Nea's world's end.

After that, Nea was never whole again.

Grief is not just sadness. It is absence. It is emptiness. It is the cruel, unshakable truth that nothing will ever be the same again.

I wanted to scream, to cry, to collapse under the weight of it, but instead, I just sat there, stunned, hollowed out.

Because how do you hold the knowledge that the person who had always been there, the anchor, the constant, the unshakable presence in your life, is now just… gone?

People tell you grief softens with time, but they don't tell you how long it lingers in the spaces between. How it settles in the marrow of your bones, how it reshapes you in ways you won't understand for years.

It took me fifteen years to heal from that loss.

Fifteen years to accept that there are wounds that don't close neatly, that some grief becomes part of you, carried like an old scar that only aches when the weather changes.

And even now, after all these years, I still hear his voice in the wind, still see him in the slow bend of the river, still feel him in the quiet moments when I least expect it.

Because love—real love—does not die.

It lingers. It endures. It remains.

Even when everything else has changed.

CHAPTER 61

The Call to Come Home

Grief is not a singular event. It is a slow decay, an erosion of everything you once believed to be unshakable. It had been three years since my father's death, and the weight of it had settled into my bones, calcified into something I could not shake. It did not fade. It did not soften. It lingered like a wound that refused to close, threatening to swallow me whole.

It nearly did.

The loss of him was more than a death; it was a rupture, a breaking of the world I had known. Emotionally and spiritually—I had never recovered. Some days, I was barely holding myself together. Some nights, the grief became something else entirely—an unraveling, a hollowing out. There were moments I questioned my very sanity, moments where the pain no longer felt like something I was carrying but rather something that was carrying me.

I needed to go home.

Not to Ottawa—Ottawa had never been my home. Not really. It was a place we had built, a life we had carved out carefully, but it was never where my soul belonged. My spirit needed to be back in BC. The land. My family. My people. I needed the mountains, the river, the trees that had witnessed every version of me before this one. I needed my mother. I needed to stand where my father had lived, breathed, and had been.

But Aleksander refused.

"We built a life here."

"My career is here."

"I don't want to move."

His words were iron bars, locking me inside a reality that felt smaller with every passing day.

Neither of us would relent.

I begged. I cried. I needed him to understand that I was drowning here.

But he couldn't.

Or maybe he just wouldn't.

I spent the next year in a haze of grief and resentment, watching our marriage shift beneath my feet, no longer something solid but something brittle, something beginning to crack.

CHAPTER 62

The Breaking Point

The fights circled the same battlefield, over and over, the same words slamming against each other like dull blades, wounding but never cutting deep enough to end it.

Aleksander refused to move. I refused to stay.

And so, we stood in the wreckage of what had once been **a l**ove that felt unshakable.

"Find a job that pays more—permanent, good benefits—and I'll consider it."

A challenge.

A lifeline.

For six months, I pushed harder than I ever had. If he wanted proof, I would provide it. If he wanted stability, I would create it.

I scoured job boards. Networked. Manifested a way out.

And then, against the odds, I did it.

It's an amazing university job. Permanent. Full benefits. A future.

I accepted the offer, packed my bags, and moved home to Vancouver.

Aleksander? He was furious.

"I'm staying in Ottawa to sell the house."

Fine.

I left.

Two months passed in a blur of back-and-forth flights, tense phone calls, and a distance stretched further weekly.

And then, one night—exhausted, frayed at the edges, sensing something I could not name—I flipped through our phone records.

A number.

A recurring number.

My stomach twisted, my pulse hammering in my throat. I stared at it for a long time.

Then, with hands that were suddenly unsteady, I dialed.

The line clicked.

A woman's voice, soft, startled.

"Hello?"

I swallowed. My voice was steady, but my blood was boiling beneath my skin.

"Who is this?"

A pause. Then—caution.

"Who is this?"

A shift in the air. A knowing.

I exhaled sharply, the words like acid on my tongue.

"Why are you calling my husband all the time?"

Silence.

A sharp inhale.

And then—screaming.

"I have no relationship with you! Call Aleksander and ask him!"

Click.

The silence that followed was deafening.

And just like that, the final crack became a break.

CHAPTER 63

The Showdown Over Salmon & Wine

The moment the phone rang, I already knew. Some truths arrive before they are spoken, slithering through the silence, coiling in the gut like an omen.

Aleksander answered, his voice clipped, careful.

"What the fuck is going on?"

Silence.

Then a lie.

Then another.

And finally, the truth.

I was already on a plane home.

That night, we sat across from each other at the dinner table, the storm outside rattling against the windows, pressing against the walls like it wanted to be let in. Between us, a plate of salmon, a bottle of wine—a mockery of normalcy, a ghost of all the quiet, comfortable dinners that had come before.

Tension settled into the space between our breaths, thick and impenetrable.

"*How long?*"

A pause. Then, too easily—too casually:

"*Months, over a year.*"

Something twisted inside me.

Two years. That's how long it had taken me to trust him. Two years to believe he wouldn't be like the men who came before him.

The fathers we had grown up watching.

The fathers who had left behind legacies of secrets, whiskey-soaked betrayals, broken-hearted women pretending not to cry in the kitchen.

Cheaters.

Liars.

In recovery.

Aleksander had sworn he wouldn't be that man.

He had promised.

He had lied.

The wine in my glass sat untouched, and the salmon on my plate was cold. The air in that room was no longer something I could breathe.

I pushed back my chair, the sound scraping against the hardwood floor. I yelled. I cried. The storm inside overwhelmed me, leaving only wreckage in its wake.

The next morning, I flew back to Vancouver.

And this time, I wasn't looking back.

CHAPTER 64

Aftermath – Numbing the Pain

Grief has a shape. It shifts, stretches, and takes form in the hollowed-out spaces where love once lived. And betrayal—betrayal carves its kind of wound.

After Aleksander, the fight, and Victoria, nothing was left of the life I had built. There was no home, partnership, or family dinners where we laughed over burnt rice and discussed our futures. No illusions of permanence.

Everything had shattered.

Mom moved in to help with the kids.

I should have been grateful. I was grateful. But her presence, the way she watched me with quiet concern, her eyes tracked the weight I was losing, the exhaustion in my face—suffocating. She never said it out loud, but I knew what she was thinking.

"She's slipping."

And she wasn't wrong.

So I did what I had to do.

I threw myself into work, into running, into survival.

If I could keep moving, I wouldn't have to feel.

5K runs to Totem Park every night.

It became my ritual. I ran like I could escape it all—the memories, the rage, the ache that lived in my ribs. Through the damp, salt-laced air, past the towering cedars that had stood longer than any marriage, longer than any promise. I pushed my body to the edge, lungs burning, legs screaming, welcoming the pain because it was the only thing that felt real anymore.

When I reached the edge of the park, I'd stop and stare at the ocean, the sky bleeding into the water like ink on wet paper, and I'd think:

I should be happy.

I was free. I was back home. I had my daughters. I had a job I loved.

But my mind was a wasteland of what-ifs.

What if I had never left Ottawa?
What if I had fought harder to save us?
What if I had seen it coming?

And worse:

What if I had never met him at all?

I spent long days at the university, losing myself in research.

If my body wasn't in motion, my mind had to be.

I took on more projects and more responsibilities. Stayed later but home in time for dinner. Answered emails that didn't need answering. Let academia swallow me whole because thinking about anything else was unbearable.

If I could spend eight, ten, or twelve hours wrapped in deadlines in the office early everyday and research papers, maybe I wouldn't hear his voice in my head, perhaps I wouldn't see the ghost of us in every quiet moment, maybe I wouldn't feel the raw, festering wound of knowing that I was alone again.

Maybe.

And then, at night—

Wine.

Three glasses, sometimes four. Poured too fast, swallowed too easily.

To silence the screaming in my ears. To drown the visions of them in my bed. To numb the pain of losing the life I had fought so hard for. The first sip was a relief, the second a necessity, the third a surrender. By the time the bottle was empty, my thoughts were dull, my body warm, my grief momentarily sedated. But in the morning, it was still there.

I reeled in pain and betrayal for months, after 10 months of nightmares and looping thoughts I finally found a hypnotherapist who helped pull me together. If it wasn't for Kaleen I would not have made it out of that period alive but the healing never seemed to be complete. As the years stretched out the pain and trauma layered over each other in ways that would not heal. Although I moved on slowly I knew I would never be the same again.

CHAPTER 65

What Had He Done?

Aleksander sat in the dark, the glow of the streetlights barely filtering through the half-closed blinds. The silence in the house was thick, almost suffocating. He should have felt at peace. He had made his choice. He was married now. Settled. A beautiful wife, a stable life, and two incredible daughters.

So why did it feel like something inside him was slowly rotting away?

The Beginning of the End

It hadn't started with lies.

No, when he met Nea, it had been **real**. A wildfire kind of love, all-consuming, a force of nature. She was unlike any woman he had ever known—brilliant, passionate, untamed. He had admired her fire, the way she threw herself into everything she did, the way she never backed down from a fight, whether it was against the government, a mining corporation, or him.

And, God, had they fought.

At first, it was about small things—where to live, how to raise the kids, and whose career should take priority. But slowly, the arguments had grown sharper, cutting into the foundation of what they had built.

She wanted to move back to BC. He wanted to stay in Ottawa. Neither of them would bend.

He knew she was grieving. Losing her father had wrecked her in ways she refused to talk about. He should have held her through it. It should have been the rock she needed. But instead, he had grown resentful. Angry that she was pulling away, angry that she was putting her family before the life they had built together.

He had told himself he was right to stand his ground.

But deep down, he knew. He was just afraid to lose her.

The Lie That Became the Truth

The first time it happened, it had meant nothing.

A business trip. A few drinks. A woman who laughed at his jokes, who looked at him like he was the most interesting man in the room.

It had been easy.

Too easy.

And for a while, he convinced himself it was a one-time thing. A mistake. Something that would never happen again.

But then there was Victoria.

It had started innocently enough. Just conversation. Just someone to vent to when things with Nea got bad. Someone who listened when discussing his frustrations, loneliness, and doubts.

Someone who didn't challenge him the way Nea did.

It wasn't love. He told himself that repeatedly.

But when Nea got on that plane to Vancouver, when she left him to move their daughters and their lives across the country, something inside him snapped.

He had never felt so angry and so abandoned.

And in that moment, the lie he had been telling himself for months became the truth.

Victoria wasn't a mistake anymore.

She was a choice.

The Marriage That Meant Nothing

Aleksander stared at the ring on his finger, twisting it absently.

It should have felt like an achievement. Stability. A second chance.

Instead, it felt like a prison sentence.

He had married Victoria because it was easier than admitting he had made the biggest mistake of his life. Because going back to Nea, admitting everything, facing the wreckage of what he had done, would have destroyed him. She even said she would never trust him again.

So he did what he had always done.

He lied to himself.

He played the role of a devoted husband and a responsible father. He convinced himself that Nea would be fine without him, that she didn't need him anymore. That this was the better path.

But no matter how often he told himself that, the emptiness never disappeared.

Victoria was perfect on paper.

She was calm where Nea had been wild. Predictable where Nea had been chaos. Safe where Nea had been passion and fire.

And God, he hated her for it.

He hated the way she never challenged him. He hated the way she needed him a way Nea never had. I hated the way he had thrown away the only woman he had ever truly loved for something that felt so goddamn hollow.

The Only Happiness Left

The only thing that made sense anymore was his daughters.

When he was with them, he could almost pretend he was still the man he used to be. He could push down the regrets, the self-loathing, the ache that never seemed to fade.

But at night, when the house was quiet, and Victoria was asleep beside him, it came creeping back.

The what-ifs.

The should-haves.

The memories of Nea—her laughter, her anger, her touch.

The truth he could never admit.

That he had made the wrong choice.

That he had thrown away the love of his life.

And now, it was too late to get it back.

PART 4
Echoes of the Ancestors

CHAPTER 66

The First Meeting—Hé Sá

The pub hummed with the easy, familiar rhythm of after-work drinks—the low din of conversations, the clinking of glasses, the occasional burst of laughter that cut through the music playing overhead. Nea sat at a high-top table, laughing with Rochelle and Jillian, a half-finished cocktail in front of her, fingers tracing the rim absentmindedly as she leaned back in her seat.

Rochelle was mid-story—some gym drama, a trainer hooking up with a client, the usual gossip—when her face suddenly lit up.

"Oh my God, *Hé Sá!*" she called out, voice high with excitement.

Nea turned at the sound of the name, catching sight of him just as Rochelle hopped off her stool and pressed her hands all over the man's broad chest and arms. He was big—*really* big—the kind of body that came from dedication, discipline, and maybe a little vanity. He wore a fitted black T-shirt that clung to his muscular frame, dark jeans, and a thin silver chain that disappeared beneath the collar of his shirt. His hair was cropped short, with a fresh fade that lined up to his sharp cheekbones and a strong jaw.

She expected him to be just another gym guy, all ego and no substance. But when he turned toward her, she felt the shift in the air. His eyes were *piercing*—not just the color, a sharp, steel-gray with hints of amber, but the intensity behind them. Like he was the type to see things, other people missed.

"Hey, Rochelle," he greeted smoothly, arms flexing as he returned the hug, but his eyes flickered to Nea.

"Oh, sorry! You guys should meet," Rochelle gushed, her manicured nails lingering on his bicep. "Nea, this is *Hé Sá he works at a corporate law firm here downtown.*"

He grimaced, just a flicker, before offering a tight smile.

"*Haysha*," he corrected, anglicizing the pronunciation like it was second nature.

Nea arched a brow. "Lakota?" Another corporate lawyer. Just what the world needs.

His lips twitched at that, something flashing in his gaze—surprise, maybe interest—but he only nodded.

"Yeah, half," he said. "But I don't really—"

"—get into all that," Nea finished for him, already knowing exactly how this conversation went.

His smirk was slow like he appreciated that she'd called him out.

"I take it you do?" he asked, voice edged with amusement.

She tilted her head, considering him. "I grew up on the land, ceremony, the whole deal."

"Ah," he nodded as if that explained everything.

Before he could say more, his gym buddy Peter stepped in, slapping him on the back.

"You two talking history already?" he teased. "C'mon, Hé Sá, let's get drinks before you scare her off."

Nea laughed, shaking her head. "He'd have to try harder than that."

Rochelle clapped her hands together. "*Shots!*"

And just like that, the night spun into chaos. Hé Sá ordered whiskey pickle backs, grinning as Nea scrunched her nose at the combination.

"Don't knock it 'til you try it," he challenged.

She held his gaze, grabbed the shot, and tossed it back—brine and burn, salt and fire.

And then came another round.

And another.

And another.

Suddenly, Nea was being pressed against the leather seats of a cab, Hé Sá's lips against her neck, the heat of his hands on her thigh, her fingers tangled in the chain around his neck.

The Morning After

The first thing she registered was warmth. His bed was *too* warm, the blankets twisted around her legs, and the faint scent of whiskey, cologne, and something *undeniably male* clung to the air. The second thing she registered was the pounding in her skull.

Fuck.

She cracked one eye open, blinking against the soft morning light filtering through the blinds. Everything in the room was dark—black dresser, curtains, and sheets—of *course,* they were black sheets.

Why do dudes always have black sheets?

It was a *thing.* Like some universal *player handbook* said: *Step One: Get a gym membership. Step Two: Buy black sheets to hide your sins.*

Her gaze flickered to the other side of the bed.

Hé Sá was still asleep, face turned away, his broad, olive-colored back exposed above the sheets. Tattoos crawled up his arms, disappearing beneath the blanket, muscle cutting hard lines down his spine.

Double fuck.

She squeezed her eyes shut.

There was no way she was doing *this.* The awkward morning-after, the weird small talk, the polite *I'll call you* lie. She needed to leave *before* he woke up.

As carefully as possible, she slid out of bed, grabbing her clothes off the floor, trying not to trip over her damn boot. She tugged on her jeans, fumbled for her shirt, and snatched her jacket off the chair.

One last glance over her shoulder—he was still asleep, perfectly at peace.

With a quiet exhale, she grabbed her boots and slipped out the door.

The Next Day

Her phone buzzed just after noon.

Hé Sá: *You left before coffee. I wasn't done with you.*

She stared at the message, biting her lip.

Nea: *I figured whiskey picklebacks weren't on the menu.*

A moment later:

Hé Sá: *Could've been. You'll have to come back to find out.*

She rolled her eyes, shaking her head.

Nea: *Also, black sheets? Seriously? I think it's a player thing.*

Hé Sá: *Maybe. Or maybe I like the way they look.*

Nea: *Uh huh. Sure.*

Hé Sá: *You sound skeptical.*

Nea: *I'm just saying… statistically, every dude I've ever met with black sheets was bad news.*

Hé Sá: *Statistically, huh? That sounds like bias. Maybe I should prove you wrong.*

She smirked, leaning back against her couch.

This could be interesting.

The Slow Burn & The Black Sheets Again

For weeks, Hé Sá played the long game. He didn't push, didn't crowd. Every few days, a text would come through—just enough to keep him in her orbit but never enough to demand anything real.

Hé Sá: *Hey, trouble. What are you up to?*

Nea: *Not much, just at work.*

Hé Sá: *Too bad. I could use a distraction.*

Or—

Hé Sá: *Whiskey pickle backs round two?*

Nea: *Hard pass. You're evil.*

Hé Sá: *Yeah, but you like it.*

It was always flirting, always playful, and when she didn't bite, he didn't chase. That was the part that got to her. *He didn't chase.* He was just *there*, like a gravitational pull, and eventually, she found herself falling into it.

The first couple of times she went over, it was fun. Low-key. A movie, drinks, then inevitably, the black sheets. He was a good time, and *damn*, was he good in bed. But after a few months, it started to feel… *off.*

Every meet-up was the same.

Hé Sá: *Come over.*

Nea: *Let's do something different—coffee, a hike?*

Hé Sá: *Yeah, maybe. Let's figure it out later.*

And then it would always default back to *come over*.

She wasn't stupid. She knew what this was shaping up to be. And yet, she let it ride—until the lunchtime jog.

Seeing Him with the Ex

She wasn't even thinking about him when she ran past the little café downtown, music pumping in her ears. But then she saw him.

Sitting at a table. Laughing.

With *her*.

His ex. The one he'd been with for ten years.

Nea didn't break her stride, but something twisted in her gut. He looked over just as she ran by, their eyes locked. For the first time, he looked uncomfortable. He looked away suddenly.

She thought so; he could *go for coffee*. Just... not with her.

The realization sank in. *This is not where I want to be.*

She ignored his texts for the next few weeks.

Black Sheets, Round Two

It should have been over.

She had gone *weeks* without answering. But then, out with Rochelle, he *was just there*. Another bar, another night, another whiskey-fueled bad decision.

The next morning, she woke up in *the same* damn black sheets.

Except this time, he was awake, sipping coffee at the edge of the bed like nothing had changed.

"Hey," he said casually, tilting his head at her. "Don't mention this to Rochelle, okay?"

She blinked, still foggy from sleep. "Why?"

Hé Sá hesitated just long enough to make her stomach drop. Then, with a half-shrug, "Well, we used to date after my ex and I broke up last year."

Her mouth went dry. *Oh.*

She had no idea what to say, so she said nothing.

Instead, he followed up, easy, *too* easy—

"I like being around you. Wanna keep this low-key, you know?"

Something in her locked up.

He wasn't lying. That was the worst part. He *did* like being around her. But this wasn't going anywhere. He wanted her in his orbit—a warm body in black sheets.

She mumbled something vague, pulled herself together, and exited.

What the *fuck* was she doing?

Reeled In

It happened fast. Too fast.

Nea had held strong for weeks, keeping her distance, trying to shake whatever spell Hé Sá had over her. She knew better. She had seen the signs and had told herself she was done with it.

And then he called. *Twice.*

FaceTime. Not texts. Not the usual flirty bait he used to keep her hooked. He looked ragged. His voice was rough.

"Can you come over? I need a friend tonight."

She sat up straight. Concerned.

Christmas was approaching, and this time of year was particularly challenging for everyone. Perhaps he genuinely needed a friend. Maybe she could hold space for that without getting sucked back in.

Four minutes. That's all it took.

His place was too damn close, and before she could talk herself out of it, she was standing at his door.

He had been drinking. Whiskey, for sure. The scent of it mixed with something deeper—grief.

She sat beside him, and he pulled her into him before she could say a word.

"My sister…" His voice cracked just enough for her breath to still. "She passed away in a skiing accident. Twelve years ago today."

His grip tightened.

"This is the worst day of the year."

She felt it then—*the weight of it*. The waves of sadness rolled off him, the quiet ache behind his words. He wasn't crying, but he didn't have to. She could *feel* it.

Instinct kicked in. She didn't think, didn't hesitate. She wrapped her arms around him and let her forehead rest against his.

Healing mode.

She didn't have words to fix it, so she didn't try. Instead, she called the light how she always did when someone broke apart. She surrounded them both in a field of warmth, letting Universal Love radiate out, filling the room, filling *him*.

They fell asleep curled together on the couch, the steady rhythm of his breath evening out against her own.

And just like that—*she was reeled in again.*

Fuck.

The Slow Burn & The Breaking Point

It started gradually.

After that night—the night he pulled her into his grief, the night she let herself fall back in—the calls and texts became *regular*. Not just the usual flirty bait but *honest conversations*.

FaceTime. Late-night check-ins. Good mornings.

They started seeing each other twice a week. Then three. Then four.

It wasn't just the heat between them anymore. *It was more.*

He started confiding in her, telling her about his ex and how he *still* had feelings for her. Nea listened and gave advice, knowing she was getting deeper into something that would lead *nowhere*.

But she didn't stop.

I didn't *want* to stop.

They had this *thing*, this deep friendship, this electric connection that hummed under her skin every time they touched. They had become close friends, with a deep trust. When did that happen? And then there was *the pull*. The *unreal* pull. Sometimes, she felt powerless to it, like he had cast some unseen tether around her, drawing her in no matter how often she told herself she should walk away.

Some nights, she fell asleep thinking about him kissing her.

Some mornings, she woke up *missing him*, aching for the weight of his arms wrapped around her, the feel of those strong, tattooed arms locking her in as if she *belonged there*.

Like she could stay there *forever*.

And then—*he changed the rules*.

It started with little things.

"Hey, I have to work early—5 AM."

Then again.

And again.

At first, she ignored it. But after eight or nine months of this—of being *his*, or *almost his*, or *whatever the fuck this was*—it started to sting.

This night was the third time.

Nea sat up fast. *Too fast.*

She grabbed her clothes, pulling them on with sharp, jerking motions, her heart hammering in her chest.

"I'll call an Uber," she muttered, *pissed off.*

She didn't look at him. I didn't *want* to see whatever excuse was on his lips.

She was almost to the door when he ran after her.

"Nea, come on—"

He pulled her arm, turning her around, her eyes burning, *hating* that she was already crying.

"Do I look like an escort to you?" Her voice wavered, but she forced the words out, *forced the rage forward instead of the hurt.* "This is the *third* time you've done this. Please leave. I work early."

He scoffed. "Do you *think* you're a hooker?"

She stopped cold.

I stared at him for *one long second* as the Uber approached the curb.

"You're an *asshole*," she hissed. "Don't even bother with the reverse psychology."

Then she got in the car and left.

The Final Cut

Like *clockwork*, the texts kept coming.

Flirty. Casual. Acting like nothing had happened.

She ignored them for months. She said *no* every time he pushed.

And then, finally—*she snapped.*

She typed fast, furious, letting the words spill before she could stop herself.

Listen, you must have plenty of chicks on speed dial. I'm done with this.

I talked with Rochelle. She told me you two were involved while you were still with your ex and that you destroyed that poor woman with your cheating. Many women, not just her.

I'm just sorry I didn't talk with her sooner.

Plus, Rochelle had feelings before you moved on to me. You destroy any woman who loves you, and I don't want to be next.

So just fuck off. Please.

Then she hit send.

And finally—*she was free.*

The Return & The Unraveling

Months turned into seasons.

At first, there were fleeting thoughts of him— Hé Sá. A memory of his arms, a whisper of a dream. But nothing more.

Eight or nine months passed. She was *fine.*

And then—*the call.*

Janelle.

Her husband had died the month before after a brutal battle with cancer.

"Can we meet for bevvies?" Her voice was small. "I can't be home alone tonight."

Nea *jumped up immediately*.

When she arrived at the restaurant, she froze.

He was there.

Of course, he was.

This town was too small.

Janelle's husband, Brian, had been one of his best friends. They were *both* grieving, and the drinks flowed heavily.

How could she be *angry* at him in this moment?

Another night. Another round of *picklebacks*.

And the next morning—*his arms around her again*.

The Words She Wasn't Meant to Hear

He kissed her ear, barely awake, his voice a sleepy mumble.

"I love you."

Nea *froze*.

Her breath hitched, but she drifted back into sleep before she could process it.

He held her tighter the second time she woke, his lips against her temple.

"I love you so much."

Her heart slammed against her ribs.

What the hell?

Did he think she was someone *else*?

His *ex*?

Oh. *My. God.*

She lay there, staring at the ceiling, thoughts *spinning*.

When she finally sat up, he was still asleep. She took a long shower, letting the water *scald* her skin, hoping to wash away the confusion curling around her like smoke.

When she stepped into the kitchen, she barely looked at him.

"Coffee. Please."

The Final Crack

He didn't answer right away.

She turned—and *he looked mad*.

"Hey," he said, his voice low, measured. "I talked to Rochelle."

Nea blinked, confused.

"She said she never said anything bad about me to you."

A sharp headache pulsed behind her eyes.

She *sighed*.

"Are you *serious*?" she said, rubbing her temples. "Every week since she found out, it's been a *diatribe* about what an asshole player you are. I've never once lied to you; you know me. If anything, I'm *too honest*."

She shook her head.

"You're going to believe her over *me*?" She laughed, but there was no humor in it. "Unbelievable." Nea was pissed, offended.

A beat of silence.

Then, softly—

"Well, it's not like I've heard from you either."

She froze.

Something in his voice…

He *stopped himself* mid-sentence.

And then—

"I had cancer."

The words *dropped* between them like a stone in still water.

Nea turned slowly.

"Oh."

Her heart *stung*.

"I'm sorry," she said quietly. "Are you okay now?"

"Yes."

But his *expression didn't soften.*

He still looked *mad.*

Nea stood there for a long moment.

Then—she turned, got dressed, grabbed her bag.

She looked at him once before walking out the door.

"I can't do this."

And this time—

She didn't *look back.*

The Final Break & The Cord That Wouldn't Cut

Two weeks later, Janelle called.

Her voice was *off*—tight, raw.

"Nea, Hé Sá is sick. *Sick.*"

Nea *froze.*

"I—what?"

"I can *see* he cares about you," Janelle pressed. "Did he say anything? Anything at all?"

Nea swallowed hard.

"Yeah," she said slowly. "He told me he had been sick but was *okay now.*"

Janelle *sighed.*

"No," she said. "We have close family friends. They said…he's *dying*."

The world tilted.

Nea stood there, speechless, her mind blank and racing at the same time.

She fumbled for her phone, her fingers moving on instinct.

Her first text:
Are you okay?

Her second:
I heard you're still terminal. Please answer me.

Her third, her fourth, her fifth—
Nothing.

But the *realization* slammed into her like a brick wall.

Oh my God. I love this man.

She had *loved* him all along.

And if he was sick—if he *was* dying—she *wanted* to be with him.

Not out of pity. Not out of obligation.

Because *she loved him*.

She picked up her phone. Called once. *No answer.*

Called again. *No answer.*

One more time. *Voicemail.*

She inhaled sharply and left a message.

"Hey, babe. Please, will you tell me if you're okay?"

Her voice *wavered*, but she forced herself to continue.

"You know my Dad died suddenly of cancer, and I don't want to lose you. But if you're sick, I *want* to be with you. And if you're *not* sick, I *still* want to be with you. Because…"

She swallowed hard.

"Because I love you."

Silence.

"Just text me. Even one word. Let me know if you're okay."

Weeks passed. Then *months*.

And *nothing*.

Not one text. Not one call.

At some point, the weight of it *broke* something inside her.

She grieved his death—whether it was *real* or not.

Somehow, she *moved on*.

She dated. *Not seriously*. Because he was *still* in her heart.

A Year Later—The Panic Call

She had just started *feeling normal* again when the phone rang.

Her breath *hitched* at the name flashing on the screen.

Hé Sá.

She answered immediately.

"Nea, *please*," he rasped. "I need you. I need a friend *again*."

Her heart *leapt* and *plummeted* all at once.

She *rushed* to his place.

Was it his *cancer*?

When she walked in, her stomach *dropped*.

His eyes were *bloodshot*.

Whiskey bottles—*26ers everywhere*.

He grabbed her—*clung* to her, his fingers digging into her arms.

Tears streamed down his face.

"Nea, I'm *so* sorry for hurting you," he *choked*. "I'm *lost*. So lost."

She *held* him, trying to steady the tremors in his body.

"I—I'm going into detox tomorrow," he whispered. "I love you. I don't even want to *live* another day."

Nea's breath *hitched*.

She *cradled* his face, pressing her forehead to his.

She *kissed* him—tried to *take away* the pain, the sadness, the years of *breaking and breaking and breaking*.

They fell asleep on the couch, curled together.

For the first time in *years*, she felt a sense of *hope*.

And in the morning—

He was gone.

She texted him.

A few times.

Did you make it into detox?

Are you okay?

Nothing.

Then—

A single response:

"You're a temptation for me. I can't talk to you. Don't text. Don't call."

Her heart *cracked*.

She had *invited* him to a ceremony to *heal* with her family.

And instead—

He had shut her *out again*.

The Cord That Wouldn't Cut

It had been *five years* now.

Five years of this push and pull.

The love that never entirely *broke*.

The *pull* in her heart that *wouldn't let go*.

Nea finally called Grampa Oliver and Mom.

She told them everything.

"This whole love," she whispered, "has gone *wrong*."

She *knew* what she had to do.

She had to *journey on it*.

She had to *cut the cord*.

And this time—

She had to make it *stick*.

CHAPTER 67

The Love He Couldn't Keep

(Hé Sá's POV)

Hé Sá never wanted to love her. There were times he hated her.

At least, that's what he told himself.

Nea had been a wildfire from the start—untamed, unwavering, fierce. She walked through life like she belonged to the Earth itself, her presence magnetic, impossible to ignore. He'd met plenty of women before and slept with more than he'd care to admit, but she was different. And she was older, close to his age. Most of the women he had around were younger.

But she saw him.

Not the gym-sculpted body, not the calm, detached persona he'd crafted over the years. She looked straight through him, into the raw, broken places he never let anyone touch. That should have been enough to make him run. And yet, every time she pulled away, he reached for her, caught in a game he didn't know how to win.

The First Pull – Lust and Fascination

At first, it was simple. Lust. Curiosity. Fun.

She was beautiful, sure, but it was more than that. There was something about the way she laughed with her whole body and didn't care about impressing anyone, least of all him. She wore makeup, but not as much as most women he dated. She was natural, with no fake nails, no extensions, no fake eyelashes, and no fake breasts; she was also smart and a career woman. Hé Sá was used to women fawning over him, eager to please, desperate to be chosen.

Nea didn't need him.

And that made him want her even more.

Their nights together were electric, the chemistry undeniable. But she had this way of looking at him too deeply, seeing things he didn't want her to see and pulling out all his stories and secrets.

He kept things casual. Or tried to. Until the first time she walked away.

She had called him out—on his avoidance, his walls, the way he never let her in. He'd let her go easily, or so he thought. He had women lined up, ready to take her place. But when he was alone at night, when the whiskey burned in his throat and the distractions faded, he thought of her.

And before he knew it, he was texting her again, drawing her back in, just close enough to feel her warmth but never close enough to let her see the whole truth.

When She Left – And Meant It

She told him the truth one night —a brutal, cutting truth.

"You destroy every woman who loves you."

It shouldn't have hurt.

But it did.

Because he knew, deep down, she was right. For that, he was furious and wanted to hate her. I tried to hate her for months and months.

His ex had loved him, and he had broken her. His past was littered with women who had given him their hearts, and he had thrown them away, chasing something he couldn't even name. And now, here was Nea, looking at him like she had finally figured him out like she had no intention of playing his games anymore.

So he let her walk away.

Not because he didn't care. But because if he held on, he'd ruin her, too. And he didn't like this feeling; he wouldn't lose control.

The Cancer

When the diagnosis came, he told very few.

Only his family, not his friends, and certainly not Nea.

He didn't want pity, didn't want to be the dying man people tiptoed around. And most of all, he didn't want her to come back out of obligation.

But somehow, she found out.

Her texts came relentlessly, her voice breaking in his voicemail.

"Are you okay? I heard you're still terminal; please answer me."

Then, the one that shattered him:

"If you're sick, I want to be with you. If you're not sick, I want to be with you because... I love you."

Hé Sá couldn't breathe when he heard it.

He sat in the dark for a long time, listening to her words repeatedly, his knuckles going white as he gripped his phone tightly. He almost called her back. Nearly told her the truth.

But he didn't.

Because if he let her love him now, she would watch him die.

And that was the one thing he couldn't do to her.

So he did the only thing he knew how to do. He ghosted her.

The Breakdown – The Love He Couldn't Run From

He should have left her alone forever.

But when rock bottom came, when he made it through cancer but when the whiskey wasn't enough to numb him anymore, when the addiction had him in its claws, there was only one person he could think of.

Nea.

She answered on the second ring. He hadn't expected that.

"Please, Nea... I need you."

She was at his door in minutes. The second he saw her, he broke.

"I'm lost, Nea. I don't want to be here anymore."

And when she held him, when her light wrapped around him, he felt safe. He felt seen.

That night, in the haze of whiskey and regret, the words spilled from his lips before he could stop them.

"I love you."

She froze but didn't pull away. She didn't question it.

She just held him tighter.

For the first time in years, he slept without nightmares.

Recovery & The Unspoken Distance

The next morning, he was gone before she woke up.

A text. *I'm in detox. Please don't contact me.*

He needed to do this alone.

And he did. Seven days in detox, then straight into recovery, the 12-step program, the meetings, the self-righteous distance.

He convinced himself that avoiding her was part of his healing, that it was the only way to stay clean. But if that were true, why did he still feel the pull?

Why did he still crave her warmth like he craved whiskey?

So, he did the next best thing. Distraction.

Blonde, fake-boobed, tattooed Instagram hotties. Porn.

It wasn't sex. It wasn't cheating.

At least, that's what he told himself.

It was just harmless fun. It's just a quick ego boost, a hit of validation. He wasn't touching them, wasn't breaking any rules. And yet, deep down, he knew.

It was a lie.

Because even when he was sending flirty messages to a half-naked model, the face that haunted him at night wasn't hers.

It was Nea's.

The Goodbye He Never Wanted to Say

It was inevitable.

The final cord cut. The moment she realized she was done waiting.

He could feel it long before she even told him.

And yet, when the Blood Moon came, when she did her ceremony and released him, he felt the shift like a blade slicing through his ribs.

A void where something warm had once been.

For the first time in his life, Hé Sá knew what regret tasted like.

It wasn't very pleasant. It was endless.

And it was entirely his fault.

Final Thought: The One Who Got Away

He sometimes wondered if Nea ever thought about him.

He knew she had moved on, at least on the surface.

But sometimes, late at night, he could still feel her in the empty silence of his own making.

The love he had turned away. The light he had let go.

And in those moments, he knew the truth he had been running from for years.

He had never stopped loving her.

And he never would. She would still text him occasionally, but he wouldn't give in. He was in recovery and following the program. He didn't need her; he convinced himself of this. There was someone else out there for him; there had to be.

CHAPTER 68

The Women Who Showed Me the Way Back

I would not have survived without them, Nea thought to herself. The women. The ones whose voices echoed in my soul when I had no words left. The ones who held my hands when they shook, steadying me when I had no ground to stand on. They were the ones who saw me—not as a fighter, not as a warrior, but as something raw, something fragile that still carried the fire of the earth inside it.

I had always been taught that strength was something you had to prove.

You had to fight for it. You had to claim it. But they showed me that true strength wasn't always about bearing the weight alone. Sometimes, strength was found in allowing yourself to be held. To be carried when you could no longer hold yourself.

The grief had hollowed me out. It came like a storm, devastating everything in its path. The love I had built—burned. The betrayal I had felt—stung deeper than I ever thought possible. And in that wreckage, I was lost.

Untethered. Adrift. I thought I had lost everything that mattered. I thought I had lost *me*.

But then, they found me.

The past: the matriarchs. The women who had walked this earth before me, their feet tracing ancient and alive paths. The medicine women.

The healers. The wise ones who had seen beyond what was visible and understood the land's language in ways I hadn't yet learned to speak.

They had always watched over me, even when I couldn't see them. The women who whispered prayers over my cradle, who planted seeds in my heart before I knew I needed them. They had known who I was before I had any understanding of it.

I remember the first time I heard my grandmother speak of the old ways before she passed away, of the wisdom that flowed through our blood like a river. She had told me, in the quiet way of women who know more than they let on, that the world could take everything from you.

Your home, your family, your pride. But there was one thing that no one could ever take from you, no matter how hard they tried. *Your spirit.*

At the time, I didn't understand. But I do now.

The women showed me the way back. They were the ones who held me close when I didn't know how to breathe. They listened when I could no longer find my voice, and they spoke the loudest truths in their silence.

They never asked me to be strong. They never told me to hold it together. They *were*. And in their presence, I remembered what it was like to feel whole.

There was Trina, who had been a stranger when I first arrived but whose laughter soon became a comfort. Trina had lived through loss in ways I couldn't even begin to fathom.

She had buried husbands, children, and dreams but carried herself with a quiet strength I envied. She never advised unless it was asked for, but her presence alone was a balm for the broken parts of me.

And there was Nita, a woman older than the sun, whose hands were weathered with years of prayer and ceremony. Nita had always been one to speak in riddles, but each riddle was a key to unlocking something in my heart.

"You must listen to the wind," she would say. "It knows the way to your heart. The earth whispers, too, but you're not listening." I hadn't understood then, but over time, her words began to make sense.

The present: *Now, I am one of them.*

I see them now in myself. Their wisdom is woven into my bones, passed down in ways I never anticipated. For the first time, I understand what it means to carry that responsibility. The path was never lost, but I was always waiting to remember it. And I had forgotten. I had forgotten that healing wasn't something you did alone. It was a community, a collective energy that was built and rebuilt over generations. My fight wasn't just mine—it was theirs, too.

I now hear the whispers of the land more clearly. I can feel the pulse of the earth beneath my feet, the rhythm of it flowing through me like blood in my veins. I know now that the land is not just a place to stand on but a part of us.

And those who came before us knew that the connection was sacred, that the way to survival lay not in domination, but in balance. The women who came before me, who built the fire in my heart when I couldn't light it myself, knew this. They had been carrying it all along.

I now remember the faces of the women who taught me to hold my ground in silence. How to resist without raising a fist. How to nurture without losing myself. These women—my grandmothers, my mothers, and my aunts—have always been my guides.

They were there before I was born, and they will be there when I'm gone, living on in every woman who carries the wisdom of the earth in her heart.

And the truth they showed me? It was simple. *Healing begins when you allow yourself to be whole.*

I was no longer lost. I had found the path again—not in the fight, but in the quiet moments, in the listening. The wisdom was always there, always within reach. The women who showed me the way back didn't do it through grand gestures or battles. They did it by simply being. By being there. By being whole.

Now, when I feel the world unraveling around me, when I feel myself losing my grip on the fire that once burned so brightly, I remember them. I recall the wisdom of my ancestors and the strength of the women who have walked this earth before me, and I know that I am never truly lost.

I am one of them now.

The path was never gone. It was always waiting for me to remember it.

CHAPTER 69

The Prophecy and the Path Forward

The wolf came to me in a dream.

Its fur was silver-tipped, thick with the wisdom of all that had come before. The moonlight that spilled across its coat seemed to shimmer with an energy older than time. But it wasn't just the glow that struck me but the weight in its eyes. Those eyes—full of stars and galaxies swirling in their depths—held something beautiful and terrifying. The past and the future intertwined in its gaze, as though it could see all the paths, all the choices, and moments yet to unfold.

It wasn't just a wolf. It was a messenger. A guide. An ancestor.

I wasn't surprised. I'd always known there was something more to the earth than the physical world, something I couldn't quite grasp but could always feel tugging at my heart. The wolf had come before, in whispers and shadows. Still, it stood before me, solid and real, its presence undeniable.

It told me what I already knew but had been too afraid to say.

"The world is changing," it said, its voice like the wind through the trees, deep and ancient. "The river will dry. The fire will rise. You have so little time to prepare."

I couldn't breathe. Those words—they were everything I had been feeling, everything I had been trying to understand. The earth had spoken for years, but I hadn't listened as I needed to. Now, I knew. The prophecy was no longer distant. It was imminent.

And when The Unsettling comes, I will have to choose—fight or disappear.

The weight of that choice was almost too much to bear. But it was a choice I had already been preparing for. I could no longer pretend I didn't feel the pull of something larger than myself. The land had warned me years ago, in subtle ways, in the rustle of the leaves, in the stillness of the night. The ancestors had whispered their caution in dreams, visions, and fleeting moments of clarity. But I hadn't been ready. Now, I was.

The past: It had started with a feeling, something that settled in my chest, a tightening of the heart, a sense that something was coming. I couldn't see a future, but I could feel how the air smelled before a storm. The river would dry. The earth would shake. The fire would rise. I saw it before I even had words for it. The first vision of The Unsettling—the earth shifting beneath me, the red snake in the core of earth, the spirits speaking in the wind—came to me in flashes, disjointed but so clear that I could never forget it. The land had always warned me. The ancestors had spoken, not in loud declarations but in quiet nudges, in sacred signs. Their voices weren't always audible, but they were always there. Always.

I had fought for so long and worked hard to preserve what I thought was worth saving. But now, with the wolf's words etched in my mind, I knew I had been wrong. The fight wasn't just about holding on. It was about *transformation, understanding what I was meant to protect and* what was worth fighting for.

The present: Now, I understand. The Unsettling is not just a prophecy. It is a call to action. It is a moment in time, a turning point. It is the battle I was always meant for, though I could never have prepared for it. It is not the battle of armies and fists, but the battle of the soul—of choice. What will I do when everything I know is threatened? What will I do when the land, the very earth beneath my feet, begins to break apart?

The path forward is unclear, but I have seen enough that I can no longer ignore what is coming. I am part of this. I always have been. My strength is not just in the anger but the fight alone. It's in the balance; I will bring it. It's in remembering who I am, who my ancestors are, and what they have taught me.

I hear the voices of the women who raised me, the ones who carried me through the dark times. They are the wisdom I need to face this. They are the ones who held my hands when I couldn't keep myself together. They are the strength I will call on when I'm asked to choose.

The wolf was right. The time is now.

This is not just my battle. It is all of ours. The river will dry, the fire will rise, but the land is not lost if we remember. The earth remembers, and she waits for us to rise with her. The Unsettling is coming, but it is not the end. It is the beginning of a new way forward.

And so, the story begins again.

The path is not easy. The battle will not be simple. But I know now that I am not alone. The ancestors are with me. The land is with me. And I will stand, not just for myself, but for all those who came before and all those who will come after.

This is the path forward. And I will walk it, one step at a time, with the wisdom of the past in my heart and the fire of the future in my soul.

CHAPTER 70

The Blood Oath

Mesopotamia – 3000 BCE

The air smelled of burning resin and crushed petals, thick with the heady perfume of sacrifice. The sacred ziggurat loomed high above the city, a stairway to the gods, its terraces gleaming under the desert moon. Below, the torches of Ur's royal court flickered, illuminating the expectant faces of priests, warriors, and noble families waiting for the ceremony to begin.

In the center of it all stood **Kishar**, High Shaman of Ur, adorned in robes of deep crimson embroidered with golden serpents that curled around his arms. He was young for his station—no older than thirty—but his presence was as commanding as the gods themselves. A circlet of bronze bound his long dark hair, his face hardened by years of devotion.

Before him, **Ninlil**, the newly ascended High Shamaness, struggled to steady her breath. She had once known Kishar as a gentle boy, the temple prodigy whose prayers were so pure that they made the priests weep. Now, his eyes were cold as the stone altars upon which countless lives had been offered.

"You hesitate," Kishar murmured, stepping closer to her. His fingers grazed the obsidian dagger in his belt, the ceremonial blade that had delivered hundreds of souls to the afterlife. "You cannot afford weakness, Ninlil. Not here."

Her stomach churned. She had not ascended through cowardice or blind faith. She had walked these temple halls since childhood, trained in the old ways —learning the songs of the stars, the healing herbs, and the movements of the great celestial bodies. But the blood rituals—the sacrifices demanded by Ur's rulers—had never been her calling.

"How many more?" she whispered, forcing herself to meet his gaze. "How many must die for the will of the gods?"

Kishar's lips curled into a wry smile. "The gods demand balance. Death is merely the passage to the next world."

"But you never used to believe that."

A flicker of something—pain, regret, memory—crossed his face. For a moment, he was the boy she had known, the boy who had stood beside her as they learned the sacred rites, the boy who had once sworn he would never let the temple turn him to stone.

Then, as swiftly as it came, the softness vanished.

"The gods have no patience for sentiment," Kishar said, turning from her. "Come. The sacrifice is waiting."

A hush fell over the gathered court as the acolytes led the prisoners forward—four men and two women, their hands bound, their faces resigned to their fates. They were slaves from a conquered city, warriors who had dared resist Ur's rule. Tonight, they would be given to the gods, their deaths sealing the power of Ur's new king.

Ninlil's hands clenched at her sides. She had known the moment would come, when she would be expected to stand beside Kishar and take her place in the temple's legacy of blood.

And she could not.

She reached for his wrist. "Kishar, this is not our way."

His hand tightened over hers. There was a warning in his grip, but also something deeper—something raw and unspoken. "Do not challenge me here," he said, voice low. "Not in front of them."

She had tried to reach him for a year, to remind him of the light he had once carried. But the darkness in him had taken root too deep, its grip too strong. And she knew why.

She had seen it once, in the high temple chamber where only the chosen shamans could enter. She had felt its presence in the shadows of the altar, a coiling, whispering force that wound around Kishar like a lover's embrace. **It was not the gods he answered to anymore.**

"Leave with me," she pleaded. "There are lands beyond Ur, beyond these walls. We could run."

For a moment, something in him cracked. She saw the flicker of the boy he used to be—the one who had dreamed of the stars and spoken to the spirits of the wind instead of the entities of blood and power.

But then, the darkness surged back.

He stepped away from her grasp, returning to his place at the altar. "Go if you must, Ninlil. But you know there is no escaping the will of the gods."

No. Not the gods.

She backed away. The realization struck her like a dagger to the chest. He had made his choice. He had been making it, repeatedly, with every sacrifice, every whispered promise to the thing that clung to him like a shadow.

There was no saving him.

As Kishar raised the dagger, the first prisoner was forced to their knees. Ninlil turned and ran.

Up the temple steps, past the guards who called after her, higher and higher toward the terrace that overlooked the city.

The wind roared around her. The stars burned bright above.

And as Kishar called her name, as his voice broke with something close to fear, she took her final step into the void.

For the first time in years, she was free.

The Fall of the Shaman

The temple corridors were silent, except for torches' flickering against the smooth, ancient stones. Ninlil walked carefully, the hem of her robe brushing against the cool marble floor. She knew every path, every turn, every hidden passage. This was their place—hers and Kishar. A sanctuary where duty and sacrifice faded, and only their whispered confessions and entwined bodies existed.

She had come early, anticipation thrumming in her chest like the low hum of the temple drums. The scent of burning Blue Lotus still lingered in the air, mingling with the sweet resin of myrrh. He was near. She could feel his presence in her bones.

But she froze as she rounded the final corner, the sacred antechamber in sight.

Kishar was not alone.

A figure loomed before him, taller than any man, draped in a living cloak of darkness that pulsed and writhed like a mass of moving legs. The air thickened, heavy with an unseen force that made Ninlil's stomach churn. The creature's voice slithered through the chamber, a sound that was not a voice but a whisper that crawled inside the mind, wrapping its cold fingers around the soul.

"You are strong, Kishar. Stronger than the others. Why fight what is meant to be?"

Kishar stood stiffly, his hands clenched at his sides. His body trembled, sweat beading along his brow, yet his expression remained rigid—caught between horror and temptation.

"I serve the gods," he said hoarsely, his voice barely above a whisper.

The entity chittered, its unseen legs shifting, its voice soft and coaxing. *"The gods have abandoned you, as they have abandoned all who suffer under the weight of sacrifice. But I can give you more than the gods ever could."*

Ninlil pressed herself into the shadows, fingers gripping the rough stone wall. She had seen dark spirits before, cast them out with fire and chant, and felt their hunger and rage. But this... this was something more ancient, more insidious.

"Power. Wealth. Devotion. The Queen herself. You will have it all, Kishar. And all it requires is one small thing."

Kishar's breathing was uneven, his eyes darting toward the temple's high altar.

"You must share in the bond of power with me. A single vow. An eternal promise."

Ninlil's heart pounded. *No. No, he won't.*

But as she watched, Kishar's resolve wavered. He took a step forward.

"Why do you tempt me?" he whispered. "I have everything I need."

The entity did not laugh, did not sneer. It only... waited.

Ninlil took a shaking breath, the sharp sting of betrayal bleeding into her ribs.

"You are still resisting. But you will return to me, little Shaman. And when you do, I will grant you everything you crave."

Then, the entity dissolved into the air, leaving nothing behind but the scent of rotting honey and a whisper that echoed deep within Ninlil's soul.

Kishar turned, his body still trembling. And for the briefest moment, his eyes lifted—catching the shape of Ninlil in the shadows.

Her heart splintered as she saw it.

Not just fear.

But longing.

Regret.

And something darker.

The beginning of the end.

The First Temptation

Ninlil pressed herself against the cold stone wall, breath shallow, heart hammering against her ribs. She shouldn't be here. She should turn and run, pretend she never saw, never heard. But her body refused to move, her spirit tethered to the moment like a moth drawn too close to the flame.

Kishar stood motionless, his fists clenched at his sides, staring at the space where the entity had been. The torches lining the chamber flickered violently as if they, too, had sensed the abyss in the air.

His head turned slightly, and in the dim light, his golden skin glowed with a sheen of sweat. For the briefest moment, their eyes met.

Ninlil knew that gaze—had memorized every flicker of his expression, every shadow of emotion that danced behind his dark, storm-heavy eyes. But this? This was something she had never seen before.

Fear.

Longing.

And beneath it all—something creeping, slithering, coiling around his soul like an unseen chain.

Ninlil stepped forward. She could not help it. "Kishar," she whispered.

His eyes darkened, his jaw tightening at the sound of her voice. "You shouldn't be here."

Neither should you. The words burned on her tongue, but she swallowed them.

Instead, she reached out, her fingers grazing his forearm, where the sacred tattoos of his lineage had been inked since his initiation. "What did it promise you?"

He turned away from her touch, rubbing a hand down his face as if trying to scrub away the ghostly whisper of the entity. "Nothing that matters."

"Don't lie to me."

Kishar let out a slow breath, closing his eyes. "It doesn't matter, Ninlil. It's gone."

Ninlil exhaled sharply. "Is it?"

He stiffened.

Because they both knew the truth, the entity had left no footprints, no lingering shadow in the torchlight. But it had not left him.

Ninlil's fingers curled into her palms. She had spent years studying under the Elder Shamans, learning the balance between light and darkness, walking the razor-thin edge of power and sacrifice. She had seen spirits attach themselves to the weak and whisper into the ears of those desperate for more.

But Kishar had never been weak.

He had always been the strongest of them.

Hadn't he?

"I heard what it said," she pressed, stepping closer. "Power. Wealth. Devotion. Even the Queen."

Kishar let out a bitter laugh, shaking his head. "You always did listen too closely."

"What did it mean, Kishar?"

He hesitated. And in that hesitation, Nea saw everything.

His slow unraveling.

The tiny cracks in his resolve.

The war is being waged behind his eyes.

"I won't take the bond," he said finally.

Ninlil wanted to believe him.

She wanted to believe him so badly that it hurt.

But something in the way his voice shook told her that this wasn't the last time he would hear the entity's voice. That the battle wasn't over. That maybe—just maybe—it had only just begun.

That night, Ninlil couldn't sleep.

She lay on the floor of the Shaman quarters, staring at the curved ceiling, tracing the constellations painted by the hands of ancestors long gone. The sacred symbols, the stories of gods and spirits and the eternal cycle of life and death.

She thought of Kishar's face.

Of the way his hands had once held her—gentle, reverent, worshipping.

She thought of the nights they had spent tangled together in secret, whispering dreams into each other's skin, swearing oaths that only the stars could hear.

He had been hers.

And she had been his.

But now...

Now, something else had its claws in him.

Something older than love.

Something older than devotion.

And for the first time since she had met him, Ninlil was afraid.

Months passed.

Ninlil watched Kishar from afar, unable to ignore the shift in him.

At first, it was small things. The way he withdrew from their circle, spending long hours alone in the temple's inner sanctum. The way his once-bright eyes darkened, always carrying shadows beneath them.

Then, the changes became impossible to ignore.

He was sharper. Colder. He was more ruthless in his teachings. He led the ceremonies and stood at the front of every procession. But the warmth in his voice was gone, replaced by something harder, something more... detached.

And then, one night, Ninlil saw him again.

Not in the temple halls.

Not in the secret chambers where they once held each other.

But in the Grand Hall of Offerings—standing at the altar, his hands stained with blood.

A sacrifice had been made.

One greater than any before.

And Kishar had been the one to lead it.

Ninlil's breath hitched.

The entity had returned.

And this time, Kishar had not sent it away.

This time, he had welcomed it.

The Pact with Xtotl

The chamber reeked of incense, sweat, and blood. The scent clung to the air like a thick, unholy perfume, curling through the vast stone temple like the breath of a god forgotten by time.

The room pulsed with bodies, slick with wine and oil, writhing against one another on silken cushions and animal pelts. Moans of pleasure and pain blended into the rhythmic beat of the ceremonial drums, the pounding echoing through the high vaulted ceilings.

Kishar stood at the center, bathed in the crimson light of the torches, his chest bare, streaked with the blood of the evening's sacrifice.

He was a god among mortals.

Or so they whispered.

He had led the greatest offering yet—the spilling of a hundred throats and releasing a hundred souls into the black void beyond the veil. Their life force still shimmered in the air, rising like a mist, feeding the unseen, nourishing the one who waited.

The one who had promised him everything.

Kishar staggered slightly; his fingers still curled around the obsidian blade. His pupils were blown wide, black, swallowing the usual storm-gray depths. The Blue Lotus, mixed with honeyed wine, burned in his veins, sending him into a heady, euphoric haze. The world vibrated around him—too loud, too bright, too much.

And yet, not enough.

Never enough.

A hand—delicate, painted, trembling—reached for his wrist. A priestess, one of many, her lips swollen from kisses, her thighs bruised from worship. She pressed herself against him, her breath hot against his throat.

"You are divine," she whispered, drunk on him.

Kishar tilted his head back, exhaling a slow, dark laugh.

No.

Not yet.

Not entirely.

But he would be.

The others in the chamber watched as he moved toward the altar, their gazes rapt, waiting. The air shifted, heavy with anticipation as if the very stones of the temple knew what was about to happen.

He lifted the blade.

And with deliberate slowness, he pressed the tip to his palm.

The room went silent.

The priestesses and acolytes, the warriors and council members—they all stilled, breath held, as the first drop of blood welled at the edge of the blade.

Kishar grinned.

And then—he **sliced.**

A deep, deliberate gash, straight across his palm.

Blood pooled instantly, thick and dark, dripping onto the altar.

And from the shadows—**it** came.

Xtotl.

The ancient one. The Devourer. The Web Weaver.

The shadows in the chamber shifted, curling like living tendrils, coalescing into something massive, something **hungry.**

Eight gleaming black limbs unfurled from the darkness, delicate and terrible all at once. Its body shimmered like polished obsidian, the ridges of its carapace slick with the souls it had consumed.

Kishar felt his breath catch, his mind buzzing with terror and exhilaration.

This was it.

This was the moment.

Xtotl loomed over him, mandibles clicking, its many eyes reflecting the flickering torchlight. A voice, ancient and silk-smooth, slithered into his mind.

"You are ready."

Kishar smiled, swaying slightly, blood still dripping from his palm.

"I was always ready."

"Then give yourself to me."

The room trembled. The torches flared.

The acolytes gasped, some falling to their knees in fear, in worship. The priestesses clung to one another, eyes wide, their bodies trembling with something between terror and ecstasy.

Kishar Stepped forward, lifting his bleeding hand toward the beast.

Xtotl moved swiftly—**too** swiftly. A limb lashed out, wrapping around Kishar's wrist, pulling his hand closer, pressing the wound against its shimmering black skin.

A burning pain seared through him.

Kishar gasped, arching, his entire body convulsing as fire raced through his veins, through his bones, through his very **soul**.

Xtotl **was inside him.**

Crawling through his mind, through the marrow of his being, sinking its fangs into the deepest parts of him.

Feeding. Binding. Claiming.

He heard himself laugh—a ragged, exultant sound—as the pleasure of it overtook the pain.

He felt **power**.

Pure, undiluted **power.**

And he wanted more.

Kishar tipped his head back, eyes rolling white as the entity coiled tighter around his soul, sealing the eternal bond.

The others in the chamber watched, trembling, weeping, and moaning in worship as they felt the shift in the air.

Their High Shaman was no longer simply a man.

He was something **more.**

Something **unholy.**

And in the dim red light, drenched in blood and divinity, Kishar turned toward them, lips curling into a slow, wicked smile.

"Worship me."

And they did.

The Queen's Seduction and the King's Fall

The halls of the temple were thick with the scent of burning resins, sandalwood, and the metallic tang of fresh blood. The torches flickered in a rhythmic dance as if mirroring the drumbeats of the city below. Xtotl coiled around the chamber, its many legs dragging shadows across the walls, whispering in Kishar's ear.

"The Queen is waiting."

Kishar laughed, his mouth still stained with wine, his eyes gleaming with the fire of his latest conquest. He had ascended beyond the constraints of mere men. He was power. He was divinity incarnate. The priests bowed when he passed. The warriors kissed his hands. And the people, they sang his name in reverence and terror alike.

And now, the Queen herself had come to his chambers.

She lay on his silken cushions, adorned in sheer linen embroidered with lapis and gold. Her dark eyes, lined with kohl, held a challenge—a dare. She was unlike the other women who now lived to serve his pleasure, trembling in awe and obedience. No, she was different. Regal, cunning.

"If you take her," Xtotl whispered, *"you will have the kingdom. And the king will not live to see the sunrise."*

Kishar laughed out loud, low and deep, his voice carrying the weight of the pact he had made. He had never denied himself anything—why start now?

He moved toward her, the Queen rising on her elbows, watching him as he untied the belt of his robe, revealing the sigils Xtotl had burned into his chest. She reached out, fingers grazing the ancient markings, and shivered.

"You are no longer just a man," she murmured.

"No," he agreed, kneeling over her, his lips brushing against her ear. *"And before the sun rises, I will be more."*

The night was a haze of passion, claiming, surrender, and conquest interwoven until the lines blurred between devotion and destruction.

And when the Queen lay spent, tangled in the sheets of his chamber, Kishar rose, pulling his robe back over his shoulders.

The King's goblet sat waiting on the gilded tray beside the wine cask. He reached for the vial Xtotl had given him, its contents thick and black as night, and poured it into the wine.

The King would never see another sunrise.

And by dawn, Kishar would be the one ruling the empire.

Meanwhile, Ninlil stood outside his chamber, watching the temple below. She had seen enough. She had begged the gods for signs. But they had gone silent.

The sacrifices, the blood, and the greed had drowned out the voices of the spirits.

Kishar was lost.

With one last breath, she stepped to the edge of the high temple tower. And without hesitation, she let go.

As she fell, she felt a sense of peace for the first time in years.

CHAPTER 71

The Karmic Unraveling

Nea sat in the candlelit room, the scent of copal thick in the air, the pulse of the drum grounding her as the medicine took hold. The The Peyote twisted through her veins, uncoiling like a serpent, winding its way up her spine. She had prepared for this moment, yet she still felt a sense of fear. The medicine knew where to go. She knew what she had to see.

Hé Sá had been cold, distant—his once tender words now edged with bitterness. The warmth in his eyes had long since vanished, replaced by something hollow. The ache of his rejection had cut her deeper than she wanted to admit. But it wasn't just heartbreak. No. Something *else* had its claws in him. She felt it every time he spoke, every time he turned away, every time he vanished into his cycles of self-destruction.

And now, as the visions unfurled, she was being taken back.

Mesopotamia - 5,000 Years Ago

The temple walls pulsed with torchlight, their golden glow flickering against the intricate carvings of gods who had long stopped listening.

Nea's heart pounded as she walked the winding corridors, her silk robes whispering against the cool stone. She had been coming to these sacred chambers for years, waiting for *him*, meeting in secret—stolen touches, whispered prayers, the promise of a future together.

Hé Sá had been a healer, a protector. A man of power, yes, but also of great tenderness. She had seen him fight against the darkness, resisting the weight of the sacrifices, resisting the council's demands.

But now, something was *wrong*.

She had arrived early, hoping to surprise him, but she froze as she stepped into the inner sanctum.

A shadow loomed against the wall, a massive, hulking figure draped in darkness. Its long, spindly legs curved unnaturally, its many black eyes gleaming like polished obsidian. A spider. Not just any spider—*Xtotl*.

Nea pressed her hand against her chest, forcing herself to breathe.

No...

Hé Sá stood before it, his hands clenched into fists, his body trembling. She had never seen him afraid before—not like this.

The entity's voice slithered into the room, a seductive hiss laced with power.

"You are strong, but you could be more. You are respected, but you could be worshipped. You could rule them all."

Hé Sá shook his head, his jaw tight. "I don't need your power."

Xtotl laughed. *"Don't you? Have you not struggled? Have you not bled? Do you not deserve more?"*

The words were laced with something *heavy*, something *tangible*, wrapping around him like a silk cocoon.

"You could have it all. More power. More wealth. The Queen herself. Any woman. Any man. Anyone. They will all bow before you."

Nea saw it. The moment it began. The moment Hé Sá hesitated. The seed was planted.

He turned away, running a hand over his face, exhaling sharply. "I will never bow to you."

Xtotl did not rage, did not strike him down. Instead, it merely *laughed*. *"We shall see."*

And, standing unseen in the shadows, Nea knew in her heart that she was losing him.

Ten Years Later

The air was thick with incense and the scent of blood. The torches burned lower now, their light casting elongated shadows over the temple walls.

Hé Sá sat on the grand dais, his tunic disheveled, his fingers still stained crimson. His lips curled as he tossed back another gulp of wine, his laughter ringing through the chamber.

Nea stood at the entrance, breathless, frozen in place.

The floor was littered with silken bodies, beautiful acolytes draped in gold and red, some barely awake from their opium and blue lotus haze. Their skin was still streaked with remnants of the evening's sacrifices, red smudges marking their thighs, hands, and lips.

And Hé Sá—her beloved Hé Sá—sat in the center of it all, half-naked, his chest glistening with sweat, his head thrown back as he took another long drink.

Xtotl loomed behind him, its great legs curled around the pillars of the chamber, watching and always *watching*.

Nea swallowed back the bile rising in her throat.

"What have you done?" she whispered.

Hé Sá turned, his eyes heavy with intoxication, but something else lurked beneath the haze. Power. Darkness.

He smirked. "What needed to be done."

She took a step forward, her voice trembling. "You swore to me. You swore you would never take its mark."

He lifted his hand, the fresh cut still bleeding into the goblet he held. Xtotl curled closer, its many eyes gleaming with satisfaction.

"I have embraced my destiny." The final words sealed her fate.

The Hé Sá she had loved was gone.

CHAPTER 72

Blood & Bone

The Karmic Meeting

Kishar was once a powerful Mesopotamian Shaman, a man who held the favor of the gods and the fear of mortals. He had spent the last fifteen years leading sacrifices, standing at the head of a temple where blood was currency and power was measured in devotion and death.

Ninlil, a Shamaness in her own right, had walked the temple halls with a different kind of power—a softer one that did not require submission to darkness. She had once been a pupil under Kishar guidance, their bond one of laughter, stolen glances, and whispered secrets beneath the moon.

But that was before. Before the blood. Before the darkness seeped into Kishar soul, ink was poured into the water. Before he stopped fighting against it.

Ninlil had seen the change. The hunger in his eyes. He spoke of the gods now, not with reverence, but with possession. He believed they were his to control and command.

When the High Priestess died, she was chosen to take her place as the Head Shamaness. It was meant to be an honor. Instead, it was a chain.

She stood before Kishar, the torches flickering shadows across his sharp face. He was everything she had once loved—tall, beautiful, his golden skin now darkened with the stains of sacrifice. But his eyes were not the same.

"You must join me," he said. "It is our duty."

Ninlil shook her head. "This is not the way."

He stepped closer, towering over her. "It is the only way."

She saw it then—the thing clinging to his back. A massive, shadowy spider, its long legs curled possessively around his shoulders, its fangs whispering against his ear.

She whispered, voice breaking. "You have let it in."

He did not deny it. He only smiled, the cold, detached smile of a man who had lost himself long ago. "Power requires sacrifice, my love. If you do not see it now, you will."

Ninlil heart shattered. For a brief moment, she thought she could still save him. She reached for him, pleading. "Come with me. Leave this place. Leave it all."

For a moment, he hesitated. And for that single moment, she thought she had won.

But then the spider's legs tightened, and Kishar eyes darkened. "No," he said. "I am already chosen."

Ninlil breath hitched. She turned and ran, her bare feet slapping against the temple stones. She did not stop until she reached the edge of the high temple's walls.

Kishar was behind her now, calling her name in a frantic voice. "Don't!"

She turned one last time, looking at the man she had once loved, now nothing but a vessel for something dark and eternal.

"I would rather die free," she whispered, and then she jumped.

The Seduction of Power

Ten years before Ninlil death, she and Kishar were inseparable. Their love was something whispered about in the temple halls, a sacred devotion hidden behind moonlit meetings and soft touches in the dark.

They had spent years studying under the Elders, preparing to take their place as the future of the temple. Kishar had always been brilliant, a gifted healer and seer with a natural ability to command a room. But he was also vulnerable.

Ninlil saw it in the way he longed for more—more knowledge, more influence, more power.

One evening, she went to their meeting place early, hoping to surprise him. Instead, she found him speaking with something that should not exist.

A massive, spider-like entity, its form shifting between shadow and substance, loomed over Kishar, its voice a sickly sweet whisper.

"You could have everything," the entity purred. "Power, wealth, women, the Queen herself. You could lead armies, and shape the future. All you must do is accept me."

Ninlil breath caught in her throat. She wanted to scream, to run to him and shake him free from whatever spell this creature was weaving. But she couldn't move. She could only watch.

Kishar hands clenched into fists. "I don't need you," he spat.

The entity only chuckled. "Not now. But soon."

For ten years, Kishar resisted. But the seed had been planted.

Slowly, the entity worked its way into his mind. It came in dreams, in moments of weakness. It whispered to him when he was drunk on Blue Lotus, when he was weary from battle, and when the weight of the temple pressed too heavily on his shoulders.

And then, one night, he broke.

The temple was alive with celebration. A great sacrifice had been made—fifty slaves sent to the gods in one grand display. Kishar stood at the center, drenched in blood, his mind clouded with wine and pleasure.

Acolytes surrounded him, their bodies writhing in ecstasy, feeding off the energy of the sacrifice. Beautiful men and women alike pressed against him, their hands roaming, their mouths tasting.

He laughed, drunk on power, indulgence, and the high of it all.

And then, the entity was there.

"Say the words," it whispered.

Kishar, lost in the haze of lust and blood, did not hesitate.

He slashed his palm open with a ceremonial dagger and pressed his hand to the altar. The entity coiled around him, sinking into his very being.

"I accept," he murmured.

Darkness flooded into him, filling every hollow space in his soul.

From that moment on, he was never the same.

Present Day - The Lodge

Nea gasped, her eyes snapping open, her breath ragged. The candle beside her had burned low, the wax dripping onto the dirt floor. The spirits in the lodge were silent now, watching.

She pressed a trembling hand to her chest, still feeling the weight of the vision, the memory, the grief.

She had always known.

But now, she *understood*.

Xtotl *still* fed on Hé Sá. It *still* whispered in his ear, lacing its promises with cocaine and whiskey, wrapping itself around his vanity, fueling his hunger for power, admiration, and control.

And now, it was *her turn* to face it.

She closed her eyes, reaching out with her spirit, calling it forth.

"Xtotl, I see you. I know you."

The air shifted. A long and slow hiss curled around the firelight's edges.

"You are not welcome here," Nea whispered.

A shadow moved at the edge of her vision, slick and dark, impossibly large.

"What will you give me to leave?" it hissed.

Nea inhaled deeply, exhaling through her nose, steadying herself.

"I have only love, light, and peace to give you."

The entity recoiled, its many eyes narrowing. It hissed again, this time in anger. *"No. He is mine. He has always been mine."*

Nea's heart clenched.

She could feel it. The weight of the bond. The lifetimes upon lifetimes. The choices.

"Let him go."

Xtotl only laughed.

CHAPTER 73

The Final Battle – Nea vs. Xtotl

The candlelight flickered against the lodge walls, shadows stretching and twisting like specters whispering in the smoke. Nea sat cross-legged before the sacred fire, her hands resting on her knees, fingers trembling as the Peyote pulled her under.

The drumbeat slowed.

Her breath steadied.

She had come to *an end*.

For lifetimes, Xtotl had coiled around Hé Sá like a black widow, whispering in his ear, feeding his ego, hunger, and self-destruction. And now, as Nea drifted beyond the veil, she could feel the entity waiting.

It felt smug.

As if it had already won.

"Show yourself."

A ripple through the dark.

Then—**the hiss**.

Nea opened her eyes within the spirit realm. The air here was thick, vibrating with an ancient hum, the unseen forces that ruled existence pressing in around her. Before her, Xtotl unfurled from the void, its great black legs clicking against the stone beneath them.

Eight obsidian eyes gleamed. Its slick, oily form pulsed, shifting between shadows and solid matter.

"You return, little one."

Its voice slithered over her skin, making her stomach churn.

"I told you—he is mine" said Xtotl.

Nea stood, her breath steady. "And I told you, *you are not welcome here.*"

Xtotl reared back, chittering, its fangs glistening with venom. *"Do you truly think you can fight me? You? The girl who has spent lifetimes failing to save him?"*

Nea clenched her fists, but before she could move, **light burst behind her**.

A sudden warmth, a golden force surging up through her chest, flooding the void.

They were here.

Buddha Goddess Creator stood behind her, an infinite being of light, neither male nor female, everything and nothing, radiating pure, unconditional love.

To Nea's left, the **Great Wolves** – her first guides- the white one lowered its head, silver eyes locked onto the entity, its breath slow, deep, *ready*.

To her right, **Fox**, quick, sharp, mischievous, flicked its tail, its energy vibrating with ancient wisdom.

Shiva appeared in a storm of blue light, his trident sparking with celestial fire, eyes filled with knowing.

And beside her, a force unlike any other—**Archangel Michael**, his golden blue armor gleaming, his sword alight, the embodiment of divine justice.

Nea exhaled.

"This ends now."

The light surged forward, **a tidal wave of power** crashing into Xtotl.

The entity shrieked, writhing as its form shifted violently, and it retreated, collapsing in on itself, consumed by the divine light that burned through its darkness.

Nea raised her hands, channeling the energy, **pushing, cleansing, and banishing**.

But then—**it stopped.**

The darkness did not disappear.

Instead, it *held*, thick and immovable, **rooted** in something deeper.

And then Nea saw it.

A thread of black *still connected Xtotl to Hé Sá.*

Hé Sá would not let go.

Xtotl **laughed**.

"He does not want to be free."

Nea's heart clenched.

"He loves the power I give him. The control. The strength. The beauty. The vanity. The chaos. The desire."

A Message from Angel Michael

Angel Michael looked at Nea lovingly. "My child, the beauty of humanity is the Creator gave to each of you free will. Xtotl made choices to be who she is, and Hé Sá made a choice thousands of years ago that only he can realize and undo. There may come a time when he is ready to sever ties with Xtotl, but it is not today.

In Xtotl's way she loves Hé Sá and believes she is helping him. One day, she too may evolve into, or closer to, the light and see the corruption and manipulation. Xtotl has been part of your and Hé Sá's karmic stories for thousands of years.

Xtotl is from an ancient race, ancient by Earth standards but young in the vastness of Creation. These beings first evolved on Earth millions of years ago. There are few left, but the ones that remain of this ancient clan Ascended out of the earthly plane.

To exist in the in-between, they feed off human emotions and fears. Most of Xtotl's brethren have evolved and Ascended to higher realms.

A few remain here as powerful dark entities often associated with the dark arts and shadow realm. These spirits, or what you call entities on Earth and of the shadow realm, also have free will to walk in the light or shadow. It is the right of all beings across time and space.

All of Earth is changing and evolving; you have received many light codes, many gifts, and many blessings to undo your karmic tie to the dark arts thousands of years ago; now as you move higher through ascension, as is the gift given to all spirits you will also evolve to cut these last ties to Xtotl. Still, I remind you it is dangerous, but your Spirit Team is here standing beside you.

You are one of the millions of Starseeds and Messengers to bring this knowledge to all of humanity. The shift is upon us to continue the Ascension; you agreed to these lessons on this path thousands of years ago when you first determined to come to Earth School. I must leave you now, but I am always near. All you need do is think of me or call my name.

I am the right hand of who you call Buddha Goddess Creator, and we have much work preparing and guiding all of humanity who use their free will to Ascend."

With that, he was gone, a flash of gold and deep, cobalt blue, the colors of his wings and gilded robes. His being was like many Ascended beings in the spirit realm, slightly fuzzy to the human capacity of sight made of beautiful fractals of light.

He maintained a masculine dimension, although all light beings were neither male nor female and could shift their presentation as desired.

Archangel Michael had a human-like appearance, though his fractal form was marked by olive skin and long, flowing golden blonde hair as if kissed by the sun. He was the only angel I had ever seen, but like many other light beings, he was large by Earth's standards, presenting at 8 or 9 feet.

He shimmered in every color of the rainbow, but deep, royal cobalt blue and gold with slight purple hues glistened. He wore body armor, but it was made of cobalt blue fractals inscribed with what appeared to be angelic sigils.

He did not speak in words; he had sent these messages telepathically with a type of vision, and they were sent straight to my brain. Some of the thought forms and concepts I struggled to understand are those related to karmic ties, as I do not fully comprehend the details of exactly how these ties are created or maintained.

I felt there were thousands more thoughts in what he shared that my feeble human brain could not process, but I felt this knowledge in my body as if the thoughts were known to me in another space and time. I felt that over the years, as my Ascension continued, more of the message would unlock as my Spirit could translate to my human form.

It was overwhelming, and although the messages were intended for my Spiritual self, the light code downloads of information taxed the human body and mind. I could feel great fatigue and a searing headache in my body as I began to wake; my body purged repeatedly.

No one said spiritual enlightenment and the gift of light codes were easy.

The Binding of Hé Sá

Nea's heart clenched, her breath catching in her throat.

"He loves the power I give him. The control. The strength. The beauty. The vanity. The chaos. The desire."

Xtotl's voice slithered through the air, thick as smoke, curling around her like a noose tightening, whispering the truth she had always feared. The truth she had always known.

Images flickered before her, sharp and unrelenting, each one a dagger thrust deep into the marrow of her soul.

Hé Sá standing before a mirror, his reflection a shrine to his hunger. His veins pulsed beneath his skin, swollen with the poison of steroids, his jaw sharp with the sharp, feverish edge of a man who could never be satiated.

His body trembled, not from exertion or need, but from something darker, something consuming—**a bottomless craving that would never be filled.**

Hé Sá in a dimly lit bar, the air thick with smoke and sweat, the sickly glow of neon casting shadows across his face. Before him, the glassy shimmer of cocaine lined in perfect rows, an altar to his ruin.

A woman draped over his arm, her lips at his ear, her fingers tracing patterns over his skin, but his mind was always elsewhere. His gaze was vacant; his body was present but detached, his soul drifting, searching, lost.

Hé Sá cheating, the same story told in different rooms, different beds, different hands pulling at his clothes, different mouths gasping his name. Lust without substance. Pleasure without meaning. Always searching. Always empty. Constantly feeding the void.

His wife was in their bedroom, rage curling at the edges of her grief. A woman betrayed too many times, hurt too deeply to cry quietly anymore. She threw things at him—shoes, vases, a picture frame that shattered against the wall. Her screams filled the space between them, but Hé Sá stood still, watching her, unfeeling, his heart a hollow thing.

Nea's name appeared on his phone, its glow illuminating the darkness, the unanswered call stretching the silence. His thumb hovered over the screen, hesitation flickering like a dying ember before he swiped it away, ignoring her. Ignoring the one tether, he still had to something real.

Then, the final vision—Hé Sá alone.

His body was thinner, his skin grey, and he had a bottle in his trembling hand. His once-powerful frame is now gaunt, his face pale, and his eyes sunken deep into his skull. He sat in the dim light of an unfamiliar room, the television flashing images he no longer cared to see, the hum of the world moving on without him.

Inside him, cancer grew.

The hunger that had driven him for so long now turned inward, devouring him from within.

CHAPTER 74

Climax: The Curse of Xtotl

Nea staggered backward, her breath ragged, her vision swimming with the aftershock of what she had seen. The images had been too vivid, sharp, and real—like claws raking through her mind, tearing open wounds that had never fully healed. Her light wavered, flickering against the encroaching darkness, a lone candle against a storm.

And then it moved.

Xtotl.

It stepped forward, its form shifting, stretching, expanding—a black mist thick with hunger, malice, and something beyond human comprehension. Its voice was a purr, sickly sweet, and full of triumph.

"He is mine."

The words slithered around her, wrapping tight like a noose.

"And you? You will never let him go. You will always feel him, and you will always think of him. Because I will make sure of it."

The shadows surged, pressing against her, wrapping around her like hands, dozens of them cold and slick and writhing.

Nea choked on a scream. This was not love. This was not an obsession.

This was a binding.

A curse written in blood.

The Feeding

The black thread between them pulsed.

A grotesque, living thing.

And then—Xtotl fed.

Nea gasped as it yanked at her soul, the pain sudden and unbearable, a white-hot lance of agony driving straight into her chest. Her body convulsed, her vision darkening at the edges as if her very essence was being away.

It wasn't just taking from Hé Sá.

It was taking from her.

Memories crashed over her, one after another, overwhelming and drowning her. His arms around her. His lips were at her ear, whispering her name. The way he had once loved her. The way she still loved him.

The way she could never forget.

Xtotl fed.

And she felt it.

It drank her love, swallowed it whole, twisted it into something unrecognizable. What had once been warmth, connection, devotion—became hunger. Became chains.

Her heart seized.

She fell to her knees, gasping, shaking, the weight of Hé Sá's energy suffocating her.

She had spent lifetimes bound to him, tied by something more profound than flesh, deeper than reason. And now, that love had become her prison.

The Haunting

For a year and a half after that night, Xtotl haunted her.

In every quiet moment, it whispered.

"He still loves you."

"He still thinks of you."

"You are the only one who truly understands him."

Its voice curled around her thoughts, slithered into her dreams, and seeped into the spaces between her ribs.

It twisted the love she had carried for lifetimes into a never-ending ache.

Even as Hé Sá faded—drenched in alcohol, lost in meaningless lust, growing weaker, dying—Xtotl still fed on Nea.

It did not care that Hé Sá was empty.

It did not care that his body was rotting, that his once-golden skin was turning sallow, that his breath reeked of decay.

It only cared that Nea still loved him.

And as long as she did—as long as her heart ached, as long as she still dreamed of him, as long as she could not let go—Xtotl would never go hungry.

But then—**The Blood Moon came.**

And the curse trembled.

For the first time since the binding, Nea felt something shift.

The question was:

Would she finally break free?

Or was it already too late?

Interlude: The Feeding

Somewhere in the depths of the city, in a room heavy with the scent of stale liquor and regret, Hé Sá slumped forward, his body a broken thing draped over the edge of a bed that wasn't his. His skin, once golden, was sallow under the dim glow of a streetlamp outside. His breath was shallow and uneven, a whisper of life barely clinging to flesh.

And then—it came.

A ripple in the air. A tear in the unseen. The temperature dropped, and the shadows thickened, pulsing with something not of this world.

Then Xtotl emerged.

It moved like oil spilling into the room, slick and impenetrable, formless yet vast, its presence pressing against the walls like an entity too large for this reality to comprehend. And then—it solidified.

Fangs. Long and glistening.

Talons black as obsidian, curling, twitching.

It bent over Hé Sá, its breath a soundless whisper, a death rattle before the body had even gone cold.

Then—it sank its teeth into him.

Hé Sá barely reacted. His body jerked once, the faintest shudder, a distant flicker of awareness before he melted back into the void of his stupor. The feeding had become routine. His will had long been broken.

Xtotl's jaws locked, its dark body convulsing, drinking, devouring. The veins in Hé Sá's arms, in his neck, bulged—black lines crawling beneath his skin like worms. His body withered in increments, his muscles thinning, his skin drawn too tight over his bones. He sighed—not in pain or protest, but in surrender.

It would take what it needed.

It always did.

But this was only the first course.

The real feast lay miles away.

Nea stirred in her sleep, trapped in a dream she had dreamed a thousand times—the forest at night. The river was black as ink. The feeling of being watched, hunted.

Then—the air thickened.

A shift. A presence.

Not a dream.

Something here.

Something wrong.

Her breath hitched. She tried to move, but her body was no longer her own. A crushing weight settled over her chest, a force pressing her into the mattress, invisible but heavy, like unseen hands pinning her down.

And then—it was there.

Xtotl.

Creeping into her room, its form shifting, flickering between smoke and shadow, beast and void.

Its eyes gleamed, liquid and depthless, its mouth curling into something too wide, too knowing. It moved slowly, savoring the moment, dragging out the horror like a lover prolonging the inevitable.

Then it lunged.

Nea felt the puncture, the deep, vicious sinking of fangs into the back of her neck.

She gasped a choked, strangled sound, her body convulsing as the pain roared through her. It was feeding.

Not on blood.

Not on flesh.

On love. On memory. On every part of her that had ever belonged to Hé Sá.

She could feel it being drained from her, siphoned away like lifeblood, like air. Her mind blurred, images flickering in and out of her vision—Hé Sá's face, his voice, his hands on her skin, how he once loved her, how she could never stop loving him.

She tried to fight.

She tried to scream.

But she was slipping.

Then—**A force. A push. A presence.**

Not alone.

A flash of blue light ignited the room.

Archangel Michael.

His sword slashed through the shadows, a golden arc splitting through the black.

Then—another force, another being.

Shiva. The Destroyer.

The earth shook, a soundless roar vibrating through existence itself as his third eye blazed open, sending ripples of light crashing into Xtotl.

It hissed, its form shuddering, wrenching back from Nea's body.

And then—another.

The Buddha. The Goddess. The Creator.

They stood together, pillars of light against the crawling darkness, their presence both gentle and immeasurable.

Xtotl writhed.

It fought.

It clawed.

But it could not win. Not tonight.

It receded, slinking back into the abyss, but not without taking something with it.

Nea gasped as the weight lifted from her body, her lungs burning as she sucked in the air. She was free—but only just.

She was weaker.

It had taken more this time.

And it would be back.

Each time, she felt herself slipping further.

Her guides had to fight harder each time to keep her from being consumed.

And each time, she wondered—

How much longer could she last?

How much more of her was left to take?

The Blood Moon was rising.

And soon, there would be no more time.

The Final Cord Cutting – Blood Moon Ceremony

Nea stood within the sacred lodge, the fire burning high, the drumbeat steady, deep, final.

Her family surrounded her—her mother, her cousins, the Elders. River stood at her side, silent but firm.

She had done everything she could. She had fought. She had loved. She had prayed.

And now—she would let go.

Nea lifted the black cord before her; the representation of 5,000 years of karma, of love, turned to bondage, of devotion twisted into suffering.

The Elders chanted, their voices rising with the fire, a prayer of release, liberation, and finality.

She raised the ceremonial knife, her hands steady.

One last time, she closed her eyes, whispering into the void.

"Hé Sá, I love you. I forgive you. I release you."

The cord snapped.

The fire roared.

And in that moment, across time and space, Nea felt the weight finally lift.

Xtotl shrieked, recoiling, hissing, its connection severed.

It was over.

Interlude: The Ceremony of Light

The darkness came as it always did—creeping, slithering, a black tide rising from the abyss. Xtotl is hungry, patient, and confident of its dominion. It had fed for centuries, weaving itself into bloodlines, into memories, into love itself, twisting devotion into chains, turning longing into a prison.

It had never been lost.

But tonight—tonight, it would be met with something greater.

A force it could not consume.

A love that could not unravel.

A light it could never extinguish.

The fire burned high in the lodge, the sacred cedar and sage twisting into thick, fragrant smoke that curled toward the rafters. The drumming started, slow and deep, like the earth's heartbeat.

Outside, the Elders gathered, their breath visible in the cold night air, their eyes alight with purpose.

Grampa Oliver. River. My mother. My cousins.

They stood at the lodge's edge, hands pressed to the earth, voices low in prayer. They knew what was coming. They had felt the shadow at the edges of their family for lifetimes, whispering through the generations, binding their men, poisoning their love, taking and taking and taking.

Not tonight.

Tonight, we would take something back.

And in the spirit realm—

They came.

The ones who had always been with me.

The Wolf. The Silver-Tipped Grizzly. The Ancient Ones.

They emerged from the folds of time, their presence expanding, shimmering, radiant in their knowing. Their love was not just felt—it was seen, touched, and breathed. Infinite. Endless. Unbreakable.

The Starchild stepped forward, eyes glowing, a cosmic tether linking them to the galaxies beyond, to the knowledge of worlds forgotten, to the wisdom of those who had walked before and those who would walk after.

Buddha. The Goddess. The Creator.

They did not fight. They did not need to.

They were.

Their presence alone sent ripples through the darkness, making Xtotl flinch and recoil, knowing it was outmatched.

And then—

I felt it.

The shift.

The unfolding of my spirit.

My feet lifted from the ground as my form took shape—no longer just woman, Nea, but something more.

Eagle wings unfurled from my back, golden and vast, edged in bright light that cut through shadow.

The drumming in the lodge reached its crescendo, the voices of my family lifting in song, their strength a tidal wave, an immovable force pushing Xtotl from the earthly realm, severing its grip with every verse, every beat of the drum, every stomp of their feet.

They were my warriors in the world of flesh.

And I—I was their warrior in the unseen.

At the helm of the battle, Archangel Michael stood tall, his sword glowing, his eyes fierce, a guardian carved from celestial fire. He struck, and Xtotl shrieked, its wail echoing into the void and a thousand souls screaming as it was forced back.

I stepped forward, light pouring from my hands, from my chest, from my very breath. I did not fight it with rage. I did not fight it with hate.

I fought it with love.

With infinite, immeasurable love.

Love for myself.
Love for my ancestors.
Love for Hé Sá, even in his ruin.
Love for all cursed before me, bound before me, taken before me.

I fought with the kind of love Xtotl could never comprehend.

And with each step forward, it lost.

The darkness recoiled.

It shrank.

It screamed.

And then, it was gone.

The lodge fell silent.

The flames flickered lower.

I exhaled, my body trembling but still standing.

The battle was over.

For now.

Then, **Michael turned to me.**

The Archangel, the warrior, the guide who had fought beside me for lifetimes, who had watched as I fell, rose, and stumbled back to power.

His gaze held something deeper than victory.

"You are ready."

In his hands, **a sword.**

It gleamed silver and white, its hilt carved with symbols older than time, glowing with the light of every battle I had ever fought, of every lesson I had ever learned.

A weapon not of war but of wisdom.

A blade forged not in blood but in **truth.**

Michael extended it toward me.

"You have earned this. Use it well."

As my fingers closed around the hilt, **I felt it—**

The shift.

The ascension.

The next step in **a 5,000-year war.**

And I knew—

This was just the beginning.

EPILOGUE
Peace

For the first time in lifetimes, Nea felt light.

The weight of the world, the burdens of endless battles—both seen and unseen—had finally lifted. She awoke to a stillness she had never known, her breath easy, her spirit untangled. There were no whispers of doubt anymore, no longing that gnawed at her heart. For the first time, there was only quiet. A peace she hadn't thought was possible.

The battles she'd fought and her sacrifices had all led to this moment. She had won, not by destroying what stood before her but by choosing to rise above it, to transcend it. The years of grief, loss, and fire had forged her into someone unbreakable, someone who could stand firm in the face of whatever the world had left to throw at her.

And Hé Sá? That was now his battle to fight alone.

Her heart, once so intertwined with his, was now a distant echo. Their paths had split irreparably, and though some of her mourned that loss, she knew it was necessary. He would have to find his way. She had found hers.

The Phone Call

Hé Sá sat in his darkened apartment, staring at his reflection. The lines on his face looked deeper now, the weight of his failures pressing down on him like a physical burden. He hadn't seen the man he was a year ago—strong, proud, determined. The reflection before him was someone broken, someone who had lost everything. His wife. His money. His reputation. His body was failing him, worn out from the stress of his ambition and the bitterness that came with it.

And Nea? He had lost her, too.

Her absence was like a hollow space inside him. A gaping wound he couldn't seem to stitch up. The world felt heavy with the emptiness she had left behind. She had been his anchor, his equal, the only person who ever made him question his choices. And now, she was gone, walking a path he could never follow.

His phone vibrated on the table, breaking the silence.

The name that flashed across the screen made his breath catch. **Nea.**

He hesitated. He had often thought about her, but he never reached out and asked how she was doing. It felt wrong now, after everything that had passed between them. But he couldn't ignore the pull, the need to hear her voice one last time.

"Hey," he answered, his voice hoarse.

Her voice was soft, careful. "I had a vision… and I was worried about you. Are you okay?"

Hé Sá scoffed, running a hand through his cropped hair, the weight of sarcasm creeping into his tone. "Jesus, Nea, still with the woo-woo neo-Shamanism?"

She didn't flinch. She exhaled slowly, her patience unwavering. "You're half Lakota, Hé Sá. Whether you believe it or not, this stuff runs through your blood."

He didn't answer right away. Her words lodged themselves in his chest, gnawing at him like a small, insistent thing. There was truth in them, a truth he had never fully confronted, something in the very marrow of his bones he couldn't escape.

A silence stretched between them, thick and uncomfortable.

Finally, her voice cut through the stillness. "Be careful, okay?"

And just like that, she was gone.

Her words lingered, heavy and unresolved. He stared at the phone in his hand, the finality of the conversation hitting him harder than expected. She was right to worry, but it was too late. He had made his choices and now had to live with them. Nea had moved on and found her path. And he was still lost, waiting for something to shake him awake.

The Path Beyond the Fire

The wind carried the scent of cedar and sage, weaving through the last embers of the sacred fire. It was a night unlike any other. Ancient and unyielding stars stretched across the sky like sentinels, watching over the gathering below. The air hummed with the quiet rhythm of something old, something eternal.

The battle had been fought. The choices had been made. The storm was over—for now.

I stood at the edge of the lodge, the weight of the white sword still heavy in my hands. It was more than a weapon; it was a key, a guide, a symbol of everything I had learned and embraced. But no one in the earthly realm could see it. It pulsed softly, a living thing humming in tune with the universe's heartbeat. It wasn't a blade of destruction but a blade of truth. It severed the old bonds, illusions, and lingering chains of the curse that had held my ancestors captive for too long.

Across the fire, the Elders watched in silence, their eyes full of knowing. Grampa Oliver, my mother, River, the cousins—each one carved from the same stone as our ancestors. Their faces spoke of strength, wisdom, and battles fought in the seen and unseen realms.

Grampa nodded once, a slow, deliberate motion. His expression was unreadable, but there was something in his gaze—a weight of understanding, an acknowledgement of the journey I had just completed.

"It is done," he said.

But even as the words settled in the air, I felt the truth that came with them.

No.

It was only beginning.

The Gathering of the Guides

Beyond the flickering firelight, just beyond mortal sight, they waited.

The Ancient Ones stood tall, cloaked in the very fabric of time itself. Their presence was vast, eternal, untouched by the smallness of human years. Their voices were not heard but felt—in the slow bending of the trees, the whisper of the wind curling through the valley below, and the distant call of the wolf that echoed in the mountain ridges.

The Silver-Tipped Grizzly sat at the edge of the clearing, massive and immovable, his breath slow and deep, filled with the patience of stone, the certainty of rivers that always find their way home. He did not speak, but his presence was a reminder: I was never alone.

The Wolves watches from the ridgeline, their fur silver in the moonlight, its eyes locked onto mine. There was no fear in those eyes—only understanding and recognition. The Wolves did not need to move. Their gaze alone was enough. *You are ready. Now, you walk with us.*

Above them all, stretching across the sky, the Starchild pulsed with an iridescent glow. It was a tether, a bridge between the earth and the cosmos, between past and future, between what had been and what was still to come.

They were all here. All of them. Waiting. Watching. For me.

The Leaving

I turned from the lodge, the warmth of my family, my roots, lingering behind me, but the unknown stretched ahead. This was the path I was meant to walk. There was no hesitation in my heart, no lingering doubt. The choice had already been made.

I walked forward, my feet light against the earth, my body filled with something more than power—something unshakable—a quiet, unrelenting purpose.

With each step, the world began to change. The forest grew deeper and vaster, the trees towering into eternity. The sky darkened and filled with stars I had never seen before. The veil between what was real and what had only ever been imagined seemed to fall away, and I stepped through.

I was not alone.

The wolves loped beside me, the Grizzly just behind, its massive presence comforting in its silence. The Starchild hovered above, its light pulsing gently, guiding me forward. And the voices of the Ancient Ones whispered along the wind, their words faint but clear.

In my grip, unseen to the mortal world, the white sword pulsed, its energy tethered to my spirit. It was more than a shield. It was a key—a tool to open the doors to unknown realms.

Ahead of me, a path stretched into the unseen—one I had always been meant to walk.

And in the distance, beyond the darkened horizon, The Unsettling was coming.

But this time—

I would be ready.

And I would not be afraid.

The story continues in Of Spirit and Bone: Shadow of the Grizzly.

Made in the USA
Monee, IL
30 June 2025

20246709R00263